Crash Course

Crash Course

PIPER LAWSON

BERKLEY XO

BERKLEY XO
An imprint of Penguin Random House LLC
1745 Broadway, New York, NY 10019
penguinrandomhouse.com

Design by Suki Boynton

Text set in Laurentian Pro

Library of Congress Cataloging-in-Publication Data is available.

First published in the United States of America by Berkley XO, 2026

Manufactured in United States of America
BVG

ISBN 9798217238583
1st Printing

The authorized representative in the EU for product safety and compliance is Penguin Random House Ireland, Morrison Chambers, 32 Nassau Street, Dublin D02 YH68, Ireland, https://eu-contact.penguin.ie.

For the ones who refuse to stay in the passenger seat.

1

Shay

I DON'T HEAR the car coming.

One second I'm walking, lost in my music and my own head, and the next the world lurches sideways.

Porsche 911 Turbo.

Recognition hits me at the same moment as the impact. I go sprawling toward the pavement in front of the vehicle. My hands shoot down to break my fall, pain streaking up my side as my hip slams into the asphalt.

My headphones fly off my ears, the plastic shattering, but that's not the worst part. Somehow, I'm on the road and the car is still moving toward me.

I've been under plenty of cars, and on a good day, there's nowhere I'd rather be. Nothing compares to the feeling of control, the rightness of knowing every component is doing its part.

But it's a lot easier to appreciate those things when the car over me isn't in gear.

My stomach plummets. Ground clearance on a Porsche 911 is about six inches, hardly enough for it to drive clean over me like some Vin Diesel movie stunt. Not without taking a strip of my face and tits with it. I like those parts of my body, at least enough to want to keep both intact.

Instinct has me reaching to grasp my necklace under my jacket, the cool ring attached digging into my flesh. *Is this what it was like for my parents? Their final moments before being engulfed in fire and metal—*

The burning tang of gasoline fumes cuts through my panic as the Porsche grinds to a halt. My feet are nearly under the front of the car, heat rolling off the engine and scorching my skin.

"What the fuck?!" The exclamation, alarmed and male, comes from someone I can't see. "Are you—don't move the car—ah, hell!"

Shoes scuff the asphalt. A moment later, their owner appears over me, haloed by the sun.

I've never been religious, but I swear he's an angel.

Wavy dirty blond hair. Square jaw. Symmetrical face. Full mouth. An unbuttoned dress shirt and jeans that hug his legs to perfection.

Do angels swear? Today they do, I decide as he holds out a hand.

I grab for it, and he pulls me up. My feet find the pavement under me, my legs still shaking.

"Are you hurt?" His concerned gaze drops to my hand.

My palms are studded with gravel from the road mixed with my own blood. They don't hurt yet thanks to the adrenaline cocktail pounding in my veins.

"It looks worse than it is. You should see the other guy." My bravado's returning.

Kind blue eyes search my face. He looks to be my age, maybe a little older, as he bends to grab the pieces of my headphones off the pavement.

"I'm Theo."

I know. Everyone in this town knows him and his family, plus half the country and a good part of the planet. I start to say the words but stop just in time as I take the headphones with my good hand. "Thanks."

His handsome face twists with regret, as if he can repair the broken plastic with contrition alone. "I'm sorry about—"

"Theo!" A sharp voice cuts him off.

If Theo's an angel, the guy leaning out the driver-side window has fallen from grace.

Dark hair falls recklessly across a lean, impatient face. Sunglasses cover his eyes. He's James Dean in a Porsche.

And he's *pissed*.

Well, so am I. "You ever driven a car before?" My shout comes out like a gasp as I spin to face him, my good fist banging on the hood.

The devil behind the wheel yanks the sunglasses off, leaning an elbow on the door. "You ever walk down a street before? The road's not your fucking catwalk."

His eyes are steel blue, fringed with dark lashes and narrowed in accusation. He's striking, like the frozen river behind my house—cool and smooth, right up until you stick a foot through the ice.

I fist the broken pieces of headphone in my hand. "We'll see what the cops have to say."

"No." It's one word, a low command over the purr of the car, delivered in a voice even colder and more assured than the rest of him. "You won't tell a soul. Not the police. Not your best friend. Not whatever townie hookup gets you off Friday night. Keep this to yourself as long as you live."

I brush dirt off my jeans, which only makes the gravel burrow deeper into my palm. "So, not long if it's up to you."

His eyes narrow as he shoves the driver's door open.

"You're going to the academy?" My rescuer reaches for my book bag, which also wound up on the road, and holds it up. The "A" for Ashford Academy is embroidered on the front in white script.

The driver's knuckles go white on the doorframe.

"I'll walk you there," Theo says, shouldering my bag as he leans toward my ear. "But let's take the sidewalk."

❖

It's only a few blocks to campus and its main building. I'm momentarily speechless as I lay eyes on the two-story wonder of glass and metal that's every bit as unique as what's inside.

"At least they're not Bose," Theo offers as we head past a front parking lot toward the doors. "The headphones," he goes on at my blank expression.

"Right. Cheap to replace. Too bad I can't get new hands," I joke.

"I'll hook you up with new ones."

"Hands?"

"Headphones." His eyes glint. It's probably a trick of the light, because there's no way Theo is flirting with me.

In high school, I was voted most likely to spend prom night covered in grease stains in her garage. I was never the person who joined sports or cheerleading or even band. Not the one who hot guys looked at like . . .

Well, the way Theo's looking at me right now.

Attractive people walk in and out of the front doors in groups of two or three, the Ashford logo emblazoned on bags matching the name on the front of the building.

I bet they're talking about important things. I bet their hands don't look as if they were victimized by a cheese grater.

Ashford Academy is nothing like a regular college. This elite school training drivers, engineers, and mechanics for the global F1 circuit only opens its doors to a select group of prodigies: people in their late teens and early twenties who eat, sleep, and breathe cars. Nine out of ten applicants get turned down. If you're accepted, it means Ashford Racing Inc. thinks you have a chance in hell of helping them do one thing.

Be the fastest on the planet.

"I'm sorry about my brother." Theo's words jolt me out of my head. "He's . . ."

"A threat to public safety?"

"I was going to say charming." He chuckles. "So, we've established that I'm Theo. You are?"

"I didn't say."

"Okay, New Girl. I like a mystery."

More than a few passing students look over at us, whispering to one another as if the fact that we're even standing together is news.

Theo doesn't notice or doesn't care.

"This is where I leave you." He shields his eyes from the sun. "But you should get checked out by a nurse."

"I'll keep that in mind."

"That sounds noncommittal."

"Noncommittal is my specialty."

He laughs before handing me my bag. Neither of us seems ready to move but I'm still looking for a reason to keep him at a distance, like I keep most people.

"Are you going to say the same thing your brother did?" I ask finally. "Not to tell anyone?"

He sighs. "Give me your phone."

I can't think of a good reason to refuse, so I reach into my bag for it and pass it over. He types a few keystrokes before handing it back.

"My number. If you need anything."

"In case I need to call Theo Ashford," I echo, the doubt clear in my voice.

This time, he grins. "So you *do* know who I am."

"Obviously." My lips curve too, and somehow, I'm a little breathless. "Your name's on the building."

The Ashfords represent exclusivity and speed and prestige. But one of them is standing in front of me with a disarming smile as if we're equals. No, it's more than that—as if the fact I'm talking to him is as much his privilege as mine.

"I hope your day gets better, New Girl." With a wink, Theo turns on his heel and heads for the parking lot, where the Porsche now sits in front of a RESERVED sign.

The driver's getting out, his sunglasses back in place. I can't know if he's watching, but I'd bet on it.

2

Shay

THE ASHFORDS.

Of the possibilities I imagined for my first day of the semester, meeting them was not on my bingo card.

Though I've watched four-time F1 champion driver Luca Ashford race on screens my entire life, this is the closest I've come to his family. Photos and video clips hardly do Luca's sons justice. I've never seen anyone so beautiful in real life.

Shaking myself, I turn for the building and walk straight into the glass doors.

I manage to avoid falling on my ass but catch sight of myself reflected on the surface. Brown hair escaping its messy ponytail. Lined eyes looking more haunted than edgy. Chapped lips always in need of lip balm. Thank fuck for my leather jacket—without it, I'd probably have a hole in my long-sleeved T-shirt, courtesy of the Porsche.

"I ran into them my first day," a slender girl with wavy black hair appears in the reflection next to me.

"The Ashfords?"

"The doors. They scrub them sparkly clean every hour." She smiles, her teeth bright against flawless golden skin. "I'm Megan."

"Shay." Her warmth is a lifeline. I breathe in for what feels like the first time all morning. "Is it that obvious I'm new?"

"I clocked it fifty feet away." Megan holds out a hand and I hold up mine. Her gaze lands on the angry red skin. "I'm guessing that's not from the door."

As much as I'd like to defy Theo's brother, I hesitate to volunteer the details to a stranger. "I fell."

Megan seems to accept it, opening the offending door and motioning me through. Her pink sweater billowing in the breeze, she looks as out of place as I feel.

"I'm supposed to be in class." I pull up my schedule on my phone.

She looks over my shoulder. "Wait. You're second year, like me." She blinks, flashing bright blue eyeliner.

There are a million questions on her face, but I only answer one. "I'm a transfer. I was taking mechanical engineering at Ohio State."

"Wow. Okay." Megan looks as if she wants to press but relents. "Well, going late to class is worse than skipping, so we might as well clean that up. I've got Neosporin."

She ushers me down the hall and into a huge bathroom. "So, I can already tell you're an overachiever. It's your first day and I saw you talking to an Ashford outside."

"Technically, I've met two." I extend my right hand over the sink, hissing at the sting of the cool water rinsing away the gravel. "Nice guys."

Megan's lips twitch as she rummages through her bag for

first aid supplies. Everything inside is pink. I even glimpse a pink torque wrench. "Theo, maybe, but not Jameson. They're used to people falling over them. Everyone in this building wants to fuck an Ashford. You might have a shot with Theo."

His grin flashes in my mind, along with those dimples, that athletic body, the warmth of his hand in mine when he helped me up.

"I'm not interested." I ignore the little shiver that runs through me as I lay the gauze pad she passes me across my palm. The sting of pain is sharper than I expect.

"If your heart or panties are set on Jameson," she misreads my comment, "you're out of luck. Unless you're driving at least a V8 engine, big brother won't give you so much as the time of day."

Ice blue eyes appear in my mind without permission.

"If you're smart, you'll stay out of their way." Megan grins. "Tell me you're a smart girl, Shay."

"Can I get back to you?"

She laughs and hooks an arm through mine as she leads us back into the hall. "I knew we were going to be friends."

Surprise has me blinking. Her easy acceptance throws me nearly as much as getting hit by the Porsche.

It's politeness, not interest, I decide. People are not my strong suit. I've always had trouble reading them, understanding what they want, what I should want from them in return. Cars are predictable. They feel like home.

"I'm going to walk you around the building. Then we'll grab terrible coffee and I'll get you to your second class. Thank goodness you're technical track, like me," Megan says. "I can tell because engineers look at a car like it's a puzzle."

"And the drivers?"

Her eyes sparkle, or maybe it's the blue eyeliner. "They look at a car like it's an animal to tame."

There's nothing subtle about Formula 1. It's a sport that pits the twenty fastest drivers in the world against one another in ungodly fast cars. Picture teams of the most brilliant engineers, designers, and mechanics, all financed by the deepest pockets.

They do it at demanding tracks in glamorous locations, with millions of fans.

Still, every one of those drivers and engineers had to start somewhere.

Ashford Academy is exactly that kind of place.

The building is somehow even more beautiful inside than outside. It's shiny and modern, full of glass and pale wood. Doors off the main hallway lead to classrooms and labs, most of which appear to be occupied.

"We're one of the only schools that has both drivers and engineers. PR touts it as a new model of education blending science and sport. Really, though, it's a talent incubator for ARI's empire." Megan launches into tour guide mode.

"Ashford has a racing-federation-sanctioned track at the ARI F1 garage about ten minutes west of campus." She points out a massive window cut into the side of the hallway toward the manicured greens outside.

"Driver candidates get their licenses through sim hours, safety exams, and races." She sounds like she's reading off a brochure as we pass another open door with a dozen new, state-of-the-art sims inside.

"What's down there?" I ask. The hallway intersects another wing, this one even wider with lockers flanking either side.

"Garages. For mechanical classes and special projects."

Megan shows me how to find my classes and tells me where to park once I get my pass so I can skip the awkward bus trip that let me off eight blocks away.

She walks me down the garage hallway to another that doubles back in the direction we came. We wind up in an open space that's huge, round in shape, and taller than the rest of the building

"This is the atrium. It's an F1 fan's wet dream," she says.

It's definitely mine.

The vaulted ceiling is filled with skylights that let sun slice down to decorate the marble floor. Benches line the perimeter, and a few students occupy them. The walls are decorated with memorabilia and televisions with video feeds from past races.

On a pedestal in the middle sits an F1 car. I don't need to look at the plaque beneath it to know it's Ashford Racing's first world-championship-winning car. Even motionless, it steals my breath. Although the technology and chassis design have changed in the past two decades, it feels unnatural to see it contained like this, on display instead of on the track.

A huge image on one screen shows this year's team standing around their race cars. Front and center is driver turned CEO Luca Ashford, an arm each around two men in fire suits.

"I'm sure you know ARI's drivers," Megan prompts.

I nod. "Navarro is first in the driver's championship standings. Dekker's fallen back."

Of the twenty total drivers across ten teams in F1, ARI's are top shelf. Between the two, I prefer Dekker. While he's not the flashiest driver, he consistently scores points and podiums, and always brings his family on the road with him.

"It's the worst numbers game of any pro sport. Thousands of potential drivers competing for twenty seats. Most of them will never see the inside of an F1 car."

"And the Ashford brothers will?" I think of Theo and Jameson.

"No guarantees, but they have a head start."

We end our tour in the dining hall, where students are pouring through the doors. A glance up at the clock tells me the first class has let out.

"Those are the drivers." Megan points to tables opposite us, occupied by attractive, intense-looking students. "F1 is supposedly a team sport—drivers working with the engineers and mechanics and strategists—but if you ask them, they don't need us."

My attention is pulled to the far entrance as the Ashford brothers stride in with the kind of slow-motion confidence that needs its own soundtrack.

Theo is ahead, running a hand through his blond hair. Looking every bit the dark prince, Jameson follows. They take seats on the far side of the dining hall with other drivers.

Some people are talked about like possibilities, others as certainties. No one needs to tell me what category I fall into, or that the Ashfords are the chosen ones. You don't end up in the driver's seat of a multimillion-dollar car by accident.

Megan shows us to a table with two other technical students, who introduce themselves as Raj and Zane.

"I trust everyone's up on the Ashford summer holiday drama," Megan starts.

"Theo partying in the Riviera again?" Raj leans in.

"A pregnancy scare. Twins," Megan confirms.

"He got a girl pregnant with twins." Zane sounds doubtful.

"No, I heard he got twins pregnant. It's been taken care of, and no one will ever be the wiser."

"Jameson punched a paparazzo in Monaco."

I try to keep up as gossip flies around the table, feeling as if I'm on the outside looking in. My gaze drags toward the oldest Ashford. He's taller. Cooler. Utterly confident. It must feel good to have your future all but promised.

"What's he like?" I can't resist asking. "Jameson, I mean."

"He's twenty-two, just over a year older than Theo." Zane plays with the collar of his shirt. "Impeccable record ever since he raced karts. Never makes a mistake behind the wheel."

Except he did this morning.

Jameson Ashford's eyes land on me from across the room and I feel it. The scorching cold. A pretty girl next to him tries to get his attention, finally pulling at his arm before he acknowledges her.

"They couldn't be more different." I force my attention back to our table.

"Well. You know what they say," Megan goes on. "They're only half brothers. One of them is . . ."

"Illegitimate?" Raj offers helpfully.

Curiosity tugs at me.

"Theo seems kinder." My attention finds him again and Megan laughs.

"Oh, he'll still eat you alive. You just might enjoy it more."

His number burns a hole in my phone.

I've dated a handful of guys, but it's always been more about curiosity than connection. Sex might be a diversion, but it's also underwhelming. It's possible I'm just bad at it, though I'll give the guys their share of the credit, too.

Or maybe I've never met someone I felt compelled to be closer to in that way. In *every* way.

"Before you worry about missing their pretty faces"—Megan interrupts my thoughts—"there's an applied strategy class—tomorrow and Thursday—that both techs and drivers have to attend."

"Have to?" Zane challenges.

Raj leans in. "Going to class matters more to the engineers than the drivers," he explains. "We're the ones who need to stick out all three years and get good grades if we want our degree. The drivers are just here to get their licenses and catch the eye of an F1 team."

"So it's more like an audition," I say.

He nods. "They don't need to stack accreditations. They need to win."

All too soon, it's time for the next class. I find myself sitting with Megan, Raj, Zane, and a couple dozen other students as the instructor runs through first-week-of-school admin.

"If you ace my class, along with the others, and graduate, the best of you have a hope of working on an F1 car," he informs us at the end.

It sounds like a dream.

What I haven't volunteered is that I'm not here to pursue a career in F1. I need to be local, and my aspirations are more practical. In a few years, I'll be spending my days fixing Subarus and Toyotas, not tweaking high-performance engines.

The rest of the morning I take notes, trying to focus despite the throbbing in my hand. After class, I'm on the way down the hall when a voice has me pulling up.

"New Girl."

I turn to find Theo Ashford smirking and leaning against a fountain, looking like a sexy Cheshire cat. "How's the hand?"

"I heal fast."

"Good. Around here, that's very good."

His stare sends sparks of anticipation through me. Damn, it's like his attention gets converted to dopamine at a cellular level.

"Why are you talking to me?" I blurt. "Is it because your brother ran me over and you want me to keep your secret?"

"Or because I like you."

Murmurs draw my attention. A few people look toward Theo with curiosity, adoration, or undisguised lust as they pass us.

"Doubtful. Apparently, you're some kind of god and I'm merely mortal."

When he throws back his head and laughs, it's a fascinating sound, warm and rich and way too affecting. Before I can get too caught up, my phone rings.

"Boyfriend?" Theo asks as if he might care.

My nose wrinkles as I see the number. "Dad."

"He must be proud of you being here."

It's my turn to laugh.

"I wish."

3

Shay

MY NEW SCHEDULE is a choreographed dance.

Get home from school. Stash my books. Lie to my dad about where I've been and where I'm going.

At least I was spared the last part tonight. After getting home from campus, I found my dad passed out on the couch in our two-bedroom house, his foot elevated at the end. I tucked a blanket around him, quietly showering and grabbing leftovers from the fridge before swiping the overdue bills from the mailbox and hiding them before I headed out again.

The drive takes twenty minutes in the dark. My vintage Mustang rumbles under me, the deep forest-green paint flashing along the edge of the hood as I pass beneath the streetlights. The '67 Fastback is temperamental, but I love it. It's one thing in my life that no one can touch.

When my adoptive dad gave me the car for my sixteenth birthday, I insisted we fix it up together. It was a thrill using my own tools—the wrenches with padded handles, the custom welded breaker bars—to bring it back to life one piece at a time.

I might not have inherited his genetics, but I got my love of cars from him.

The ARI garage is humming when I pull up. I type my code into the keypad by the door, the Ashford "A" above the nine digits.

"MacDonald. You're five minutes late," calls Keane as I step inside.

"I'm sorry." It's on the tip of my tongue to mention I put in a full day on campus, but I don't want to give our shift supervisor any excuse to send me home.

In the break room, I open the locker with my name on it. My dad's name, technically, and his locker too. Inside are photos and stickers from F1, artifacts of his career spent working for ARI.

No less prominent are photos of me doing things he was proud of. Losing both my front teeth at once so I whistled for an entire month when I spoke. Making my first pancakes, which I forgot to add eggs to but he ate them with a smile anyway. Getting my driver's license while he paced in the back of the DMV, wringing his hands the entire time.

Dad's only ever been based here at headquarters, in contrast to the traveling engineers and mechanics who work on the F1 grid. Each week, the mobile city builds their garages, kitchens, and data centers at a new track to race Thursday to Sunday. Then they tear it all down and go to a new country. It's glamorous and grueling.

When I burst into his world sixteen years ago, Dad was a race car mechanic without the first clue what to do with a little girl. We figured it out together.

The first time I went into our home garage, I wanted to know what all the pieces were that made up a car. How they fit together. What made them break and what made them fast.

Dad would try to shoo me out, but I always snuck back.

I shrug out of my jacket and hang it up. In the smudged mirror inside the locker door, the necklace around my neck glints in the fluorescent lights overhead.

"Keep working on this." Keane gestures to the aluminum chassis in the corner housing a direct-injected Mecachrome V6 engine. It was damaged in a race before the summer break but wasn't a high priority to fix.

"What're you working on?"

"Something above your pay grade." The shift supervisor has ten years on me but looks even older with his full beard and crinkled eyes. He waves before disappearing through a door I've never noticed—probably leading to a different section of the garage.

When Ashford HR called the house to tell Dad he couldn't take the medical leave he requested after his knee replacement surgery, there was no room for the anger I felt knowing he'd worked there his entire life, yet there was no protection for him when he needed it.

I did what I had to do: promised the shift would be covered.

I didn't volunteer that it would be a different MacDonald showing up to work for a month.

Now, I pop an antacid from the roll in my pocket before reaching for my headphones only to remember they're broken. I grab a seat and get to work fixing the F2 car. It's a standard make, and I know what parts go where.

At night, the garage at headquarters is quiet and climate controlled. These vehicles get shipped off to races, then shipped back when they fail. We don't see the excitement of the track, but we make what goes onto it.

It's peaceful. Here, I can block out my dad's bills. The emptiness I feel when I think about the parents I barely knew. I can figure out what's wrong and set to putting it right.

Engines make sense. A car doesn't try to hide why it's broken. With a little patience and skill, you can always, *always* put one back together.

"What you're doing is gonna come out," Bo, one of the other mechanics, grunts as we both head for the break room a while later.

"Only if you say something," I counter as he digs cigarettes from his locker while I fix a coffee. "Keane hasn't." I'm grateful our shift supervisor's had my back so far.

The TV in the corner is on, the volume turned down to a low buzz, replaying footage from last weekend's race at Monza in Italy. F1 recently came back from its summer break. There's fallout from the previous race in Zandvoort, and Dekker is giving an interview, an ARI media person at his side.

"Your performance has fallen behind your teammate since the break," the broadcaster notes. "Were there changes to the car that would account for this? Or is it simply an issue of your teammate having a better feel at this point in the season?"

Dekker's usually lighthearted, but his lips thin. "No. I'm at least as fast, and I'll prove it at the next race."

Unease ripples through me at the interviewer's implied dig and Dekker's defensiveness, but I shake it off. There are always storylines coming out of the summer, and it's usually just media trying to get attention.

I turn away from the TV and follow Bo outside to the railing that overlooks the on-site racetrack. Part of the industrial complex that makes up their Michigan headquarters, the ARI garage is close enough to Detroit to get shipments to and from the airport.

"How is the old man?" Bo asks, the end of his cigarette glowing in the dark.

"Getting pissy. I didn't realize his knee replacement would leave him with such a sparkling personality."

"Sounds about right." He snorts. "Thought you were supposed to be back in college this fall? Some fancy engineering degree."

I lean both arms on the railing. "I was. But he needed surgery and I couldn't see him taking care of himself while he recovered."

Bo takes a long drag. "He wouldn't want you working here."

"He wouldn't want us to lose our house, either," I counter. "One day, we're going to open our own garage. It might not be as thrilling as working on race cars, but he'll be able to take a holiday once in a while. And it'll give him a retirement in another decade."

"Your dad on board with this plan?"

Not entirely. "He said as long as I finished college first."

Bo nods. "He's lucky to have you."

"I'm lucky to have him."

He's everything to me. What I know of my birth parents is limited to a few memories and an account of how they died. Even that's patchy and my dad doesn't like to talk about it.

A car wheels onto the track from a different part of the garage.

"What Keane's been working on all week." Bo nods to the car.

Sure enough, our supervisor steps out and confers with a driver before the car goes out on the track. Keane watches from farther down the railing as the car picks up speed. My heart accelerates with it.

It's beautiful. A silver chassis, smooth fenders, sleek curves. It flies around the track.

I hear the tires light up the pavement, smell the rubber laid down on the road with each pass.

My fingers grip the railing. "Is that what I think it is?"

"Next year's F1 model," Bo confirms. "Association made some changes to regulations and everyone's playing catch-up."

The car sails past. "It looks fast."

"Not fast enough." Keane's voice edges into my thoughts as he moves next to us. "New season starts in six months, and we need more speed if we're going to compete with Ignite. They'll be the team to beat."

My knuckles are white on the railing beneath the bandages on my palms. "And if we can't get more speed out of it?"

Keane clears his throat. "Corporate might start laying off mechanics."

His words cut through my haze of awe.

Firing mechanics. Like my dad.

I'm feeling sick as the car rolls to a stop in front of the garage, its driver shifting out in a smooth, athletic motion.

I know who it is before he takes off the helmet.

Jameson Ashford's dark hair shines under the fluorescent

track lights and the nearly full moon overhead. His body is dangerous—his muscles clear through his suit and every movement precise. Aggression leashed in service of performance.

Of course it had to be him driving like the car was built for him. He carves up the track, putting his car in exactly the right position.

It's one more reminder that this world runs on selection, not merit. People like him are chosen. People like my dad and me scrap our way into the edges. We're the last ones to earn a seat at the table, the first to be cut.

One of the most vivid memories I have of my mom is her reading me a story about a princess locked in a tower and promised to a haughty prince to save the kingdom.

I told her I'd pick the dragon every time. Entitled pricks have always been my least favorite brand of asshole.

I'm preoccupied enough I barely notice when another man walks out onto the track and says something sharp to Jameson, stabbing a finger at his chest.

Luca Ashford. Though I've never seen him in person, I recognize him immediately.

His long wool coat obscures most of his suit, revealing leather shoes that aren't designed for the dirt. He has the same build as his son, but where Jameson is icy cool, Luca is all fire.

Luca raises his voice, angry.

I wait for Jameson to snap back. Instead, his shoulders tense and, eventually, he nods.

Though reading people might not be my strong suit, the relationship between them looks anything but easy.

I'm leaning over the railing, straining to hear details of their conversation, and perversely grateful we're close enough to see their faces.

Which I would've done well to remember when Jameson turns this way.

4

Shay

JAMESON ASHFORD *CANNOT* see me. He'll recognize me, and he'll end my future without a second thought.

The Ashfords are too important to care about my dad, but not too important to ruin him—and me—if they decide to.

I double over, ducking behind the railing and tugging the hat down over my face.

"What's wrong?" Keane prods.

I search my brain and blurt the only thing I can think of. "Cramps."

Both men groan in sympathy, or maybe it's the sudden desire to be anywhere but here.

"Might have a couple leftover Percocet from when I split that tooth last year," Bo grunts.

I would laugh if I wasn't panicking. "I don't need Percocet. But thanks."

When I risk a glance up again, Jameson's walking toward the parking lot with his father as mechanics wheel the car back toward the garage. My dad might not be the only person I need to worry about finding out what I'm up to.

I think about it all night and into the next morning when I get to campus, using my new parking pass to park in the lot in the back designated for people whose names didn't make the building facade.

"Did you hear?" Megan drops into the seat next to mine as we wait for our first class to start, waving her phone in front of me. "ARI's second F1 driver is out."

I blink, scanning the headline: ASHFORD DRIVER FIRED IN MIDDLE OF SEASON.

The air evaporates from my lungs. "But Dekker was on a long-term contract."

"They're saying he violated it. Didn't get enough points to meet his performance requirements." Raj claims the seat next to Megan, and Zane the one next to him.

This is massive news, the kind that will rock the entire grid. A driver with Dekker's reputation racing for the world's most famous team getting cut in the middle of the season is shocking. It'll change the face of F1 for the rest of the year or more.

"That for me?" Megan nods to one of two coffee cups I set on the writing desk attached to her seat.

"I stopped at The Junction on the way to campus. You said you didn't like the coffee in the dining hall."

It's such a small gesture, but she beams. "Thanks. You're the sweetest."

I manage a smile in return but caffeine feels trivial in light of this ARI revelation. The entire class is buzzing with it.

I thought I knew from the media how callous Luca Ashford was, but this throws me. If he's this impatient with his drivers, he's probably one step closer to firing mechanics like my dad.

I'm still thinking about it as the professor in our racing

strategy class walks in. I'm surprised to see it's a woman in her fifties, with gray hair pulled back in a short ponytail. As she arranges her books on the lectern, Jameson and Theo Ashford enter, locked in conversation with a few other drivers.

Theo looks like he just rolled out of bed, probably not alone. His hair is messy and his shirt is unbuttoned, his bright eyes full of mischief and humor. I take a second to enjoy the view. His brother could be on his way to a photo shoot, his shirt perfectly tailored, not a hair out of place. Or maybe to a funeral, judging from his grim expression.

Theo nods to the professor, a sheepish smile on his handsome face, and takes a seat in the second row. Jameson claims the end of the row. Probably in case he needs to make a quick escape to mow down more unsuspecting women.

"I'm Professor Vogel." Her voice carries a light European accent. "If you think I'm going easy on anyone because of your course load or your name"—her gaze lands on the Ashfords—"you're mistaken. You want to work on the fastest cars in the world? The Ashfords have the fastest car on the grid."

"Not the fastest," I say under my breath, thinking of last night.

Jameson cuts a look this way, as if he heard me.

"Are there questions?" Vogel asks, scanning the crowd.

A hand goes up from a guy a few rows ahead of me. "What's happening with Dekker?"

"Who'll get the seat?" someone from the driver's side asks.

Vogel's arms fold. "I can't comment on ARI decisions. This is a racing academy. I suggest you focus your attention on learning and forget the gossip."

Excited murmurs start up.

I raise a hand.

"Yes, Miss . . ."

"MacDonald. Shay."

I swear her lips purse. "Miss MacDonald."

"How can we help make them faster?" A few chuckles go up and I ignore them. "That's what everyone wants, isn't it?"

Theo Ashford grins in my direction as if I said something charming. Jameson's gaze lingers on me. I feel it down to my toes.

"You wanna go fast, I'll help you out," a guy near Theo tosses.

"Shut your mouth, Knox," Megan says, too low for him to hear across the room. "God knows where it's been."

Raj shushes her and Zane just shakes his head.

"You don't have the first clue what it takes to put together a race car." Jameson Ashford shifts back in his seat, but somehow it feels like aggression, not retreat. His jaw is razor sharp, his lips pressed into a hard line as he stares me down. "You're some math nerd who squeaked through on an entrance exam."

A hush falls over the lecture hall.

The heat in my stomach is the kind no antacid can touch. Knox's lewd comment was irritating, but this high-handedness from the rich asshole who drove into me is worse.

You won't tell a soul. His words from yesterday come back, whispering along my brain like poisonous fumes.

"You're right. I do like numbers." I pause. "Like six-forty. The horsepower of a Porsche 911 Turbo."

Jameson opens his mouth, but I speak first, rattling off specs I know by heart.

"Two-point-five seconds. That's how long it takes to get from zero to a hundred."

I'd never talk this much about myself, but quoting car stats in front of the class feels easier.

"Last but not least, six inches."

I'm on a roll now. Everyone's watching but a freight train couldn't stop me.

"The maximum ground clearance. Although I'd say yours is . . ." I hold up my hand, eyeing the distance between my spread fingers. "Smaller."

The classroom erupts with hollers and gasps.

"Enough!" Professor Vogel shoots us both a look and returns to her lecture.

Jameson stares holes in me for the rest of the hour.

When class wraps up, Jameson is out the door first, flanked by his posse.

Theo walks over to my row. "Were you waiting for the right moment to call my brother's dick tiny?"

"No," I admit. "It just happened."

His eyes crinkle. "Well, it was the most entertaining class in recent memory. Thank you."

He disappears out the door after his friends.

"That was legendary," Megan crows.

"It's going to come back to bite you." Zane's checking his phone with one ear on our conversation.

Raj shakes his head. "Are you afraid of anything?"

"Spiders. Terrified." I don't have to fake the shudder.

For my eighth birthday, I wanted to spend the entire weekend in the garage in a tent with my stuffed animals. I woke up with a spider on my face and screamed so loud my dad thought I'd lost a limb.

Megan packs up the pink notebook and pens into her Ashford bag. "What are you doing tomorrow night?"

"Sleeping." My body aches from the accident and all my shifts. Dad has the night off, which means no one's expecting a mechanic at the garage. I'm planning a scalding hot shower, to rest my injured hand, and face-plant into my bed for at least ten hours. It'll be heaven.

"Incorrect. The Ashfords are having a party. It's Theo's birthday and Luca's out of town."

"I doubt I'm invited."

"The whole school is invited. It'll be a bigger deal if you *don't* go. Especially given how Theo keeps looking at you," she continues.

A ripple of awareness hits me as I shoulder my bag. Given the choice between drinking and smoking pot and flirting with cliquey assholes, I'd rather be under a car. Still, part of me is curious.

"Don't you want to check out the Ashfords' mansion?" Megan dangles the possibility in front of me.

A party is objectively a bad idea, especially after the scene I caused in class. I need to fly under the radar. Get my education and get out. But maybe if I go, Theo Ashford will be there, sexy grin and all.

And that just might be worth losing sleep over.

❖

CHOOSING CLOTHES FOR the party is harder than I expected. Theo Ashford spends his summers on European beaches with models. I'm way out of my depth.

"You look hot," Megan says from the driver's seat when she and the guys pick me up, eyeing my black leggings and heeled boots paired with my leather jacket. Raj echoes his approval.

"It's very 'cat burglar chic,'" Zane corrects from the back seat as I slide into the front.

It's too late to second-guess my clothing choice. I flipped through my closet for something without grease stains. A little mascara and lip gloss and I looked like a woman at least a few hours removed from the garage. Whatever my mom didn't pass down to me, I got her curves.

"Any statement from Dekker?" Megan's attention flicks to the rearview, where Zane is swiping on his phone.

"Nothing public. He's probably too busy getting drunk and hoping he'll wake up and find out it was all a bad dream."

"Or maybe he lawyered up." Megan cuts me a glance.

"ARI's still tied for first in the team championship. And Navarro's having a good season. Does Luca really think a reserve driver will help them?" Raj muses.

"I don't know." I think back to the other night at the ARI garage. "Luca seems like someone who only cares about winning."

When we get to the Ashfords' mansion, we're greeted by flashing lights outside the gate.

"Cops?"

Zane follows my gaze. "On Ashford payroll."

We head up to the house, if you can call it that. The sprawling manor is all columns and stone. I expect to see a gargoyle or two, but there's nothing when I head in the doors.

Megan said the entire school was invited, and there must be a hundred unfamiliar faces at least. The girls are in short skirts and heels. The guys in dress shirts and shoes that probably cost more than our mortgage payment.

A massive chandelier takes up the foyer, highlighting a double staircase. Like at school, photos line the walls. Unlike the ones on campus, there's a uniformity to these. It takes me a moment to put my finger on it. They're all win pictures. At the center of each photo is a trophy, an award, a bottle of champagne mid-spray.

No sweat or blood or sacrifice. Only the prize matters.

"Please tell me you didn't come to the party to look at twenty-year-old pictures," Megan chides.

But my eyes find one photo in particular, a group of men and a woman accepting an award. I squint to make out the faces.

"Good evening, ladies and gentlemen!"

Theo Ashford's cocky voice rips my attention away. Our host appears at the top of the stairs, barefoot and grinning. His shirt hangs open, rolled at the sleeves like he's headlining a rock concert.

"Thank you all for coming. I hear it's all downhill after twenty-one, so I'm glad we can have this last time together."

A drunken chorus goes up.

"Before going any further, we have an important tradition."

That's when I notice Jameson, a shadow at his brother's back in a collared shirt and dress pants. If Theo's a sexy rock star, Jameson's giving Dracula: prince of darkness, terrible sense of humor, not above sacrificing small animals in service of living his best life.

He scans the crowd and jerks his chin once. Four drivers from school join the Ashfords on the stairs.

"Where?" one asks.

"Harmon Ave." The road in front of the house.

Theo's gaze lands on me, warming appreciatively. "You came." The slow scan down my body makes me feel like maybe I'm not underdressed after all.

The guy who gave me a hard time in class, Knox, follows Theo's gaze.

"Look. It's the girl who wanted to get some." He leers. "I'll let you ride with me, baby."

He's closer to me than Theo is, and when he reaches out to grab my waist, I'm too startled to stop him. His breath smells like liquor, and his grip is surprisingly firm. I try to pull away, but he holds fast.

Disgust and apprehension twine in my stomach. It's not fear of him hurting me, but fear of being out of control. Of not acting on my own terms.

The next second his hand is gone. Someone new steps between us.

Jameson Ashford.

The back of his shirt brushes my lips and I inhale sharply, the scent of Knox replaced with Jameson's subtle cologne.

He fists Knox's shirt to lift him up on his toes.

"What the hell, Jamie?" Knox tosses, unrepentant.

Jameson lifts a flask out of the guy's pocket. He turns it upside down and shakes, finding it empty.

"You know the rules. Get the fuck out."

Quiet falls over the crowd. Someone's cut the music, every eye in the room on this showdown.

When Jameson releases his classmate, Knox slinks off,

muttering. I wrap my arms around my body, hating the relief I feel, the confusion hot on its heels.

Knox was drunk. So? It's a party.

That's when I realize both Ashfords look surprisingly lucid. *What are they about to do that they have to be cold sober for?* A deeper foreboding sets in.

"Shotgun," Megan explains, suddenly at my ear and pulling me back toward her. "It's a race. The drivers each pick a girl, and she rolls the dice. Whatever turns up is how many shots she drinks before getting in the car. The passenger side, of course," she goes on at my expression.

"My big brother's right. The birthday boy picks first," Theo announces, scanning the crowd. His dancing eyes land back on me. "New Girl."

I look around, surprised. Some other girls are giving me dirty looks.

"You're lucky. They're the best drivers in the world," Megan says at my shoulder.

"Debatable." I think of Jameson running me over.

But I wouldn't be riding with Jameson, I'd be riding with Theo.

Maybe if Theo likes me, Jameson will stop hating me. The way he looked at me after class, I might need a protector.

I nod without being quite sure what I'm agreeing to, and hollers go up. The rest of the drivers pick their copilots. I don't see Jameson make his choice, but a blond girl who looks like a model appears at his side.

Dice come out and the girls take turns. I roll mine and come up with a three.

Three shots appear next to me, and I take a steadying breath as the scent of vodka hits my nostrils.

I can hang on to the dash. Just brace myself in the passenger seat and pray for it to be over.

Until a butler appears with a tray bearing keys and Theo lifts a set. I see the Ducati logo glint before he tosses them at his brother.

"Plot twist." He grins, and my tentative optimism evaporates.

We're not racing cars.

We're racing bikes.

5

Shay

CARS GIVE YOU the illusion of safety.

Motorbikes don't pretend.

Once the girls have had their shots, we're down at the road. I'm regretting my heeled footwear, but at least they're boots and not stilettos, like most of the others are wearing.

Theo gets on a BMW, passing me a helmet before fastening on his own. "Trial by fire, New Girl."

"Thought I'd already survived that." The comment earns me a grin as I strap mine on.

Looking at the superbike, the moon shining off the titanium, makes my stomach lurch.

Jameson gets on a Ducati Panigale. The girl wrapped behind him is wearing a short skirt, and her long bare legs have me thinking this is an even worse idea than I originally thought. She catches me watching and rests a possessive hand on Jameson's leg.

Yeah, I'm not fighting you for that one.

I go to Theo's bike, reaching for his shoulders. His body is hard and warm through his shirt. Maybe this won't be so bad after all.

Until I feel Jameson's moody eyes on us. He rocks back, pulling off his helmet and tossing his dark hair off his face. "Change of plan. Switch girls."

"What?" My heart thuds against my ribs.

Theo considers, frowning. "Do it."

No fucking way.

"I chose the route and made him drive my bike," Theo explains. "He gets to pick an advantage."

My lip curls as I eye up Jameson on the Ducati. I want to get on behind him as much as I want to cuddle with a bucket of live spiders. But everyone's watching and waiting, and drawing attention to myself isn't the best idea.

His copilot looks even more unhappy than me but she peels herself off Jameson, evidently deciding Theo's not a bad second option. I wish I felt the same about mine as I cross to the Ducati. Each step feels heavy. The music and cheering in the background might as well be happening in another universe.

While Theo's wearing the same shirt from inside, Jameson grabbed a leather jacket along the way. It should look like shit with the dress pants. Somehow, it doesn't.

"If vomiting on your head is an advantage, you're more twisted than I thought," I offer.

"Save the sweet talk." Cold eyes flash from under the helmet as someone holds up a phone with a countdown.

Three.

I scramble to swing a leg over the bike, shifting on the seat.

Two.

I scoot forward an inch. How much space can I leave between us without going flying off?

One.

"I suggest you hold the fuck on." His voice is the last thing I hear before the sound of an airhorn rips through the night.

Arrogant pr—

The bike leaps forward. I cling to Jameson, my hand still rough from the accident the other day.

My thighs are spread to accommodate his hips, and it feels startlingly intimate. His body is hard, his chest and abs a wall I suddenly wish I wasn't forced to hold quite so close. He always looks cold and composed, but this is the first time I clock that he's a living breathing person.

We're accelerating. The wind whips over us, our tires bumping across the road. I expect the front of the bike to lift, but he keeps it level. We fly along the pavement, and my shock recedes, replaced by adrenaline. When I crack my eyes open, I see the other four bikes are eating our dust.

Alcohol makes my stomach lurch. We're neck and neck with the BMW I should have been on.

Come on, Theo. I want him to beat the asshole who treats everyone, including me, like crap.

We head into a turn. I work my body closer, acting in self-preservation. Theo falters and we pull ahead an inch.

That's when everything changes.

My body was already on alert from the game and the thrill, but some new part of me is waking up.

It's not fear, or nerves.

It's want.

This part lives deep in my chest, nestled between my ribs, and it's competitive.

I'm longing to pull away from the other bikes and watch the other drivers' faces fill with dismay.

The nausea is gone. So's the pain in my hand, crowded out by adrenaline. My face is pressed into his jacket, and I can smell leather, cold night air, and something sharp and masculine underneath.

Cool. Dark. Mysterious.

My hands fist in Jameson's shirt. His abs flex underneath my grip. He might be an epic asshole. He's also a mind-blowingly good driver.

Right now, he's mine.

Faster. My arms tighten around him, my thighs pressing against the backs of his.

His heart thuds under my hand, quickening as if I willed it to. Like in this moment, we could be one person.

Our lead's growing. We're going to win.

Then the superbike hits a groove in the pavement, and my weaker arm loses grip.

I slide.

A millimeter at first, then another.

Shit. Panic surges through me. If I eat asphalt for the second time this week, it's not going to end with a scraped hand and a few bruises.

Jameson reaches back and grabs my hip, his bare hand hot through the thin fabric. His strength anchors me in place, and I'm so grateful I can forgive the way his fingers dig into my ass.

Now he's driving with one hand. If I wasn't so close to catastrophe, I'd be impressed.

Theo pulls even with us. Jameson cuts a look toward his brother.

We can still win. But at the last second, the Ducati eases off. Theo hits the finish first. I'm still shaken by the development when both bikes slow to a stop. Theo gets off first, hollering in triumph.

"You're my good luck charm," Theo calls to me, grinning.

One of the girls threw up during the race, and at least a couple more do it on the return journey, one opting to walk, her heels in her hands. Everyone heads back to the house, this time with new stories and bragging rights.

"Can I tell you a secret?" Theo asks as he follows me inside.

"Yeah." I press a hand to my chest, my heart rate starting to slow.

"That's the first time I've beat him at that. Had to take his bike to do it, too." His grin fades a little. "Don't go anywhere. I'm getting you something better to drink."

Forget that. I'm in the Ashfords' house. It's my chance to find out about the family my dad has worked for all these years.

Now I have time to study the photos from a generation ago. Luca is commanding. Powerful. Magnetic. One photo where he's looking straight at the camera leaves me cold. He's obviously a man who could let go of hardworking mechanics without a second thought. Cut loose a driver for missing a few points over a hard season.

Luca Ashford's origin story isn't a secret, but he takes every opportunity to remind the world how he fought his way up the ranks as a teenager but was passed over for a seat because there were already two British drivers established in F1. How he ultimately found a spot driving for an American team, and how he rewarded them by winning multiple world championships.

My gaze flicks to the next photo, a group shot of a bunch of men in suits standing around a race car. The two in the middle have an arm looped around each other, a trophy between them.

The man on the right is Luca Ashford. If I hadn't seen him last night, I'd recognize him from the media.

But it's the other figure that has me inhaling sharply.

My dad.

My heart kicks against my ribs, a dull alarm. Despite working on Ashford cars his entire career, he told me he barely knew Luca.

Here, though, they could be the best of friends.

"There you are." I turn back to see Theo Ashford, handsome and grinning. "This is for you. Shay," he adds, saying my name like it's a trophy as he passes me a lowball glass full of amber liquid.

The first sip tastes sweet on my tongue, chased by a low burn in my throat.

I turn back to the photos, but Theo's already steering me to the kitchen with a rallying cry of "More shots!"

❖

I'M ALREADY BUZZED when I wander outside to get some air. I can still feel the caress of Jameson's hand on my hip, hear his scornful voice in my ear.

The race comes back to me, my body thrumming with the echo of adrenaline. Do the drivers play games like Shotgun because they can get away with it? Or is that the only way they can blow off steam?

Maybe it's to feel invincible. Not made of flesh and blood, but speed and ambition.

My fingers trail along the hedge that borders the pool. In September, no one's in it. As I watch, a leaf drops off a tree and sends little ripples along the surface.

Movement on the other side makes my pulse accelerate, but whether it's the alcohol or what I've already been through tonight, I'm not afraid.

Not even when Jameson Ashford moves out of the shadows, a drink in one hand. He's graceful, measured, his body perfect under the dress pants and shirt.

"Why did you let Theo win?" My voice carries over the music echoing from the house. "Was it brotherly love? A birthday gift?"

Jameson drains the drink in a fast gulp. "Stay away from Theo."

The alcohol is definitely blurring my brain, because it sounds as if he's being protective.

"*He* chose *me* tonight."

Jameson stops opposite me across the ghostly ocean of blue, setting the glass on a nearby table with a clink. "He'll get you out of his system and we can get back to the family business."

I take a step toward one end of the pool. "Unless I get under his skin."

"Like a disease?" His scoff echoes off the concrete.

"Like a drug."

I take another step. Jameson does the same.

"You'd enjoy that," he predicts. Despite the darkness, his attention is sharp, a laser slicing through me.

"He might like it too."

I'm not sure I even believe the words, but I've never needed to prove someone wrong so badly—about this or anything.

When I reach the end of the pool, he paces a circle around me. The jacket's gone, the top button of his shirt unfastened so I can see the muscles of his throat work. The fabric clings to his strong shoulders, the hard abs I felt beneath my fingers.

"There's no happy ending for you and my brother." His voice is composed, and I wonder if it's his default setting when he's not running over classmates or threatening them.

I tilt my chin up. "You wouldn't know a happy ending if it ran you over in a Porsche."

He steps closer and I back up without thinking. The backs of my legs hit something solid.

The diving board.

When I don't move fast enough, my breasts crush against the hard planes of his chest. He's unyielding, the scorching heat from his body seeping through the layers of our clothes.

His woodsy, intoxicating scent is invading my senses again, slipping beneath all the reasons I hate him.

My body reacts instinctively, and it's not the repulsion I felt when Knox grabbed me. This is being lit up by an electric current, one that makes me want to press closer. Just like that, I'm feeling the wind racing over my back on the bike. Jameson at my front, his intensity and competence.

Our faces are inches apart. All I see are the hard lines of his mouth, the drawn brows under the fall of dark hair. I feel his heartbeat like I did on the bike.

"You don't belong here," he whispers, his breath caressing my lips, sending a shiver up my spine.

His hand comes up suddenly. He grabs me, yanking me close. Not by my neck. *By my necklace.*

"The only place you'll end up," he says, each word softer than the last, "is under an Ashford car with tire tracks up your back."

All of it hits me—the fear, the doubt, the shame. I'm alone and completely out of my depth.

My hand covers his and it's his turn to stiffen.

As if just my being here, refusing to back down, is destabilizing to him.

Laughter pours from the direction of the house, a voice I vaguely recognize as one of the other drivers. "Jameson? Where the fuck are you?"

I take advantage of his surprise to pry myself loose and run along the pool deck and out the gates.

The Ashford house is a glowing promise of sanctuary, but I don't want to face my classmates, so I stumble through the darkness, reaching for my phone to find it dead.

Damn it.

If I can get to the road, I can get a ride. But the farther I walk, the more outraged I get at Jameson Ashford. His arrogance, believing he can take what he wants and control everyone else. Exactly like Luca. Judging from the photos in this house, my dad was even more important than I thought. Yet his job was at risk for taking a few weeks of leave.

The modern, single-story rectangular outbuilding I come across is bigger than my house, with a garage door on one side, and a standard door next to it.

No signs of life, but maybe there's a phone I can use. I try the door handle, relieved when it turns. I push it in, feeling along the side for the lights.

The building hums to life, a cascade of fluorescents illuminating several cars. The closest to me is the Porsche 911 Turbo.

Jameson's Porsche 911 Turbo.

No one is guarding it. They probably don't even have security inside their gates because no one would dare touch their things.

I glance over my shoulder in the direction of the house. There are no windows in this garage. The stainless steel workbenches on two sides are equipped with tools.

Blood throbs in my veins.

I'm supposed to fly under the radar. Go about my business, collect my Ashford credits, and get out of this world that's so far from my own.

I grab my necklace, still warm from his hand.

Jameson Ashford is an entitled asshole and he's owed some vengeance.

When I crawl under his car, it's the most powerful I've felt all week.

6

Jameson

THERE ARE TWO kinds of winners in the world.

Those who win by luck. They're in the right place at the right time, and circumstance handed them a favorable coin flip.

And others who win because they're undeniable. Every move is engineered, every strength honed, every weakness eliminated until winning isn't merely probable. It's inevitable.

I spend every day of my life trying to become the second and shed my reputation as the first.

Waking up every day in a ten-bedroom estate home with staff and one of the best car collections in the country doesn't make that easy.

"Morning, brother," Theo calls from across the island in the kitchen when I enter.

The party raged until the early hours of the morning when I signaled to the staff to clear the house. Despite how efficiently they shut it down—twenty minutes and the last drunk slob was put in a cab, because we might be indulgent, but we have a name to protect—I couldn't sleep.

Thousand-thread-count sheets are bullshit. Rest is one luxury I can't afford.

"We have media this afternoon," I tell him.

"According to who?"

His pajamas hang off his hips, his hair a mess that makes me itch to smooth my own. There's a half-eaten bowl of cereal in front of him. An entire staff waits ready to make him a protein shake or custom breakfast, but he eats Cheerios.

"According to our calendar."

My head thuds dully. The sunlight that cracks in the window doesn't help.

Most traces of the party are gone, except for a shot glass on a table in the hall that I collect myself.

"You're not dressed," I point out.

"I'm wearing my weekend best," he counters, snapping the waistband on his plaid pajama pants.

I resist the impulse to look down at my own clothes—chinos and a button-down.

We're only a year apart in age, but some days it feels like more.

Most days.

Considering we share a house, a father, and an intended career path, we're starkly different. Driving is all I've ever wanted. Since we started in karts as kids, it called to me. When you lock in and find the right braking point in a turn, accelerate around a curve . . .

It's holy.

I love being on the track. Love every moment of the effort, the intensity.

Not a day goes by that I'm not practicing driving, or at least thinking about it. It's an obsession. Without driving, I would be nobody.

Theo, by contrast, enjoys the thrill the same way he enjoys spending money or having sex. He thinks responsibility is below his pay grade. He has no business being as fucking fast as he is.

When I took a development year after karts—simulator work, private testing, no classes—Theo moved straight through.

Do I resent how easily it comes to him? Sure.

My path to an F1 car might be more direct than most thanks to my family, but it's still not guaranteed. ARI is a billion-dollar company with a ruthless streak and competition for every job. I need the strength, focus, reflexes, and stamina that most people will never possess to have a chance at it.

I cut a look toward the stairs. Knowing my brother, some girl's going to come down any moment and disrupt our peace.

"No." He shakes me off with a dismissive wave. For a partier and a dilettante, my brother can be oddly perceptive.

I scratch my abs and go to the coffee machine. There are scant few moments of peace and quiet, and I value these. I pull a double espresso the way my brother likes it best and slide it over. "For the birthday boy."

"You're hoping I forget that I won at Shotgun." Theo grins, the same charming smile that endears every living creature to him, myself included.

"Impossible."

"You liked it." He takes a drink, watching me over the rim.

My arms fold across my chest. "What?"

"You were enjoying yourself. I've never seen you enjoy losing before."

"Trick of the light."

People are always coming up with ways to divide us. I suppose the narratives write themselves.

Two brothers.

One prize.

Our family legacy is the most lucrative one on the grid. Endorsements, media, it's all part of a giant machine we've been entwined with since birth.

It's like being royal, if crown princes had to pull 5Gs as part of the job description.

But at the end of the day, we're still blood. We've always been able to come together despite our differences.

Until now.

Since the news about Dekker's firing, everyone's talking about him. But the only thing I can think of is who will be the new driver.

"Have you heard from Dekker?" Theo's thinking of it too.

"No." I've met ARI's second driver a handful of times, but I did watch his brief media appearance, tight-lipped monosyllabic answers about his performance and whether he saw it coming.

"Don't look so worried. It'll be you. We both know it."

A noise outside has my brother moving to the window. "It's here. Let's go."

I follow him outside. If he's self-conscious being in front of the delivery people in pajamas, he doesn't let on.

They unload the car. A sporty red Lambo.

"She's something else, huh? Happy birthday to me."

"Luca's favorite sons." Parker's voice has us turning.

"His only sons," Theo counters.

Our father's business manager looks impeccable as always. Parker's a stand-in for Luca. He dresses as if wearing the most expensive suit will make us forget he's not actually our father.

"Luca's sorry he missed last night." Parker crosses to Theo and gives him a pat on the shoulder. He doesn't comment on Theo's wardrobe.

"Have you eaten, Parker? There are Cheerios inside," Theo offers graciously.

"I have, thank you." To his credit, Parker doesn't blink.

"Busy with what?" I prompt.

He hesitates. "You've heard that Dekker is out."

"Everyone's heard," Theo says.

"How will he be replaced?" I ask.

Parker's smile flickers. "That's what your father is discussing with the board."

Our father could pluck a driver from any other team, drop a lucrative contract at the most successful team in the sport.

Or he could decide it's my time.

I'm twenty-two. I have the super license I need to race.

Still . . . before the firing, I figured we had another season, possibly two, before there would be a job opening on the family team. Now, it looks like the timeline is moving up.

Adrenaline surges through me, possibility chased with determination.

I've wanted to drive my entire life. Luca knows it. I'm faster than Theo, sharper, more mature.

And I'm ready.

❖

"I'LL DRIVE," THEO decides as we head to the garage.

"No." I hit the power button on the garage door and it lifts, revealing the Porsche.

"It's my birthday."

"And you can do whatever the fuck you want after media."

I shift into the car and start the engine. The hairs on my neck lift.

Theo's jabbering on about something. "Jamie, are you even listening?!"

No, I'm listening to my car. It's talking more than normal. Whispering something I can't quite hear.

I shake it off and drive the route from memory.

My shoulders knot as we pass the spot on the road where we had that showdown. Theo doesn't comment on my route, or the girl we hit.

We.

Because we can argue behind closed doors, but in public, one Ashford stands for all of us. Twenty-first-century goddamned Musketeers.

Theo had to walk her to campus. Because, as my luck would have it, she goes to the academy too.

"She's something else." Theo pulls out his phone as we reach the end of the street. I glance over to see the name New Girl at the top of a text chain.

She made an impression on my brother. I knew it the moment he helped her up, how he smiled at her in class while she eviscerated me, the way he grabbed on to her at the party.

"A stray dog," I reply.

It took more effort than usual to scare her off.

"This time, you're wrong." He shoots me side-eye. "You don't think she's hot?"

Flashbacks of the party hit me. Her defiant eyes, pointy nose, and full mouth. The messy hair falling past her shoulders and the all-black clothing clinging to her slow curves.

She didn't want to switch bikes, but then surprised me by not only hanging on but leaning in. I remember the feel of her thighs against mine, the weight of her body pressed to my back.

You wouldn't know a happy ending if it ran you over in a Porsche. Her words replay in my mind. So does the way she lifted her stubborn chin, the rebelliousness as she refused to look away.

I shake myself, realizing my brother's still waiting for an answer.

"A lot of girls are hot. That doesn't make them worth your attention."

"She definitely deserves my attention." The humor in his voice irritates me. "What you mean is she doesn't deserve yours."

The hairs on my neck lift again.

I punch the accelerator, a move that's couched in years of practice. The car barely picks up.

No.

I try again, certain it was a glitch. Same response.

"What the fuck happened?" Theo looks over at me.

I ease the car into the parking lot at ARI headquarters. My hands are shaking on the wheel as I kill the engine.

"You coming?" Theo asks. "You're the one who wanted to be on time."

"In a minute," I snap.

Theo shrugs and steps out of the car, heading for the suit-clad PR person designated to meet us by the front doors.

My head falls back against the headrest. In the midst of the most important week of my life, someone's been inside my car. Under the hood. Touching things they shouldn't.

My teeth grind like bad gears.

This isn't a setback.

This is war.

7

Shay

"SHAY?" DAD CALLS out the door. "Where are you going?"

The biggest problem with lying isn't the risk of getting caught. It's that lying gets easier the more you do it.

"The Junction," I toss. I'm stopping by the diner on my way to school, so it's not an outright lie.

"I made breakfast." His voice and the sound of his shoes scuffing the doormat have me looking back. He's leaning awkwardly to the left as if trying to distance himself from the slow, painful healing around his new artificial knee.

Oof. Dad guilt, next level.

I shoulder my backpack—heavy thanks to the second Ashford bag inside it along with my laptop and books—then check my phone. I have time, but barely.

Ducking back into the house, I grab two plates and drop into a seat at our small kitchen table. Eggs and bacon are already laid out. My pancakes are cut into stars, like he's done since I was a kid and never stopped.

Dad's always been sturdy, and it never occurred to me that at fifty-five he was less than superhuman until his doctor showed us a scan of exactly how wrecked Dad's knee was from decades working in the garage.

Now, I can see more of his graying hair than usual.

Dad's gaze falls to my scraped palm, regret flickering across his face. "A smart girl like you should be in college, not burning your hands on coffeepots."

"I'm exactly where I should be."

By the second week of the semester, I'm starting to get into a rhythm. Popping antacids, lying to my father. It's easy to forget that each moment could be the one I slip up.

When the surgeon's office confirmed the timing for Dad's knee replacement, I asked if I could take a semester off my college automotive engineering program to stay home and take care of him. The administrator at Ohio State told me they don't do semesters off and couldn't promise to hold a spot in my program. "You're in automotive engineering. Why don't you transfer to Ashford Academy, since you're in the area?" she suggested.

I think she was joking, because it's nearly impossible to get in. I applied anyway without telling a soul. When I got accepted, I read the email on my cracked phone screen in my bedroom, nerves and excitement colliding in my stomach.

There was only one downside, and he's seated across from me.

"How well do you know the Ashfords?" I ask Dad now, pushing my eggs around my plate.

Dad bumps his drinking glass. "Enough to know they're trouble."

"They can't be that bad. You've worked for them for two decades."

"Just because I work for them doesn't mean they're good people. Least they haven't stopped sending a paycheck while I've been off.

"Speaking of the garage," he goes on, "I should call my supervisor to check in."

"No!" I clear my throat, alarm rising up. "Keane knows you're on the mend and when you'll be back. He doesn't need daily updates."

"Maybe you're right." Dad winces, probably from a twinge in his knee, but relief sags through me.

It's harder than I figured keeping two secrets from him.

"It'll all be worth it when we can open our own garage," I remind us both.

"Only once you finish college."

I roll my eyes.

Since I was young, we watched racing together on TV, but he refused to let me into his work at ARI. He was every bit as resolute the handful of times I mentioned Ashford Academy.

I was allowed to love F1, to be a fan with him, to mess around with cars in our own garage once he realized he'd have to padlock the door to keep me out. But anything more serious was off-limits. When I joked in high school about going to the academy, his reaction took on a new edge.

"That world is not for you," he said in a shaky voice I'd rarely heard him use. "Racing is dangerous. Full of greed and ego and . . ."

"Toxic masculinity? I can handle it."

He thinks I picked up a few day shifts at the diner. He'd never approve if he knew the truth.

Now I finish my toast and cut a look at the clock. "Okay, now I really have to run." Our stomachs full, I grab both our plates and drop them in the dishwasher.

I collect my bag, but before I can head for the door, Dad's out of his seat and waving me in for a hug.

"They would be proud of who you've become," he murmurs, the strength of his arms making up for the shakiness of his legs.

He's been weirdly sentimental lately, but I hug him back, my left elbow stiff. It's so subtle I barely notice it anymore, but on a cold day, or when I've been working a lot, the ache is still there.

I jump in the Mustang and head into town, making a stop on the way.

The Junction is a local institution, a diner dating back to when kids drag-raced Chevys on the main street. They've kept the uniforms and the jukebox, because there's no point messing with perfection.

"There she is! I was starting to think you were dead." Bree's expression brightens as I swing in the door.

As familiar as The Junction is to locals, that's how Bree feels to me. When I started first grade, I struggled to fit in. When one of the boys broke a strap on Bree's backpack, I helped her fix it. She told me I would be her friend and that we'd make our own games from then on out.

"I miss your face. I should see it more since I'm supposed to be covering for you." Bree moves seamlessly between the kitchen fridge and the pass-through, tattoos peeking out from under her short sleeves.

"You will. Once I get caught up with school." I duck behind the pass to pour two coffees.

At Ohio State, I'd never felt behind, even as a freshman last year. After just one week, it's like I'm running just to keep up.

There are only a scattering of patrons and Bree keeps one eye on them while we work, her blond braids bobbing.

Bree has my back on scheduling, and if Dad called The Junction looking for me, she promised to let me know so I can call him back.

I finish pouring the coffees, wincing as my right hand stings. I turn over my palm to the red burns that have faded but not disappeared.

"Shit. What happened?" Bree demands.

I glance around to ensure no one's in earshot, then lower my voice. "Jameson Ashford hit me with his Porsche."

"You met Jameson Ashford!" She blinks. "I mean. Please tell me you're okay."

"Fine." I laugh, and it eases an ache in my chest. I didn't even realize how much I needed the relief before now.

Bree inspects me, satisfied I'm not irreparably damaged. "Is he as gorgeous as he looks online?"

My mind's already conjuring an image of him, tall and dark and welcoming as a storm cloud. One with a square jaw and accusing eyes, and sure, the kind of body it was impossible not to appreciate when I was forced onto the Ducati.

"He's an asshole."

"Not what I asked."

My phone buzzes with a text and I glance at it.

"Is that the prick who ran you over?" Bree's knuckles flex.

"No. It's"—Theo's name flashes up at me, and my heart speeds up—"his brother."

I reread our message chain, right up to the newest one.

THEO: Thanks for coming Friday night.

SHAY: I should have brought a birthday present.

THEO: Your presence was enough of a gift.

THEO: Actually, scratch that. I want to see you again. That'll be my gift 😉

Bree gasps. "Theo Ashford has your phone number."

Without waiting for an answer, she pulls out her phone, typing furiously before turning the screen. A social media account that can only be described as a shrine to Theo Ashford boasts dozens of photos.

His golden hair and that eighth-wonder-of-the-world grin. His lean, strong body and easy charm. That unbuttoned shirt and just-fucked look in nearly every photo.

"This Theo Ashford? Sexiest man under twenty-five Theo Ashford?"

"Didn't realize you were a stalker." The way her eyes are shining, I'm only half joking, but she has a point.

"No, I just don't live under a rock." Bree shakes her head, bewildered. "You've slept with two guys in your life. Your idea of a date in high school was talking some boy through repairing his car in the movie theater parking lot. Now one Ashford hits you with his car and you're practically dating the other. Who are you?"

"I'm nobody," I insist. "Same as last week."

But that's not entirely true. I feel different—more alive. As if for the past year or more, I was going through the motions until I was shaken conscious.

I start toward the door but pivot as I have a thought.

"On Friday, I saw pictures I've never seen before of Dad with Luca Ashford."

"So?"

"So they looked almost . . . cozy." I huff out a breath. "He's worked in the garage at HQ for two decades, but he never let on that he knew Luca personally."

Bree frowns. "Let me teach you about priorities. Finding out why your dad knows Luca Ashford." She holds one hand flat at her waist. "Getting railed by the most beautiful guy you've ever met in real life." The same hand shoots above her head.

I can't stop the eye roll. "He does have an amazing smile," I concede, heading for the door.

"All the better to eat you with!" she calls after me.

❖

"GREATNESS ISN'T BUILT from the ground up, but on the shoulders of those who came before," Luca Ashford intones from the stage.

In case we didn't know it was Legacy Day at Ashford on Monday, the flying banners proclaiming it in ARI colors would clue us in. It feels less like a school and more like a medieval castle hosting a jousting tournament.

"If tradition is so important, it's a wonder we aren't still racing horses instead of cars?" Megan whispers to me as we stand a few rows deep in the massive crowd, along with Raj and Zane.

Going to Ashford these first few days has been a wild ride, but my new friends make it better. Raj is an eternal optimist who brings his electric scooter everywhere he can and a few places he shouldn't.

Zane loves designer clothes almost as much as the novelty socks poking out above expensive loafers in class.

Megan's love of cars is only rivaled by her obsession with K-pop. The lockers we have near the garage at the academy are for storing our books and gear, but hers is filled with posters of her favorite groups. From the way she talks about her siblings being the "good children," I'm guessing she's the black sheep of her family.

And by black sheep I mean rainbow sheep dipped in glitter.

"Dekker's not here," Raj notes. "The drivers always participate in Legacy Day," he fills in for my benefit.

Navarro, the other ARI driver, who presumably still has a job, is standing offstage talking with execs wearing suits.

"He's probably just sore about being fired." Zane glances around.

My attention drifts to where Jameson and Theo flank their father onstage. Bookends, but hardly matching. Today, they're both in suits. Jameson's wearing a tie, Theo's shirt is open at the collar.

Theo catches my eye and winks.

He does have an amazing smile.

All the better to eat you with.

Does that mean his mouth is good at everything? Hypothetically, of course. I chew on my lip like I'm pondering a serious scientific question as my gaze reluctantly lands on his brother.

If Theo is the golden retriever, Jameson is the black cat. Prickly, untouchable, beautiful in the way that icebergs and diamonds and other things that could kill you are beautiful.

Here's hoping that he hasn't noticed my handiwork from Friday. I'm not proud of what I did, but I was angry and the Porsche was *right there.* Perfect. Tempting.

"And in a few short months, we'll be passing the torch to one worthy new driver," Luca continues. "And, we have an exciting announcement. Our new driver . . . will be someone in this room."

A buzz rips through the crowd and Theo cuts a look at his brother. *He didn't know.* From this angle I can't see Jameson's face to gauge his reaction.

"ARI is sponsoring an exclusive three-race series." Luca raises his voice to be heard over the exclamations. "The Challenger Championship is open to driver-track students at Ashford Academy holding a racing license. The top ten interested drivers based on lifetime F2 and F3 performance are eligible. Points will be totaled across the series and the winner will be offered a contract to drive for ARI starting next season."

The buzz escalates to gasps, shrieks, and rapid-fire conversation as Luca explains the details. Three months of racing major venues across the country, to mimic the travel of F1 while keeping the focus stateside. The first in October, the second in November, and the final race in December.

What rocks the entire school though, as well as me and my

friends, is the news that the new driver could be either Ashford son . . . or someone else entirely.

Luca waves his hands at the audience, and the noise diminishes slightly.

"Before our technical teams feel left out, ARI is also running a contest for an internship to work next year's season on the grid. Engineering track students will have until the end of this semester to make your case for the internship."

"How many spots are there?" a student calls from the crowd.

"One. A paid role, like everyone else on the grid."

I straighten. Someone will have a chance at working on the grid. Not someday, but a few months from now.

"Holy shit," Megan says numbly as we file out.

"This is unprecedented," Zane says. "I figured Luca was an asshole, but I didn't see him holding a pro-racing edition of the Hunger Games."

Once we reach the hallway, we're ushered by staff toward two lines in the foyer to pick up our name tags.

"Catch up with you guys at lunch?" I tell my friends once I get mine.

I run to the bathroom, still thinking of Luca's announcement.

Not the driver one—the engineer one. It's a dream job for someone who wants to work with F1 cars and experience the thrill and pace of the grid firsthand.

A tingling hum vibrates through my chest, filling my body.

When I emerge, the main hall is busier than before. Lunch is opposite the atrium, which is now swarmed with people.

The crowd is at my back, my front, my sides. I fall into the flow of traffic, craning my neck to see if Megan or the guys are anywhere near.

But it's not any of them I meet first. Jameson's voice at my ear is cold enough to freeze me in my tracks.

"Tell me what the fuck you did to my car."

8

Shay

THERE'S NO WAY out. Hundreds of students and ARI staff fill the space, all of them going nowhere quickly.

Jameson's tall and imposing at my back.

"I don't know what you're talking about." I pray for the crowd to move faster, my pulse racing.

No such luck.

"You put a limiter on my engine revs."

My mouth falls open. "Then why did you ask me?"

"To hear you say it."

The crowd moves, and Jameson's body brushes my back. My ass.

Breathing is suddenly impossible.

"You hacked my ride, Townie." His voice is close to my ear, his words a whisper. "I know it was you. If I tell someone you did this, you'll be expelled in five minutes."

Reality slices through the haze of awareness. Getting expelled would mean no engineering degree. No garage with my dad.

I fist the strap of my book bag in my hand, my palm healing

but still rough. My finger brushes the ring hanging from my necklace. Deep in my chest, the sensation I felt Friday night starts up again. The rebellion that had me breaking into his car in the first place.

No. I'm not going down like this.

"But what a fascinating five minutes it'd be." I sound more confident than I am. "I'm sure the administration would love to hear how you hit me with your car. Probably the police, too."

There's a beat before he responds. "They won't arrest an Ashford."

I shrug, and that tiny movement has my shoulder rubbing his chest through our clothes. I clock every spot we touch.

"Either way, it'll make for a fun chat given the ARI seat your father just announced is up for grabs. Is it smart business to put a driver with an accident on their record in the fastest car in the world? One with sponsor names covering every inch? I bet they'd at least like to see photos of my injuries."

It's a calculated bluff. I pray he can't tell, that the heart hammering against my ribs doesn't betray me. I've never threatened anyone in my life and it's either the bravest or the stupidest thing I've ever done.

From the sharp inhale at my back, his chest pressing into my shoulder blades, it worked.

That's right, asshole. You don't run the world.

But before I can move, he grabs my shoulder and spins me to face him. My toes bump his and any semblance of personal space is as laughable as it was on the Ducati Friday night.

Jameson grabs my wrist and yanks up my sleeve.

"This injury?" His fingers press against the faded two-inch scar on my elbow.

My body jerks. Forget the subtle crowding of the hall. The way he's touching my skin feels like a brand.

Any borrowed courage evaporates and I yank my arm back, my heart hammering against my ribs.

"That is none of your business."

I don't have time to appreciate the surprise on his face before I shove through a nonexistent gap in the crowd and take off toward the lunchroom.

❖

THE AFTERNOON IS a blur.

Through the lectures, demonstrations, and games with my friends, I'm rattled by my confrontation with Jameson, but that's not the only thing on my mind.

There's a bonfire on the campus quad scheduled for the end of the evening—a final chance to remember the glory of the past before we refocus on the future, according to Luca. Megan, Raj, and Zane are across the quad talking to some other engineers.

I could be there too, but instead I'm staring into the fire by myself. It's easier than confronting how everyone is obsessed with where they came from.

Maybe if I hadn't lost all of that years ago, I could relate.

My throat burns from the smoke. I should be making a plan for how to handle Jameson's threat but can't focus. I spot a few other students around the perimeter of the fire, each wearing their own name tag proudly as if it means something.

"This is bullshit," I mutter to myself, peeling off my name tag and tossing it in the fire.

"That sticker you just turned into barbecue was recyclable, you know." Theo Ashford's amused voice has me wiping a sleeve over the corner of my eye. I'm not sure how he got here, but as he moves to stand next to me, I'm not mad about it.

"So let me guess," I start. "Your dad didn't tell you about this championship series?"

"Nope. He didn't even tell my brother."

I cock my head. "You're surprised."

"That's an understatement." Theo sizes me up. "Jamie's the son he always wanted. I'm not even supposed to be here except my mother got pregnant and fucked everything up with the most inconvenient timing."

I feel his hurt, even if he's smiling through it. "That's on your dad. Not on you."

"He doesn't see it that way. I'm his backup in case of emergency. A crude copy of his perfect son." Theo leans in. "But it's hard to be upset about that now I'm here with you."

Somehow, I feel the same about him. Now that Theo's here, I can almost believe we could be any two people on any campus in the world, enjoying a bonfire.

"Tell me, did Jamie warn you off?" he asks.

I can't help laughing, mostly at the idea of anyone daring to call Jameson "Jamie." "Something like that."

Theo shakes his head. "He wants to keep me out of trouble."

"And he thinks I'm trouble," I guess.

"Yup. And I'm trying to get into you." This time, we both grin. Theo inches closer to the fire, closer to me.

"I can't let that slide," I groan. "I'm sorry. That's a terrible innuendo."

"You're right. I take it back."

"The words or the sentiment?"

He cocks his head, looking so roguish I'm starting to think he practices it in front of a mirror. "Which do you want me to take back?"

My arms fold as I study him. "I'll get back to you."

Theo nods approvingly. "You do that."

I don't feel self-conscious. Theo's like the sun and I didn't notice how cold I was until he turned his attention on me.

A server comes by with s'mores ingredients and pokers. I build my s'more and toast it over the growing bonfire, and Theo makes one of his own. Mine is decent while his comes out a gooey mess.

"You want more?" He licks marshmallow off his thumb. It should be gross. Instead, it's sexy.

"More?"

"Dessert." But there's a glint in his eye.

"I'm good. Thanks." I turn back toward the fire, embarrassed by the sudden flush in my cheeks. I try to think of something that's not how drawn I am to him.

The crowd ebbs and flows around us. Theo acknowledges the odd person who calls out to him, but not once does he take a step back from me.

"What can you tell me about working for Ashford Racing?" I ask after a moment.

If it's a hard right, he goes with it. "What do you want to know?"

I recall the photo I saw at his house. "I think my father worked on the grid a long time ago, but he doesn't like to talk about it."

"There would be records. The administration building on

campus." Theo wipes his fingers with a napkin. "I thought you were asking for an inside scoop on the grid internship."

"Oh. I don't think that's in my future." I'm supposed to finish my degree and then open that garage my dad and I have been dreaming about. "But you must be planning to race for the ARI seat?"

"Race, yes. Win? That's another question." He laughs.

I square to face him again, the toes of my sneakers brushing his. "But you're fast. I've seen your race footage."

"I'm flattered. But fast isn't enough. Since we were kids, Jamie's always been number one and I'm number two. Not that it's all bad. When you're in second place, everyone wants to be your friend. If you're in first, you have a bullseye on your back."

I wrap my arms around myself. "Maybe the real question is whether you're willing to have a few less friends in order to be number one."

He lifts a brow like I've surprised him. The firelight dancing on his face makes him seem even brighter.

An ember darts out of the fire and lands on his sneaker. I stomp it out. The moment I do, another one sizzles into the edge of his shoe.

"Shit." Another stomp, but this time, I lose my balance.

He grabs my waist. "Got you."

Theo's gaze drops to my mouth and my stomach flips. It takes everything in me not to bite my lip. The flames suddenly feel like the second most intense heat source in my immediate surroundings.

He pulls me back a step. "Better?"

My tongue darts out to wet my lips. "Yes."

No. Because now he's filling my entire field of vision. His hair falls across his face and I'm not sure how I thought he looked like an angel because his expression is way too wicked.

"Did you decide yet?" he asks. "If you want me to withdraw my intentions."

The hairs on my arms lift. No one should be this magnetic, it's actually unfair.

"I'm giving it a lot of thought."

Usually when his mouth curves, it's quick. Reflexive.

This time, it's slow. Every second has my stomach flipping over.

"Well, that's something at least."

I'm wondering again how talented his mouth is. The tingling between my thighs might be an answer.

A student I don't recognize runs between us and the fire, bumping into us and breaking the spell.

I'm relieved and disappointed by the interruption.

"Tell me this." Theo's words are light, but there's a seriousness about him that's new. "If I win, will you be cheering in the front row?"

I nod to the clusters of students around the fire, the gazes that return to him over and over. "You already have a huge fan club."

"The thing is, New Girl . . ." He bends toward my ear, my hands grabbing for his biceps to steady myself.

"I'd rather hear you shouting my name."

9

Shay

BLOND HAIR. BLUE eyes. A cocky grin.

Theo Ashford's hard body presses against me.

His shirt's unbuttoned as always, no tee underneath. His body is ridged and muscled, and the sight of him has my throat drying.

He takes my face between his hands and I'm already breathing heavily. Those eyes cloud with longing. "I want you so fucking bad, New Girl."

Before I can respond, his lips brush down my neck.

Pleasure lights me up, an ache that's sweet and torturous at once.

I push his shirt off his shoulders, revealing hard muscles that bunch when he starts down my body. The heat of his mouth finds my shoulder, my collarbone, starts lower between my breasts.

I arch into him, my eyes closing on a sigh. Theo Ashford is already outdoing every guy I've ever been with and we haven't even hooked up in real life.

A rhythmic shuffling sound cuts into my dream. *Clunk. Clunk.*

"Shay!"

I blink my eyes open and wipe my mouth. I'm curled up in the cab of my dad's truck parked in our home garage.

"Shay? You out there?" Dad's voice calls from outside.

I slam my textbook shut and stow it under the seat. A week into the semester, I have them littered all over the house in whatever hiding places I can find.

"What're you doing?" he asks, appearing in the doorframe.

"Trying to modify this to make it easy for you to drive once you're given the okay."

His eyes crinkle as he braces a hand on the doorframe, easing his weight off his bad knee. "You're too good to me. And optimistic—based on the physio schedule the doctors recommended starting in another week, I might not survive long enough to drive again. Now come inside for dinner."

He heads back toward the house and my shoulders slump in relief. Despite a couple of close calls, I haven't had any major mishaps. He still thinks I'm working at the diner during the day and out with friends at night.

I even kept my poker face through the entire broadcast of the F1 race over the weekend, the two of us chirping about race strategy, summer break gossip, and the Dekker firing.

Now my phone vibrates with a text.

THEO: Tell me how amazing I am.

SHAY: At . . . ?

THEO: Lots of things, now that you mention it. I have exceptional hands. Unbelievable stamina 😉

My dream comes back, warmth tingling between my thighs.

THEO: But today, I did a drive by the admin building. Found something interesting . . . Your dad has a file at the academy.

SHAY: You mean a file at ARI.

THEO: No. The academy.

What the hell? Why would my dad have a file at the academy? Surprise blurs with unease.

I shift out of the truck, shoving the phone in my pocket as I try to make sense of Theo's words.

I'm on autopilot as I head into the house, taking off my shoes and washing up at the sink before I dry my hands and pull my phone out again.

SHAY: What was in it?

The three dots blink up at me. Then Theo's message loads.

THEO: Got interrupted before I could explore any further.

The hairs on my neck lift.

"What the hell is going on," I mutter, my pulse kicking.

"That's what I'd like to know," Dad says from behind me, holding up my schoolbag. "Is there something you want to tell me?"

Shit.

"You've been going to the academy." Dad's voice is full of accusation. More than that, there's betrayal.

The guilt that's been simmering in my stomach boils over like acid in my throat.

"Yes."

"Since when?"

"The start of the semester. You got hurt and I couldn't go to back to college this semester."

"You could have." He makes it sound simple when it was anything but.

"I didn't want to! I figured I could take a semester of courses at the academy, then transfer those credits once you're on your feet."

He drops my bag on the table as if he can't stand to touch it.

"How many times have I told you to stay away from the Ashfords?"

Dad's clearly overreacting. I'm an adult and this was entirely my decision. "This has nothing to do with them. I'm getting credit for the semester I need to stay in town. It's not a big deal."

He exhales hard. "Did I push you into this? Make you think you couldn't talk to me?"

"No. If anything, you try too hard to protect me." I think of how I'm covering his shifts at the garage. "When were you going to tell me that you went to the academy?"

His face freezes in confusion. "I didn't."

"Then why do you have a file there?"

His eyes flash. "You're grounded."

The whiplash is getting to me more than the disagreement.

"We're not going to have a conversation like normal people?" I say it as if we aren't both better at communicating with cars.

"Not about this."

My mouth falls open. "You've never grounded me in my life!"

"Well, I'm starting now."

"I'm twenty. You missed your window."

He bellows in frustration. "Then I'm taking your car until you come to your senses."

✥

THERE'S A GOOD reason I don't walk anywhere from my house. Living on the outskirts of town, the closest destination is the gas station, which is still a twenty-minute walk. Ashford Academy is an hour-plus, and I missed the only bus that would deliver me anywhere in the vicinity.

I'm taking your car until you come to your senses.

My dad's barking voice yesterday echoes in my head as I start up the street.

The roiling in my gut isn't only anger. It's regret. A week and a half is all it took him to find out. I'm not sure how long I figured I'd keep it up, but at least until he could go back to work.

I can't remember the last time he was this upset with me. What if the idea was doomed from the start? I don't belong at Ashford. Thinking I could fit into that world was misguided.

The storm clouds overhead threaten to erupt as a text comes in from Megan.

MEGAN: Are we meeting up before class?

I consider calling Theo, but I'm too ashamed to explain. My problems are mundane compared to his—living in a mansion, racing for an F1 seat and multimillion-dollar contract.

It takes me a few minutes on the Ashford student web portal to find what I'm looking for: the drop form. A few clicks and I could be pulled out of school entirely. It'd be like I never went there.

Raindrops plop on my phone screen. I tip my face up and catch another on my nose. Then three. Then five.

There's no way for today to get worse, I think.

Then the last car I would want to see pulls up beside me, shining in the corner of my eye.

Porsche 911 Turbo.

I was wrong. What's worse is hitting rock bottom and Jameson Ashford witnessing your fall.

I force my feet to keep moving along the gravel. The window rolls down with a smooth hum.

"Where's your Fastback, Townie?"

I ignore him. Water drips off my nose onto my lips as he continues to creep next to me.

"Vogel will drag you if you show up looking like that."

I hate his confidence, and the fact that he's probably right.

"Get in." The engine revs, the driver not bothering to hide his impatience.

"I will if you let me drive."

Jameson snorts. "Never going to happen."

But when he leans over to open the door, I'm desperate enough to comply.

My shoes splash in a puddle before I shift inside and drop into the passenger seat. Water squelches against the leather. I reach for my seat belt as we accelerate smoothly along the road.

"You didn't report me," I say.

"Been busy."

He's calm. Controlled. Not like Legacy Day.

I lean forward to wipe a drop of rain off the dash. "This time next week, I'll probably be gone anyway."

His gaze flicks over me. The drop forms on my phone feel like a weight.

I've never prayed, but right now, I pray for silence. Just a silent car ride with the person I hate most in the world.

"What happened to your arm?" he asks, looking over as if he can see the neat, faded scars through my jacket and shirt.

My eyes close. I don't want to talk about this. Not with him. "A car crash when I was four. Left me with a plate and screws."

The memories are gone. The reduced range of motion, chronic stiffness, and compensation with my other arm when I'm working are mine to keep.

Seems like a fair trade.

The car hugs the pavement through the pounding rain. Jameson handles the Porsche easily, as if it's an extension of his body and not a machine. "The driver?"

I could refuse to answer, but it seems pointless because he could find out in a snap.

"My dad. He and my mom were both killed."

Trees and buildings pass outside the passenger window, forms and colors blurring with streaked raindrops.

"You should hate cars."

When Jameson speaks, it's not an apology. He almost sounds . . . curious.

"Cars aren't the problem. People are. Cars are predictable. You never have to guess with them. When I'm working on a car, everything else is quiet. It's freeing. Not that you'd know anything about that."

Jameson scoffs. "Feeling trapped?"

"I didn't say trapped."

"You said working on a car makes you feel free. Free is the opposite of trapped." His logic irritates me. "Or perhaps you meant I know nothing about the entire world thinking it understands exactly who you are and what you're capable of."

I force my attention back to the road, but I'm thinking how it would feel to learn your own father set a gauntlet for you to prove yourself against your brother and the entire school to claim your supposed birthright.

Probably fucking terrible.

Still, not as terrible as thinking I might have something in common with Jameson Ashford.

Rain beads on the window, but the sound is drowned out by the rhythmic scrub of wipers.

"How long did it take you to hack my car?" he asks.

The change of subject has me glancing over. In the driver's seat, he's perfectly still, except his eyes flicking along the road and the little tic in his jaw.

"Twenty minutes."

"Not bad."

I frown. "How long did it take you to figure out that I limited your engine revs?"

I catch myself studying his darky, shiny hair. His straight nose. His full, hard mouth.

Stop looking at his mouth.

"Ten seconds."

My system jolts.

Driving a car takes skill. *Knowing* one takes patience, dedication, humility. Not things I'd attribute to the arrogant asshole behind the wheel.

"You could've done more damage. Why didn't you?" His voice is thoughtful.

It's the first real question he's asked me—no threat, no demand. Despite my reservations, I give him a real answer.

"I couldn't destroy something so perfect."

His eyes flick my way. Down my body, back up.

Oh fuck. Fuck me.

"The car!" I flush. "I meant the car. Not you, obviously."

How much blood can pump through your face before you're permanently red? Maybe the floor will open up and swallow me so I can stop living this humiliation.

"*You* can jump off a bridge," I add.

"High one, I suppose. Choppy water."

Jameson's laughing at me. It's not a Theo laugh, the earnest kind accompanied by an easy grin, but a mocking one that's invisible to the naked eye.

It's uncomfortable, being the subject of his interest, but for the first time I don't feel the need to run away.

When we make it to school, he ignores his reserved spot and pulls around behind the building, finding a back alley. I start to unfasten my seat belt, but his hand closes around my wrist.

"I'm going to give you some advice." His voice is stilted, as if he's wrestling with his own judgment. "Fuck them."

"Who?" I'm so focused on the feel of his strong fingers against my skin that I forget to flip him off, which is the appropriate response when Jameson Ashford deigns to meddle in your life.

"Everyone who stands in the way of what you want."

Electricity shoots up my arm and settles into a low throb in my chest.

I don't know who's more startled, me or him. But when he blinks, I realize those eyes framed by impossibly dark lashes actually aren't steel blue. They're not purple blue like cornflowers either, nor the green blue of the ocean in a travel ad. Instead, they're the warm, bright blue of a sky that's cleared after a storm.

The thought comes out of nowhere, settles between my ribs like a second heartbeat that drowns out the first.

Faster. Stronger.

My gaze drops down to where we're touching. He follows my gaze, hesitating a moment before he releases me.

I swallow and get out of the car. There's an awning overhead, but I'm more vulnerable than when I was walking to campus in the pouring rain.

10

Jameson

IT MIGHT BE the middle of September, but nobody at the academy is thinking about classes.

The first race is in less than three weeks, with a full circle of media. Despite Luca's grandstanding at Legacy Day that next year's ARI seat could be won by any driver in school, I'm determined to come out on top. I have the best race record, the best lap times in testing. My strategy is to do what I usually do, only better.

Still, everyone at ARI and the racing world has assumed for years that I would be the natural fit when there was a spot. Me included.

So what the hell is he playing at?

I won't give him the satisfaction of asking.

EDEN: Heard about the race series. You worried?

JAMESON: I'll handle it.

EDEN: You always do. But if you need a meme of Luca with his hair on fire, I'm here.

At least Eden's texts gave me a laugh. Of the three of us siblings, she's got the right idea being halfway around the world instead of living in the same house as our father.

Being the only one of us without any intention of participating in the family business helps.

She rarely comments on ARI except when it directly impacts me or Theo. So when I get another text, it has me blinking.

EDEN: Anything to these rumors that Dekker was pushed out?

JAMESON: You know I don't follow the gossip.

EDEN: This wasn't public. I heard it through my contacts.

I'm about to ask who her contacts are—Eden's eighteen, and as far as I know, my sister doesn't come close to racing if she can help it—but it's probably nothing.

JAMESON: His performance dropped this season.

EDEN: All of a sudden.

JAMESON: You're too clever to have this much time on your hands.

EDEN: You're absolutely right ☺

I have enough to think about without entertaining rumors about ARI's former driver, so I brush off her words and focus on my job.

Anyone who thinks driving a race car isn't a sport can go back to their boring Volkswagen lives. The human body isn't built to withstand the pressures of F1 racing. Not the g-force, or the heat, or the repetition. Not the mental clarity and quickness to make split-second decisions, to remake them again and again under pressure from twenty other drivers who are also equipped with impossible speed and the singular desire to be the first one across the line, no matter the cost.

That's why every week includes strength, cardio, reaction time, and mobility training. Our gym takes up an entire wing of ARI headquarters, with every machine and training implement known to man.

I'm on my second hour of pull-ups, rows, push-ups, and shoulder presses when Theo trudges in.

"You're late," I point out, glancing at the clock.

"He said it was okay." He hitches a thumb to our trainer, who follows him in.

Now I do a double take.

Theo usually skips working out with a trainer, opting to follow his own half-assed regimen.

A few other drivers come in after him.

"You missed out last night," Knox says as Theo takes up residence on the treadmill.

I start to respond that I had other things to do, but Theo's the one who answers.

"Figured I'd have an early night." My brother hits the incline and starts to run.

Theo skipped a party for a good night's sleep? There's a first.

Thirty minutes later, we both move to the Batak board.

"After you," Theo says, gesturing to the vertical panel with light-up targets arranged in a grid.

I hit the button for sprint mode, where you have to hit as many as possible in thirty seconds.

"Remember when we raced karts?" he says as I start my session, my brain focused on slapping the buttons as fast as possible when they light up. "You won every time."

"It wasn't every time." I finish, my score displaying across the top as I catch my breath.

"Sixty-two," Theo reads. "Nice."

We switch places.

He starts and he's slower. But he builds.

When the buzzer goes, the display says sixty. I blink as the smile spreads across his face.

"You usually come in the fifties," I say.

"I've been coming here all week to practice. Winning at Shotgun on my birthday reminded me that all I need is one win."

I finish my workout and head for the sauna. Knox follows me to the dry sauna in the corner. The window has a view of the rest of the gym, and I watch Theo continue to work diligently.

"It's weird, right?" Knox says.

I tilt my head back, ignoring the bead of sweat tracing its way down my face.

"Someone got in his head," Knox says, and I know immediately who it was.

Townie.

I spotted her walking in the rain, her hair plastered to her face, steps heavy with defeat.

I'd been angry with my father for how he was handling things, and feeling out of control, and when I saw her trudging along the road miles from school, I didn't want to see one more person beat down by the world.

It was a mistake. I shouldn't have pulled up next to her, or insisted she get in. I definitely shouldn't have told her to stay in school. Jameson Ashford, guidance fucking counselor, reporting for duty.

"She's not his type," I hear myself say. Theo's usual flings are flashy, outgoing partiers who want to see and be seen.

"I'd go there." Knox shifts on the bench, extending both legs and leaning against the wall.

I'm remembering the feel of her behind me on the Ducati again, her curves pressed against my back. How her pulse felt under my fingers in the car, accelerating under her soft wrist. My hand migrates to my abs, scratching the bare skin damp with sweat. "Got other things on my mind."

"Right. Driving first, last, only, huh?"

Knox's question is irritating, but he's not wrong. I can keep it together. Theo has nowhere near my focus. He's likely to fuck up his future over some girl, and while I'm fully intending to beat my brother for this seat, I'm not going to watch him throw away his life.

I flex and force my hand back to the bench. There's one thing to play for, and it all starts in three weeks.

I wipe the sweat off my face and get back to work.

11

Shay

"I'M NOT QUITTING school." I glance toward the passenger seat of my dad's truck as we cruise through town Monday morning.

"Yes, you are," Dad replies, irritated.

This morning marked the second checkup since his surgery, and since he still can't drive, it meant he couldn't avoid me any longer, either.

"It doesn't cost you anything." The academy might be harder to get into than college, but the actual tuition isn't that expensive.

"It's not about the money, Shay. If it was only that, we'd figure it out."

How? I want to ask. Because keeping "the money" coming right now means me covering his shifts.

Fuck them. Jameson Ashford's words from the car play in my mind, the soundtrack to every quiet moment I steal.

When he said it, it didn't feel like rebellion. It felt like liberation.

Still, it's one thing to defy haters at school, but I love my father. That's why I've been trying to formulate the right words to talk to him about the academy since he found out.

I pick at the steering wheel with a fingernail. "You can be as mad as you want, but the reality is, I want to work on cars. Now and for the rest of my life. You taught me how to do that," I reason.

Dad folds his arms, staring out the window.

"An automotive engineering degree from Ashford has to be at least as good as one from another school," I go on when he doesn't answer. "When else could I get this kind of opportunity?"

The realization struck me this weekend. Every day is a challenge, but for the first time in my life, I feel as if I'm the one choosing.

"If I wasn't here, I'd be at college doing who knows what," I press.

"I'd prefer who knows what as long as it's far from this place."

"Why? We've always watched racing together." Some of my best memories of him were cheering for ARI from our living room.

"Watching is safe. Being involved isn't." Dad takes a longing look at the driver's seat as if by getting behind the wheel, he could roll back time to when things were easier with us.

"Do you not remember what your surgeon said fifteen minutes ago?" I shut it down, hitching a thumb toward the rear windshield. "You can drive in another week. If the knee feels good."

He huffs out a breath. "I could use some caffeine and fresh air. Let's get a coffee and stop at the lake."

I don't argue. I shouldn't miss my first class, but this is about making all the other classes after, so it feels more important.

At the diner, I run in and wave to Bree.

"Doctor's appointment?" she asks as I dash behind the counter to pour the coffees.

"He can drive soon."

"God help us."

I slap a bill on the counter and head for the doors.

The drive to the lake is about ten minutes of winding roads. It's the other direction from school, and I've heard of people partying here at night, but in the day it's peaceful.

I help him out of the car and we sit on a picnic table together, both of us seated on the flat top with his leg propped on the seat.

"I'm taking the Fastback to the academy," I say. "It's my car. You made sure my name was on the ownership."

"Looks like a dumb idea now, doesn't it?" The wry edge to his voice gives me a tiny bit of hope as he opens his coffee. "I don't want you in that world."

"But you were in it," I insist, thinking of the framed photo at the Ashfords' mansion. "I saw a picture of you with the ARI team on the grid next to a trophy."

He doesn't say anything. A few birds call over the lake.

I pull my jacket tighter around me. "You never told me you won a championship."

"I went to the entire race calendar for years."

My mouth falls open. So much for being a factory mechanic who spent a few lucky weekends trackside.

"It was a part of my life best left in the past."

His meaning is clear: He's not interested in talking about it.

There's no making sense of that. If I'd spent that much time on the F1 circuit, working on the fastest cars with the fastest drivers, I'd never shut up about it.

I have so many questions. "Was it a total thrill?"

He shifts back on his palms, staring out into the trees. "It was unbelievable, Shay."

Anticipation thrums in my veins.

I picture being trackside for all those races, a different landscape every week. Working with the most talented engineers, mechanics, drivers. Everyone pulling together for a common goal. It doesn't matter where you come from or who your friends are. What matters is who you are on that day.

I think of Jameson that night at the ARI garage, the way the car ripped through the track, how my heart galloped off with it.

"But you walked away." I turn toward him.

He scans the scenery as if he'll find the answers there, but I sense his mind is somewhere else entirely. "The team and I encountered differences we couldn't reconcile. I couldn't bring myself to be on the grid anymore."

He's lying. I can feel it.

I bet the truth is that he adopted a little girl and couldn't keep racing at the track.

My heart aches at the thought of him missing out, but also that he's kept it from me all these years.

Birds chirp from the trees as we finish our coffees. I wait to drain the last drop before asking another question. "What about your record at the academy?"

He sets his empty cup on the tabletop next to him. I half expect him to shut me down again. He doesn't.

"I taught a mechanics course for a semester after our championship." His eyes soften a little.

"So what you're saying is that it's the best place to learn about cars. If you taught there, it must be." I'm pretty proud of my mic drop moment, but Dad only shifts forward and brushes off his hands.

"Ashford Academy might give you the education you need to work in this business," he says, wincing as he shifts to avoid putting weight on his bad leg. "But I don't want you working at Ashford."

"Dad . . ." I'm up too, steadying him.

He collects his empty cup and waves me off. "I mean it."

Landing a full-time job with the most prestigious team on the grid still feels like a wild fantasy. "You realize there's almost no chance that'll happen."

He glances back at the truck. "That's not what I'm worried about."

I MIGHT NOT technically have my dad's blessing, but it feels that way. When I drive the Fastback to campus, I swear the entire day is brighter.

I'm also giddy to see Theo, who texted me on my way.

THEO: I have something for you.

SHAY: ?

The photo loads as I slam the door and head toward the building.

SHAY: This better not be a dick pic, Ashford.

Once the photo appears, it's him wearing a white tank and a sweaty grin.

THEO: This is me getting through my workout knowing I'll see you later today.

He just happens to be in the gym, showing off seriously ripped arms.

Okay, yum. I save the photo to my phone.

For posterity, of course.

In my first class of the day, we're making ride height tweaks to optimize grip on different track conditions. The second focuses on cornering force, using software to model lateral loads through corners at Spa and Monaco.

They're a reminder that we're going to use this in the real world—if we're lucky.

"As Luca said, one student will qualify for an internship with ARI next year," Vogel says. "Your performance at the academy will form the basis for that evaluation."

I sit up straighter.

Maybe it's hard for my dad to see me here at Ashford because he doesn't realize how much I want it. Or he's afraid I'm setting myself up for disappointment.

But if I got that internship, I'd be working on actual F1 cars in a matter of months. I'm not only going to get my credits—I'm going to land this internship and make him proud after all he's given up for me.

"You okay?" Megan asks.

"I think I need another ten hours in the day to catch up." I adjust my bag on my back and fix the hair that's fallen out of my messy ponytail as we head down the hall toward lunch.

"Did you catch last weekend's race? Ignite is going to give ARI a run for their money," Raj comments as we dig into our paninis in the cafeteria.

"That's just talk. They're too new, too chaotic and undisciplined," Zane says.

"Until they aren't," Raj tosses back.

"Here's hoping ARI locks down a car for next year. I don't want to score an internship and be working on a losing team," Zane gripes.

Jameson and Theo walk by with their entourage across the cafeteria.

I've been watching a lot of footage of them racing. Theo's a straight-up street fighter. Everything is instinct with him; he never gets thrown and reacts to whatever chaos takes place on the track.

Jameson is sheer power and finesse. He knows what's going to happen before it does, putting the car in exactly the right position to be its fastest.

Either of them is the last person another driver wants to see in their mirror.

Sometimes, I watch their films a little longer than I have to—as Theo gets out of the car, grinning, the bleachers of impassioned fans erupting in the background. As Jameson pulls his helmet off, staring up at the screen for a replay with those icy blue eyes.

I'm still thinking about it when I head down the hall after lunch and collide with someone coming the other way. My bag flies off my arm, my belongings spilling out onto the floor.

Perfect. Why does every item in my bag roll? Note to self: Buy more things with edges.

I'm kneeling to collect lip balm, pens, and tampons when a low voice comes from above me.

"You didn't quit."

I look up to see Jameson Ashford wearing chinos and a preppy shirt, his dark hair a mess of waves that's probably the only soft part of him. After watching him on video, seeing his face up close is even more of a trip.

"You didn't have me expelled," I can't resist commenting as I reach for my phone, sliding it in my pocket as I straighten. "You're really slacking in the 'reign of tyranny' department this week."

Jameson's brows lift under his hair. "Reign of tyranny?"

I wave a hand. "Mean girl syndrome. Hall monitor on steroids. Whatever you call it."

"You've thought about this a lot."

"You keep crashing into me. It's hard not to."

He folds his arms, his biceps pulling at his tailored shirt. It's at eye level, which is the only reason I notice.

He gave me a ride to campus. He's still an asshole, I remind myself.

Hall traffic flows around us. I start to shoulder the bag when a cramp has me buckling. Jameson moves so fast I don't see him, grabbing my bag before it falls with one hand, the other finding my arm to steady me.

A little zing runs along my nerve endings. It's like when he grabbed my wrist in the car, but this time, he's circling my entire upper arm. The backs of his fingers brush the side of my breast.

My eyes fly up to his in time to see his expression go blank, as if he's a computer and I pulled the power cord.

Before he can respond, two girls call his name.

"Jameson, are you coming?" One's wearing the shortest skirt imaginable and the other is in tight pants.

"In a minute."

He's back online, all systems go, "impatient" and "dismissive" modes engaged.

He releases me and I brush off my jeans. I'm grateful for the distance, and the reminder that my natural state is minding my own business and the guy across from me is a prick revered by the kind of people who revere rich pricks.

The girls head back down the hall, breaking their necks for another look at their precious idol. Neither is familiar from classes, but with the drivers around, conventionally attractive people seem to magically appear.

"Do they even go here?" I ask when they're out of earshot.

"I have no idea." He frowns, as if it never before occurred to him to consider the question.

"Hey, New Girl." Theo's voice has us both turning.

The tightness in my chest relents. He's gorgeous and smiling and that instantly puts me at ease.

Okay, not quite at ease. It's impossible to be completely relaxed when you're the focus of Theo Ashford's attention.

He reaches into his pocket and pulls out a small, shiny, blue-wrapped package.

"A present?" I'm taken aback, but also immediately appreciate that it's square, not round. "It was your birthday, not mine."

"Don't worry, I'll talk you through it. Step one, unwrap," he says, deadpan.

I tear into the package. Inside is a sleek white case containing AirPods.

"They're not Bose, but they're way easier when you're working on cars."

"Thank you." I'm not sure how much they cost but I'm assuming they're pricier than the tiny pieces of plastic suggest.

I lift one out and turn it in my fingers. "They stay in?"

"Step two." He steps closer and takes them from me, presses them in my ears.

I bite my lip. It shouldn't be sexy to have a guy put earbuds on you. But when Theo does it, it kind of is.

He hits a few buttons on his phone and it's suddenly playing music.

"I could get into this." I laugh.

I've never had a guy give me a gift before. The AirPods are generous and exactly what I need. It's as if he's still making amends for the accident even though it wasn't his fault.

I didn't know guys like this existed.

"What's step three?" I ask, probably too loudly.

Theo hits pause on the music, and I reluctantly set the earbuds back in the case.

"Step three is a few of us are going to the city for dinner and karting tonight," he says. "You should come with."

Theo Ashford is asking me out.

Theo Ashford, owner of the most devastating smile I've ever seen, is asking me out.

He's just a guy, I remind myself as a little thrill races through me. *I'm a grown-up, and why is it I want to spread my legs every time he grins?*

I press my thighs together on principle. "You want me to hang out with your friends."

"Mostly with me. We can ditch them if you want." Theo's grin widens.

Tonight is Dad's night off, so I don't have to be at the garage. "Sure. I'll meet you there."

"Great." He brushes a piece of hair behind my ear.

Theo turns and starts back down the hall, reaching for his phone. In a few steps, he's laughing on the line with someone.

"Remember the part where you were going to stay away from my brother?" Jameson's irritated voice cuts through my haze.

"Drawing a blank." I pull out my own phone and manage to connect my earbuds in a few keystrokes. "But I remember a piece of good advice I got recently."

The tiny case goes in the front pocket of my bag, which goes back over my shoulder. I pop the earbuds back in my ears.

"When someone stands between me and what I want . . . fuck them."

When I hit Play on my music, it drowns out whatever he might have said in response.

I take a beat to relish the stunned expression on his unreasonably attractive face before heading back down the hall.

⯌

BY THE TIME my last class of the day lets out, I'm longing to hang out with Theo. For the chance to forget my responsibilities and just flirt with a hot guy who, for some inexplicable reason, seems to think I'm more interesting than any other person in school.

I go out to my spot, turn on the Mustang, and wince. It's

running more than a little rough because it needs a tune-up, which I haven't had time for.

Chords blast through the speakers. I don't usually leave it on this loud.

I put the car in gear and start on the ring road that laps the building. The Mustang cruises slowly but sputters a little. "Don't You (Forget About Me)" streams out.

As I drive past the front of the building, Theo's pulling out of the lot in his Lambo with friends. Jameson's getting into the Porsche with the girls from the hall earlier. *Guess he doesn't care if they go to school here.*

I put my foot down to leave him in my dust. But when I give the Mustang gas, it backfires.

Something's wrong.

I nurse the car along the road, glancing in my rearview mirror.

Jameson pulls his glasses down, an expression of satisfaction on his brutally beautiful face.

I should've killed him when I had the chance.

12

Shay

TWO HOURS.

It took me two hours of my night off to figure out what was wrong with my car. And less than a second to know it wasn't an accident.

Jameson Ashford sabotaged my car.

A loose distributor cap isn't a big deal if you know what you're looking for. But it can wreak havoc with your engine and put you out of commission fast.

"How was your date with Theo?" Megan asks when we're in line for coffee the next morning.

"Nonexistent," I gripe, recalling the apologetic text I sent him last night to say I couldn't make it. "Car trouble."

She frowns, but I don't explain.

Jameson must hate me, or at least hate the idea of me anywhere near his brother. No matter how I imagined he might be human the day he drove me to school, I'm still dirt compared to his precious Ashford blood.

"Well, you'll have the chance to see him in action tonight at Test Track." Megan's voice brings me back.

"I thought the Challenger series didn't start for another couple weeks?"

She shoots me a look. "This race isn't sanctioned."

⁂

"TEST TRACK IS a big deal," Zane calls over the noise of engines and cheering.

"It's more fun with vodka," Megan says, grinning as she holds up a flask.

I take it and toss back a sip, mostly to keep warm against the biting wind that slices through my bomber jacket.

It's the first time I've been to the facility where Ashford Racing Inc. practices at night as a spectator.

And next year's new ARI driver is on this track.

Music pounds through the speakers people have brought for the occasion. The participants might technically be in college, but it has the intensity of the real thing.

"So if this isn't official, what's tonight for?" I lean in.

Zane flashes his teeth. "Psychological warfare."

"And the best parking spot on campus," Raj adds.

I frown. "I thought that was Jameson's?"

"Only because he always wins. Knox nicked it one time and his car got trashed. Jameson had it back in a week," Raj confirms.

The drinks are flowing trackside. It feels good to blow off steam. Everyone is dressed in their best streetwear, except for the drivers, who are already in their fire suits at the garage.

My friends and I line up along the railing as Metallica rips from the speakers.

The cars roll onto the track. The F2 chassis are the same ones I've been repairing in the garage.

"Everyone gets one lap. Winner gets bragging rights and the parking spot," Megan calls over the noise. "Still can't believe all three of my brothers went to law school instead of this."

I cock my head. "Seriously?"

"My mom says this is a phase. I can't wait to prove her wrong."

The song changes. "Sweet Dreams."

Heavy synth and '80s beats shake the place, giving it a nostalgic feel. It's before my time but it's timeless.

My hands grip the railing.

The first driver out is a third year, Mateo Ferreira. He looks fast, and the lap times appearing on the screen overhead confirm it.

Next up is Ren Nakamura, a second year. He stumbles in the first corner but recovers.

Then it's Jameson's turn.

My fingers dig into the metal as if I'm holding on to the car. Or the bike, sitting behind him again.

The F2 car rolls out of the pits and onto the track, getting ready for its flying lap. When he crosses the start in front of us, my heart lodges in my throat.

I can practically read his mind as he drives. Every inch, every turn.

He's so skilled, so cool. Controlled but lethal.

"God, he's good," Megan says.

His time gets posted and I gasp.

Two seconds faster in the same car.

"He drives so clean. Practically a machine." I frown.

It doesn't look fun for him. It looks necessary.

"You say that like it's a bad thing," Zane offers.

The music changes to a K-pop song as Knox gets ready to start his lap.

Megan crows, both hands in the air as she sings along despite my blank look.

"BLACKPINK?" Raj laughs, delighted. "Tell me you hacked the playlist without telling me you hacked the playlist."

"Lisa is such a bias-wrecker," Zane says.

Knox finishes his lap, catching a wheel in the dirt. We all gasp as he nearly spins out.

Theo is up last.

He's fun, a little reckless. Cutting corners and braking late. It's almost like if he spins out, he'll just laugh and try again.

"He's faster!" I grab Megan's arm and point.

We're all invested as if it's our future on the line as he finishes his lap in a blur of tight turns and aggressive braking.

Theo's lap is fastest.

Hollers of surprise go up.

A crowd descends on the garage, where the last of the drivers are getting out.

Theo catches my attention first and grins, throwing an arm around my shoulders. "You are my good luck charm."

Warmth tingles through me, not only because of how sexy he looks in his black fire suit, his hair sticking up from his helmet. It feels good to be tucked against Theo's side.

Megan and the guys are laughing and drinking. Megan's flask clearly isn't the only one on-site, as I see at least half a dozen now that the racing's over. Even the drivers and mechs are blending together.

Is this how it would feel, to fit in here at Ashford? To make friends and be part of something bigger than myself?

It's kind of beautiful.

"Glad you got your car up and running again," Theo murmurs, tugging me to face him. One palm rests lightly on my lower back.

"Just had to get the rat out from under my hood."

Nearby, Jameson's surrounded by drivers and girls. You would think he'd have less fans given how dismissive he is of them, but somehow, he seems to have more.

"You still owe me a date," Theo decides.

"This doesn't count?" I glance around us, teasing.

"Mmmm. No. I want you to myself."

He steps closer, his chest brushing my breasts.

"And have you thought about what we'd do on this date?" I manage.

"I've thought about a lot of things." His eyes dance with heat. "But since we're here now . . ."

Theo grabs my hand and tugs me after him toward the F2 car back in the garage.

"You want me to get in?" I laugh.

"I know you want to."

"I do, actually." I've been in a sim but never sat in an actual race car. The flask is forgotten on a table nearby as I shift inside the car, sliding my legs inside the cockpit and angling my body down into the seat. It's a tight fit.

Theo's called away by some other drivers and I let my eyes drift closed, my fingers wrapping around the wheel.

Instantly, I'm flying down the track. I can feel the power. Nothing can touch me; the whole world is a blur.

I've worked my entire life on these cars, only imagining how it feels to go that fast. This is the closest I've ever been.

I want more. Want everything.

"Don't get too comfortable. You won't be there long." I blink my eyes open to see Jameson leaning against the wall, the top half of his fire suit around his waist and the black layer beneath plastered to every line of his chest and abs. The two girls from the hallway flank him like slinky bookends.

"I think I get it. Why you have a problem with me and Theo," I decide. The girls exchange an uneasy look. "You don't know how to enjoy yourself unless you're winning. You're afraid your brother will beat you, claim the seat, *and* have more fun doing it."

Jameson's eyes flash like I've hit a nerve. He lifts the flask between two fingers, inspecting it. "Bet you always imagined getting into one of these because you deserved it."

He crosses to the car, still toying with the flask.

"As opposed to what?" I shouldn't ask, but can't resist.

When he drops the flask in my lap, the remaining vodka splashes on my shirt and the car. He ignores my sharp inhale of surprise, leaning close to murmur in my ear.

"Being the latest in a long line of people my brother wants to fuck."

13

Shay

I WAS WRONG.

Whatever moment of connection I thought we had the day he drove me to school, I can still find it in myself to hate Jameson Ashford.

He thinks I have to beg some guy to let me in his car? I'll show him how wrong he is.

The next afternoon, Jameson was spotted with a Porsche that clunked and rattled its way across campus, courtesy of yours truly. He babied it for twenty-four hours until he figured out someone zip-tied his driveshaft.

The day after, it took me way too long to find the two plug wires that were swapped under the hood of the Fastback. My firing order was fucked up, so the '67 started but idled like garbage, sounded worse, and had zero power.

Thursday, Jameson's Porsche didn't make it to school. The drivers had off-campus commitments and media training in town. Finding it there would be hard for someone not sufficiently motivated.

I'm very motivated.

I'd been dreaming all night about replacing the engine sound profile so the next time he revved the engine in front of school, it'd hum like a golf cart. At least until I got to my own car and saw what he did.

My cockiness evaporated into horror when I slid into the driver's seat and reached for my shifter.

Letters were etched into it with cold precision.

A-S-H-F-O-R-D.

"GOD, HE'S GORGEOUS." Bree's pencil moves over her notepad as she leans on the counter.

"Hmm?" I glance over to see what she's drawing—a guy with massive biceps and a big grin holding a wrench in one hand and lifting a girl with tattoos in the other.

She's not looking at the page, though, she's staring at the guy fixing the door. It's not a hardship; he's tall and muscular, his head buzzed and his eyes intent on his task.

"I could have fixed that," her brother says, wiping his hand on a towel as he emerges from the kitchen.

"And I would have broken it again if you had," Bree declares, flipping her blond ponytail over a shoulder.

We watch the guy work until he comes over and smiles at Bree. "All done for today."

"Thanks, Trevor."

His gaze drops to the notepad. Bree flips it closed, but from his confused smile, she was a beat late. "Anything else I can help with while I'm here?"

She stares at him as if she's genuinely trying to think of something.

". . . Or I can come back."

"Yes!" she gushes. "Yes, please come. *Back*. Come back."

"He *is* cute," I inform her once he leaves. "You going to do anything about it or stick to drawing thirsty cartoons?"

She shoves my shoulder and turns to the stack of pies she's supposed to be boxing for an order. "I'm waiting for him to ask me for my number."

"He has it. He works for you," her brother says, passing through with a bin of dishes.

"I mean he needs to ask me out."

"Or you could ask him out. Maybe he's shy. Or he doesn't want to be unprofessional."

She chews her lip. "I would be so unprofessional with him."

I laugh and start folding boxes to pass to her.

"For real though. I've been reading fantasy and my brain is running overtime." She sighs. "What's happening with you and your Ashford?"

I narrowly avoid ripping the box I'm prepping as adrenaline unloads through my veins. "You won't believe what that asshole did to my shifter—"

"Theo sabotaged your car?!" I realize my mistake too late. Her eyes narrow. "I thought you were vibing with Theo."

"We are." There's a stack of six boxes next to Bree and only four pies.

My friend gasps. "Are you thinking about Jameson?"

"No! But . . ." I tell her about the car feud.

Her eyes are gleaming before I finish. "So Jameson Ashford broke into the Fastback, your baby, and made it his."

"It's deranged."

"It's sexy as hell. Welcome to your villain origin story." Bree makes a purring sound. "Can't you picture him under the hood with his sleeves rolled up, getting grease on his designer shirt and giving zero fucks?"

I shift on my feet. As natural as it is to put the words *Jameson* and *fuck* in the same sentence, I shiver when she does.

Sure, he's gorgeous. He's also arrogant, cold, and completely insufferable.

"It's like this one book I was reading," she goes on. "We have the charming playboy brother. And the strong silent one . . ."

"Not silent enough."

"My point is, older brother's always endgame. It's practically canon."

I give her my best side-eye as a stray blueberry falls off the edge of a pie crust. I pop it in my mouth, sucking on its sweetness before swallowing.

"Not this time," I promise.

❖

TODAY, WE'RE ON a beach. He's shirtless, and he's kissing down my neck.

Somehow, I'm only in a bra and panties. It still feels like way too many clothes.

His voice hums along my skin. "You feel so damn good. Going to find out everything about you."

I'm lying in bed, halfway between asleep and awake. It's morning but no alarm yet, which means I don't have to tear myself out of this place.

I've been amped all week, my stress over school and this car feud and flirting with Theo colliding. I slide a hand down my pajamas and settle between my thighs.

Yes. Right there.

His head moves lower. He drags down my bra, lips skimming my breast. My eyes squeeze shut and I press harder against my clit.

Pleasure races through my veins. Since it's my fantasy, everything he does feels addictive.

Damn, imaginary guys are good in bed.

I feel his cock between my thighs, grinding impatiently like he wants me to feel every inch of him.

A sigh slips out of me, because I want that too.

Suddenly his breathing is harder, rougher. The playfulness is gone, replaced with intensity.

My nails dig into his shoulders, my hand fisting in his hair as he sucks.

Then he moves lower.

Yes. My teeth sink into my lip. He knows exactly how to touch me. And when he's out of control, well, that turns me on even more.

He shifts between my thighs, and every part of me is straining for contact. Except when I look down, Theo's hair isn't dirty blond but dark. When his head tilts up to meet my gaze, those slate-blue eyes burn into my soul.

"Admit it, Townie." Jameson's low voice drags along my

skin, his expression hot and knowing with a little smirk. "We both know I'd get you off better."

When the blare of my alarm interrupts the silence, I'm still staring at the ceiling like I can burn through it with my eyes.

14

Shay

"THERE IS NO racing without friction," Professor Vogel says. "It's friction between the car and the track that allows us to create speed."

Next to me in our strategy class, Megan's watching a K-pop video on mute under her textbook. Zane is taking careful notes, and Raj studies a bird out the window.

I sneak a look at Jameson on the drivers' side of the classroom. He's bored and at ease, his strong legs stretched out in front of him and his shirt rolled up at the elbows. His dark hair in waves that look as if he's been running his hands through it.

Probably after he carved *ASHFORD* in my shifter.

Vandalism shouldn't be attractive, but on Jameson Ashford . . .

It's inexplicably hot.

I force my attention back to Vogel.

Theo's absent today. He texted to say he was stuck doing media and asked if I'd take notes because Jamie had terrible penmanship.

If he were here, maybe I'd be sneaking looks at him. But no. I'm stuck with Mr. Congeniality.

My gaze shifts sideways to find Jameson already staring at me.

His moody blue gaze is charged. Like I'm a car he could take apart with his capable hands and there's nothing he'd rather do.

Awareness rocks me in my chair. Heat dances along my nerve endings, making my thighs press together.

Does he know he crashed my Theo fantasy?

I would die a thousand agonizing deaths before—

"Miss MacDonald?" The professor's sharp voice cracks my haze. "How does downforce affect cornering speed, and why does it come at a cost?"

My attention jerks toward the front of the room, where she's waiting.

I know this one. I was reading about it yesterday. But now my memory falters. "I'll get back to you."

Vogel frowns. I slump lower in my seat.

Megan, looking between us, clears her throat. "It's the friction coefficient between the tire compound and the surface. That's what lets us generate lateral and longitudinal force."

"Very good," Vogel says flatly. "But not Miss MacDonald."

"Shay knows it, too," Megan adds. "We were studying together. It was a late night."

I shoot her a grateful look, but it's still humiliating. Not because I need to get every answer right, but because of the reason I wasn't at my best.

I was up until all hours studying but kept dreaming up ways to sabotage Jameson's Porsche. It's my new favorite hobby.

Obsession?

Semantics.

After class, I pack up with my friends and start to follow them out of the room, but Vogel calls me. "Miss MacDonald, stay back. You too, Mr. Ashford."

Megan cocks her head and I make a face.

"I'll catch up with you guys."

When they leave, I force my gaze up, hoping Theo materialized out of thin air without me noticing. No such luck. She's staring at Jameson.

"Give me a moment." She steps outside when another faculty member flags her down.

The rest of the class trails out and it's only the two of us. Jameson's leaning on his desk, scrolling his phone. "That answer was in the text."

"Thank you, Captain Obvious." My tone isn't the least bit grateful.

"I would have gone easier on you this semester if I'd realized you couldn't read." He lowers his phone.

I fold my arms and lean back against the wall. "I bet it's a long walk from your new parking spot since Theo took yours."

He shoulders his bag and crosses the classroom with impossibly athletic grace. "Don't be embarrassed, literacy is a national crisis."

"So's nepotism."

Jameson's shoes brush mine when he pulls up. I try to ignore the muscled forearms folded across his chest, his lean hips, the arrogant tilt of his head.

He sighs, the long-suffering sound of a genius surrounded by idiots. "What's your problem?"

"Someone carved their last name in my shifter."

His eyes spark. "Maybe it was Theo."

I fist the strap of my bag like it's my sanity. "Theo wouldn't do something so . . ."

"Violating?" he supplies.

"Personal."

His smirk fades.

I barely have time to enjoy it because Professor Vogel is already returning.

"Shay. You're a bright young woman, but you're at risk of falling behind. All week, you haven't been yourself."

Dismay slices me. "Professor, I know I was distracted today. But I do want the internship."

At Ohio State, I would've gone to office hours and fixed this. Here, everyone else seems to already know the answer. I'm the only one pretending I do.

I'm uncomfortably aware of Jameson standing close by, afraid Vogel will tell me there's no chance in hell. Because as scary as it is to admit I want the internship, it's less terrifying than naming the truth—that I might want a place here at Ashford. A job on the grid with the best engineers and drivers in the world. That I would dare to believe I'm good enough even though I haven't been chosen the way Jameson or Theo has.

Instead, she only frowns. "Then you have work to do. There's an entire school of worthy candidates."

I'm grateful to be off the hook, at least until she speaks again.

"Jameson, you'll help Shay catch up on the material."

"No." We both say it at the same time.

"I'm flattered you want me to babysit, Professor Vogel, but I have other things to do this year." Jameson's voice sounds anything but amused.

"I've heard," Vogel answers dryly. "And you might've heard that racing is a team sport. This academy puts the best engineers and the best drivers in competition. You both need a reminder of the end goal."

"Which is?" Jameson sighs.

She levels stern eyes at both of us. "If you play your cards right, you could be on the same team."

15

Jameson

"YOU'RE LATE."

Shay looks up at the clock as she drops her books on the table next to me. "Two minutes."

There are a few other students in the library, milling about the stacks and studying in the carrels. I chose a spot in a corner away from prying eyes.

It's Wednesday and we're ten days from the first race that will decide the rest of my life, but I'm spending an hour each afternoon with her instead. The person who's been messing with my ride one piece at a time and flipping me off while she does it.

"You get that I have a seat to race for?" I pull a book from my bag and drop it on the table in front of us. "I could be logging sim time right now."

"Maybe you should." She refuses to look at me.

Not only am I spending my time tutoring her, I'm burning energy convincing myself her stubborn streak is neither intriguing nor sexy when some twisted part of me is insisting she's the most fascinating person I've met in a long time.

She's bold but defensive. Capable but uncertain.

Knox's comment rings in my head. *I'd go there.*

When he said it, I told myself I didn't see it. Truth is, I've seen it for a while, I just wish to hell I didn't.

Today, she's wearing jeans and a short-sleeved top. I can't help wondering if she wore that when she zip-tied my driveshaft.

I can picture her leaning over the Porsche, her full lips parted in anticipation and—

Nope.

If I'm going to help her, Vogel can't say I didn't do it right.

Yesterday, we covered the high-level concepts. I tried to put aside the fact that she's been taking my car apart all week and focus on the task.

It worked.

Mostly.

She knows the concepts; it's putting them together where she's weaker. Which makes sense since she transferred in and is playing catch-up while the rest of her cohort has had another year of specialized training.

Still, I'm impressed by how fast she catches on as I crack a book and start quizzing her on specifics.

When she shifts in her seat, the light slants differently across her face and I clock the dark circles under her eyes.

"Try kangaroos," I say.

"Huh?"

"If you can't sleep. Works better for me than counting sheep. Something about the bouncing. It's calming."

She lifts a brow but doesn't respond.

We get through ten minutes before she shifts in the chair

and pushes her hair behind her shoulder. Behind her, students pass, a few bearing pennants they made for the driver series.

"This whole race series is a stunt," she says under her breath. "Luca must realize you and Theo are his sons and not his PR spectacle."

"I'm not sure he does." The words slip out, and it's too late to take them back when she raises a brow.

"Come on. You're practically his mini me."

The comparison makes me wince. My father was a hell of a driver, and I intend to surpass his accomplishments on the track. But there are reasons to hope some of his wiring didn't get passed on to me.

He doesn't advertise the part of his story where his team tried to phase him out of racing at the end of his driving career, saying he wasn't as sharp as he used to be, and he responded by buying the company.

Or the part where he slept with different women every year that Theo and I were kids, causing shouting matches that echoed in the halls of our enormous house until he eventually paid them to leave. Or how he only took an interest in my younger brother when he could be used to make me better.

Luca would call himself strategic, but there are other words for it.

"I always looked up to him," I say finally, "but he used to say I took too much after my mother."

I expect that to end this conversation but instead, Townie leans in. "What's she like?"

I frown, remembering that her experience of family is probably even more limited than mine.

"Kind," I say at last.

"She doesn't live with you."

"That's none of your business."

"Sorry." She turns the page of my textbook.

I know her history. It's not a huge risk if she knows a piece of mine. "My father wasn't faithful. She loved him, but eventually realized there was nothing there to love, so she left."

The look on Shay's face has me regretting the admission.

"It's fine, Townie. I'll drown myself in Cristal if I'm feeling sentimental. Jump off that bridge you mentioned. Besides, you had it worse."

"Pain isn't a contest."

I cock my head. "Everything is."

We go to work for a bit, me quizzing her. She knows more than she let on to Vogel. Either she studied up for this or she really wasn't at her best the other day.

"This isn't enough." She leans back in her chair, stretching her arms overhead. "I can't win the internship by studying hard. There are hundreds of engineers."

"So, what's your plan?"

The little groan she makes as her shirt rides up her stomach is particularly distracting, and I force my attention up to her face.

Shay folds her arms and turns toward me. "The drivers are all distinct. Everyone knows who *you* are. I have to set myself apart."

"But your work is distinctive," I counter. "When I get into the Porsche, I know it was you."

"Not like all the other girls who fuck with your car?"

I grin. "No."

I spend my days pushing faster, harder, closer to the edge of human performance and physics. But this battle of wills with her is the most amped I've ever felt off the track. Every time I've got one up on her, she hits back harder. Getting her expelled somehow went from a priority to the farthest thing from my mind.

It's that momentary weakness that has my gaze softening on her hair, her face, the V in her shirt.

If she can tell I'm soaking in every inch of her, she's gracious enough not to point it out.

Fuck that. If she knew, she'd lord it over me. Because that's how this works.

Whatever this even is.

I don't have time for distractions. Particularly not ones in the form of sexy engineering students who have the uncommon ability to pinpoint my weaknesses.

"Yeah, well. Sabotage isn't exactly a high art," she says, arching a brow. "Any asshole can break things."

I'm still turning over her words as a few classmates brush past us, their attention on me. She doesn't look at me like they do—wanting what I am, what I have.

"Ever imagine what it's like to be invisible?" I ask suddenly.

"No," she answers without looking up. "I *know* what it's like. You, on the other hand, could never be invisible."

"Because I'm Jameson Ashford."

"Because you're too fucking good." She says it like it's a great tragedy.

I'm leaning in, my forearm brushing hers. "Too perfect. That's what you said."

There's no way I'm letting her off the hook this time. She lives to exploit my weaknesses? I get to push back once in a while, if only to keep my sanity intact.

This time, her tongue darts out to sweep her lips. "I was talking about the car."

But she knows she's been caught out, and she knows I know it too.

When the flush colors her face and neck, my fingers itch to trace the path. I want to know how far that reaction goes.

I want to know what else I could do to make her blush.

"You should pick on someone who actually wants your attention," she decides, flipping through the pages of her text.

"Like you want Theo's." My brother's name feels odd in my mouth.

When she shifts, her knee brushes mine under the table. I bite my tongue.

"My brother has been taking his workout seriously. Did you flatter his ego? That's the surest way to control my brother."

"I told him he had a chance," she says simply.

The belief on her face hits me. I'm used to having all the answers, but for a moment I'm envious of my brother, and it's not because he coasts through life.

Our conversation has veered dangerously far from racing strategy. We should get back to business, but there's one thing I owe her first.

"What I said at Test Track about you only getting in a car because Theo wants to fuck you. That was wrong."

"He doesn't want to fuck me?" Her brow lifts.

I exhale. "No. He absolutely does."

She laughs as my words settle between us.

And he's not the only one.

I don't finish the sentence, because it would break the invisible rules between us. The ones that feel sturdy but, I'm realizing with every second we're close enough to touch, are actually fragile.

I glance at the next page in the textbook, decide we've covered this one.

"Being the second son was hard on him, especially when my—our—mom left," I hear myself say. "Things were always a little easier for me. I wanted him to stay focused so he could have the things he wanted."

She leans in. "What if they're the same things you want? Like the seat. Maybe there's a one-in-a-million chance someday you'll both race for ARI, but not at the same time. Not next year. You can't both have it."

It sounds stupid but I'd never really thought much about it. Competitiveness has always been a part of my life, so it never sank in how he'd feel if I got it and he came up short. Or if he got it but I didn't. I don't love the idea of going head-to-head with my little brother, especially with stakes high enough we might hold it against one another, but there's no other option.

That's our world. Our fate. Always has been.

I start to put the book away, but it catches on the edge of the table. She grabs for it at the same time, my hand bracketing hers on top while hers is over mine beneath.

A jolt runs straight up my arm. It's childish, how much I feel it, how fast my body reacts.

But it doesn't seem childish at all.

Her gaze flicks to mine, her eyes a thousand miles deep.

I don't have to wonder if she's feeling it. I fucking know.

Before I can answer, her phone buzzes with a text. She lets go of the book first.

"I have to cover for my friend at the diner."

"The Junction?" I ask, surprised. "They have those fifties outfits. Skirts up to here." I motion.

Shay throws her pen at me. "Stop picturing them."

I duck easily. "Probably the only way to see you in a skirt."

"I didn't know that was on your bucket list." Shay reaches past me to retrieve her pen, but I hold it away.

She's leaning across my body. With her pressed against me, her breathing shallow, I suddenly can't decide where to look. Her eyes, lashes half-lowered. Her tits, warm and soft through the thin layers of clothing. Her lips, full and parted.

She smells sweet and a little spicy, and I want to drop my mouth to her throat and see if she tastes like it, too.

"Sick of staring at your ass in jeans every day," I manage.

Her grip closes around the pen, and my fingers. "At least you're finally admitting you stare at me all day."

Heat barrels down my spine. My dick presses against my zipper as if it's been waiting for exactly this opportunity.

She's looking at my mouth. I know because I'm looking at hers, and she's not pulling back.

We're an inch apart. Millimeters, really.

I brush my thumb along her knuckles because I need to touch her, and if I don't do that, I'll do something worse, something I can't take back.

In my head, the library's gone. Except the table. That can stay while I push her down on it, shut her smart mouth up with mine. The students can leave too—just fucking evaporate into nothing so her sounds echo off the walls.

A breath trembles out of her lips, and for a wild second I wonder if she's thinking the same thing.

Buzz. My phone vibrates on the table.

Buzz.

I blink and reach for it, coming back to the library and reality with it.

Theo. I don't answer but the reminder of my brother's existence sends a pang of guilt through me.

My brother, who genuinely likes this girl, who I've watched get better in the weeks since she came into his life.

Who I promised to protect and look out for with everything in me.

He doesn't deserve this.

Neither does she.

"I should go too." If my voice is rougher than usual, I hope she doesn't notice.

We pack up our bags and walk outside. It's dinnertime, and there are only a few cars still in the front lot.

I stop between the Porsche and the Mustang. "How'd you score the '67?"

"It was my dad's. Took us three years to get it back on the road."

That's a big rebuild. I'm floored she fought her way through it.

"It needs more work," I say, more harshly than necessary, my gaze lingering on the deep green paint. "Last time I was in there, it was a fucking mess."

Shay flips me off, the amusement in her eyes softening the gesture. "There are lots of things I'd love to do, but it takes time. And money."

"What's your dream upgrade?" I ask, because suddenly, it's the only thing I want to know. She gets cars more than most guys I grew up with, drivers and mechanics.

Shay chews her lip. "Supercharger. Hands down."

I groan. "Of course it is. You'd rather add chaos than fix anything."

"It's not about speed—it's about reaction," she counters. "The second you ask for something, it gives it back."

She's smart and capable. It's seriously impressive.

Though she's never come out and said it, she's also had a ton of challenges in her life, and something tells me it hasn't gotten easier since she started at the academy.

When she goes to get in, I grab her door, if only to keep her here another moment. "Vogel's right about one thing. If you get your shit together, Townie, you might actually survive here."

Her expression softens, her lips curving. "Never doubted it."

It's a lie. But my mouth lifts too, like it's our inside joke. A secret neither of us asked for.

If we were touching, she'd feel my heart speed up in my chest.

Of all the ways she's disrupted my life in a few weeks—the car failures and insults and inconvenient fantasies—what fucks with me most is that I used to be able to lie to myself, and I can't anymore.

Not about her.

16

Shay

JAMESON: Can't meet today.

When the text comes in Thursday morning, I know it shouldn't make me spiral. But disappointment rises up, a living thing wrapping around my chest.

Though I wouldn't admit it to another soul, I've been looking forward to our study sessions. Being forced to spend time with him made him more human. When neither of us could run for the door, we were forced to pull our punches.

A little.

I was right when I clocked that the Ashfords are opposites. Theo puts you at ease. Jameson challenges you until you question whether you know anything about your own life.

But my first impression of Jameson as a callous prick has been strained under the weight of what I've learned since.

I know he cares about his brother. That his mom leaving hurt him a lot, and that his feelings about his family are complicated even if he's forced to pretend publicly that they're all on the same page. That he operates in a state of constant pressure intense enough to make most people shatter.

Still, it's not only that realization that kept me thinking too much of him since the library.

Tossing and turning in my sheets couldn't make me forget his chest pressed against mine, how good he smelled, how his cool blue stare turns a thousand different colors.

He almost kissed me. If we hadn't been interrupted, maybe he would have.

I'd love to say I'd have pulled back, even before I learned how his mouth felt, before I let my hand creep up to his chest to see whether this of all things could make his heart beat faster.

The fantasies don't help.

Fantasies, plural. Because instead of coming to my senses after the first time, some twisted part of my brain seems to have decided Jameson Ashford is the only way to get off.

Talk about fucking inconvenient.

Watching seconds-long fan videos that somehow stretched to an hour on repeat probably didn't help.

I debate before texting back.

SHAY: Tomorrow?

Dots appear. Stop. Start again.

Forget car wrecks. Dots on a screen will be the end of me.

JAMESON: Busy all week.

It means nothing. Definitely not that he regretted what

happened—almost happened?—between us during our last study session.

Theo's been away all week due to commitments for the upcoming race. Jameson's probably genuinely busy too.

By noon, I've convinced myself it's better that way.

✥

THERE'S A BETTING line on the Challenger Championship.

The update hit my feed while I was scrolling my phone on my way to lunch.

I knew the world would be watching this contest, but it's surreal seeing pictures of people I know linked to that.

"Watch everyone be so focused on the races that the internship won't matter anyway," Megan says as she buys a piece of banana bread in the cafeteria. "January will come around and Luca will be all, 'Actually, we decided the drivers are more important. Forget the engineers.'"

She's not wrong—anticipation is building to these three showdowns, and the first is just over a week away.

"What if the engineers get involved with the driver series?" I muse, unwrapping a chocolate chip cookie and breaking off a piece.

"They're racing spec cars."

"So they can't be customized at all?" I press.

Megan drums her painted nails on one knee, frowning. She's not dismissive, she's thinking. "I wouldn't go that far. There's limited setup freedom. Ride height tolerances, brake bias windows, damper settings within the control ECU. Mostly tiny stuff." She glances at me. "My brothers always say they win cases on the details. I think racing's no different." Her lips curve. "And there's *so* much data nobody's touching."

I'm thinking about it while I chew my cookie.

And still thinking hours later when I go to cover my dad's shift at the ARI garage. It's been almost a month since his knee replacement, which means I only have a few more weeks to tell him I've been working his job. But I've only just got him on board with my school, and our relationship feels too tentative to strain more right now.

Usually when I'm working at Keane's, my music is cranked and I don't hear gossip. But I forgot to charge my AirPods, so that night, I overhear the guys chirping.

"You hear the rumor about Dekker?" one mechanic grunts.

"There's no way ARI tried to get him fired. And we shouldn't be talking about it," Bo tosses, glancing around uneasily.

"ARI's not careful, they're going to hand this season to another team. Ignite's been promising they're going to finish strong."

"Ignite isn't going to get to us. We're understaffed in the garage," another mechanic says. "That's the cause of all the problems."

I have my own problems, like getting noticed for this internship. That's where I focus my brain for the next hour.

"Keane," I start when I'm in the kitchen chugging coffee on a break. "How much effort do the F2 teams put into adjusting their setup?"

"Hardly any because they don't have the resources. The teams are lean compared to F1, but it's more about the drivers anyway."

"But what if the car doesn't suit a particular driver? There are some tweaks that are legal, right?"

"I guess so. Why?"

I shake my head. "Just a hunch."

"Hey, Mac. When's your dad back?" another mechanic asks.

"Soon." I chug the rest of my coffee, ignoring the kick of guilt in my stomach.

✥

"Hi, New Girl."

Theo's voice on my phone has me smiling as I shut the door of the Fastback and head toward the main building on campus.

I haven't seen Theo all week, and I didn't realize until just now how much I missed his presence.

"Are you back?" I'm scanning the courtyard as I head up the walkway as if he might appear at any moment.

"Yeah, got in last night. Media's been intense but I'm finally able to duck out for a bit. Ashford PR team isn't as fun to hang out with as you are. Or as fun to look at." My lips twitch. "I'm going into withdrawal, and you still owe me that date."

"I'm in class all day, and I have to work tonight." The regret in my voice is real.

"Then let me bring you a picnic."

A little rush of anticipation surges through me.

"You weren't joking," I say as I meet him on the grass lawn at lunch under the shade of a big tree. The end of September has been unseasonably warm, which is why I've peeled off my sweater in favor of a tank top.

"I wasn't sure what you liked to eat, and you don't post on social, so I had to guess."

The spread is impressive. Definitely enough to feed four people, possibly Keane's entire night shift.

"This is the tiniest sandwich I've ever seen." I hold up a triangle stacked with different colored fillings. I bite into one and it's delicious. "Did you make this?"

"Yes. If by 'make,' you mean asked the cook for afternoon tea to impress a girl."

I laugh. It's typical Theo, but I love it.

"How are you settling in?" he asks.

"Classes are hard, but it's fun to have everyone else love something as much as I do."

"There are perks."

"Like the finger sandwiches." I finish one and grab another as Theo laughs. "And the parking. For you anyway." In the distance I can just spot his Lambo occupying the best spot in the VIP lot.

"It does feel good being number one," he says. "Now I just have to keep it through the first Challenger race next weekend."

"There are things you could adjust."

He squints into the sun as I tell him the idea I've been working on since my talk with Megan.

"You think that'd make a difference?" he asks when I've finished.

I pull up my phone and open a map of Circuit of the Americas, the Austin F1 track. "A few tweaks can shave a lot of time off. Enough time to ensure you qualify on the front row. If you can start first, you should get off the line faster than Jamie. Then a few quick corners and he's eating your dust. What?" I prompt as I look up to see Theo staring at me.

"Jamie?" he repeats, amused.

I shake my head. "Jameson. Obviously."

Theo and I have chemistry. Forget whatever pen-stealing,

door-holding Jenny Han bullshit had me stealing glances at his brother in the library.

And as for the fantasies . . .

Yeah. Forget the *fuck* out of those.

Theo shifts onto his knees, his eyes dropping to my mouth. "You have something. Right here."

There's a moment where I register what he's about to do, but only one. Just long enough for my lips to tingle under his stare, for my stomach to knot.

Then he presses his mouth to mine.

He's warm and assured, the casual confidence of his lips sending sparks of desire through me.

It's sexy, in the way that beach days and bikinis are sexy.

He tips my face up with his fingers, making me open under him. I suck in a surprised breath.

Whatever money I'd have bet that Theo Ashford was a good kisser? Should've doubled it.

Every slide of his mouth over mine makes me want more. I'm leaning in, arching my body to press closer.

"Better?" I murmur against his lips, my breath uneven.

Theo stares up at me through his lashes, his grin lazy and satisfied. His palms splay across my hips.

"Not yet."

He tugs me off-balance until I land in his lap, straddling him. My breath catches at the feel of him pressed between my thighs.

We're in the middle of the quad in broad daylight and the expression on his face says he couldn't care less. Maybe I don't care, either.

He kisses me again, one hand sinking into my hair while the other slides down to my ass.

His tongue teases mine until I'm dizzy, grabbing the front of his shirt to stay upright.

I kiss him back until there's no room in my head for anyone else.

✥

"CAN YOU GIVE me a ride home?" Megan asks as we wrap up our final class. "I told Raj he could borrow my car tonight."

"You're a good person."

"Yeah, and it's the roommate tax."

We head to the parking lot and drop our bags inside the Mustang.

"Theo and I kissed in the quad at lunch." I blurt it as I start the car and shift into gear. "There might have been some groping."

"Oh, I know. I was waiting for you to tell me." She grins from the passenger seat.

"He brought me a picnic."

"And you had to eat it out of his mouth?"

I cruise out of the parking lot and toward the front of campus. "I like him. He's fun."

"Right. New shifter?" Megan takes in the silver knob.

The hairs on my neck lift. "It was time."

I'm not mentioning I had to replace it yesterday because the old one had *ASHFORD* carved into it, or that looking at it made me a strange combination of murderous and horny.

But our feud is over.

At least, that's what I tell myself.

There'll be no more studying with Jameson either.

Vogel wanted to make sure I was caught up. I'll tell her I am. And Jameson won't argue.

Not judging from how fast he backed out.

Fine. I don't need to spend any more time with him. Theo's the one who wants to hang out with me. The one who makes me smile.

Forget the car feud that was edging me way too hard. Surprise tea sandwiches and a sexy make-out in the grass are objectively superior to threats and felonies.

When I hit the gas, the Mustang accelerates hard.

There's a little fishtail when we launch, and I grab the wheel, forcing myself not to overcorrect.

My pulse starts to hammer as we tear up the asphalt. *What is happening?*

I press harder and it sails.

"Whoa! Don't try to tell me the shifter's all you swapped out," Megan says, impressed.

This can't be my dad's Fastback. It's responsive, alive in a way it never has been.

I throw it in park, then jump out and round to the engine, popping the hood.

Gleaming metal stares back at me.

What the fuck?

I hit a contact on my phone without second-guessing if I should. The line picks up on the third ring.

"What did you do to my car?" I demand.

"You tell me." Jameson's voice is cool.

My gaze is on the huge, shining intake housing where my carburetor used to be. There's a belt snaking around new pulleys. Wires and hoses have been rerouted, and the overall effect is tidy but dangerous.

"There's a jet engine where my carb used to be."

The sun warms the back of my neck, but it's my body that feels hot. Like I could come out of my skin.

"Technically it's a supercharger. I also tuned a few things while I was in there. It's not a big deal."

He says it casually. As if it wasn't a full day of work for a capable mechanic with the right tools.

Not to mention *thousands* of dollars.

My pulse is pounding in my veins. I brace a hand on the car, unsteady.

I might've had the upgrade on my wish list but didn't have any delusions of actually being able to get one. Today or any other day.

But while I was eating tiny sandwiches with Theo, Jameson broke into the Fastback and torqued it with staggering skill and precision.

"Why?" I demand, struggling to find words.

I'm not letting him black cat his way out of this. I need a reason that fits with the box I've assigned Jameson in my mind.

The car is secretly a bomb that's about to go off. Or he's punking me and I'm being filmed as a prank for the drivers to watch. Or he's proving a point, trying to make me realize I'll never be as good as he is.

When he finally answers, I wish I hadn't asked.

"It's like you said." His voice sounds different than I've ever heard it. "Any asshole can break things."

I wonder if he realizes his fingerprints are now on my car in a way that goes deeper than his name etched in my shifter ever did.

Because I can't think of anything else.

17

Shay

WHAT JAMESON DID for me is an ache in my chest all weekend, a flame that won't go out.

I need to respond. Not with words, but with action.

It's Saturday night when I get the idea. I spend all day Sunday working out the details, a process derailed only when I answer the doorbell to find a delivery guy with an armful of flowers from Theo.

I bring them inside, sniffing carefully.

"Who are those from?" Dad asks.

"A friend." I shove the card in the pocket of my jeans.

"Where did you meet this friend? The Junction?"

"Dad . . ."

He holds up his palms. "I just want you to have a social life. You'll never meet anyone under a car."

When I text Theo to thank him for the gorgeous flowers, he asks if we can hang out today.

I bite my lip.

SHAY: **Love to, but I'm working on a project. It's kind of urgent. Catch you at school?**

I dig through our kitchen cabinets—no vase in sight but I settle for a pitcher and fill it with water, sticking the flowers inside and taking them back to my room. They fill the space with a soft scent as my gaze returns to my computer, and my task.

I'll need more than I could access in the school parking lot. And unlike Jameson, I can't snap my fingers and get a tow truck to take it to the school's garage.

"We need to get into the Ashford house," I tell Megan when I call her.

"Are you high? If we're breaking into Daddy Ashford's compound, you owe me answers, coffee for the next month, and a get-out-of-jail-free card, because your ass is going to be right there alongside me when they catch us."

When I was wandering the property after Theo's party, I found an area where the old stone fence is completely hidden by trees. Megan, Raj, Zane, and I are there with a ladder and tools within an hour of sunset.

"If we were a K-pop group, what would our roles be?" Raj asks as we trudge toward the fence on what we judged to be the quietest side.

Zane snorts. "We don't meet the criteria."

"But if we did," Raj presses. He's still annoyed we made him leave his scooter behind.

"I would be the visual and the face," Zane says. "Megan's the leader. Shay's our main vocal. You're the maknae. Everyone babies you already."

"You've thought about this." I'm relieved for the momentary distraction from our mission.

"Clearly not enough." Megan shakes her head. "Can Shay even sing?"

"Only in the shower," I confirm.

"So what exactly are we doing?" Megan asks me when we get onto the property and inside the garage. The guys hang back to keep watch.

I pop the hood on the Porsche.

"I'm remapping the engine." I hook up the cord to my computer. I hit the Enter key with a flourish and watch as the custom mode starts to load.

"Ghost Mode," Megan reads off the screen. "Which is?"

"You'll see." It's better than anything factory, that's for damn sure.

Jameson wanted to be silent and stealthy. He's also completely fearless and brutal. I'm giving him a way to be both with the flick of a switch.

While the programming runs, I look around at the slick garage. Photos of the boys racing karts speckle the wall. Each of them holding up trophies. One of Theo pouting, Jameson's arm around him. No matter how fucked up their family is, it's clear the brothers love one another.

"What is going on with you and Jameson?" Megan pushes her shiny dark hair out of her face as she leans against the Turbo.

I shoot her a look. "Nothing."

"What I said the first day of school stands. He won't give you the time of day unless you're sporting a V8 . . ." She trails off, looking around us. "That's what this is, isn't it. Some game between you." Her dark eyes are rimmed purple today, which doesn't hide the worry. "If you're going to mess around with an Ashford, it better be Theo."

"Or what?"

She must sense I'm genuinely asking, because she sighs. "I don't know. No one's ever kept Jameson's attention long enough to find out."

When Megan and I finally finish and pack up, I text Zane and Raj, who're outside keeping watch. There's no answer. We head outside and start back across the property when a voice calls, "Where do you think you're going?"

Megan's already scrambling up the fence. Her eyes widen on me and I shoo her. "Run!" I whisper.

"Not without you." She drops back next to me and her hand finds mine.

She's willing to go down with me. There's no reason for it, but she's doing it anyway.

I'm touched by her loyalty. It's almost enough to crowd out the panic as we turn slowly.

Luca Ashford stands behind us, imposing in a dark suit. This is the closest I've seen him. I'm struck by how much Jameson looks like him, but his expression is different. Harder.

His gaze flicks between us.

"Hi, Mr. Ashford," Megan says.

"And you are?" But his attention is on me.

"Shay," I say, inching ahead of Megan without meaning to. "We're friends of your son."

His eyes narrow. Luca inspects me more closely. "Shay what?"

I start to say *MacDonald* but hesitate. "Mac . . . Alister."

Megan's hand stiffens in mine. She's not sure why I lied. I'm not sure, either. Except it's better if Luca thinks we're townies, not students at the school he lords over, where a single word from him could ruin our futures.

"You should leave." His eyes stay on me. Not Megan.

"We will." Megan blurts it first.

"Shay." He calls after us right when I swear we're home free. "Use the gate."

⁜

"THAT WAS CLOSE," Raj says as he swipes his card to pay for his coffee in the cafeteria the next morning.

"You have a twisted definition of close. He caught us." Megan grabs for the card before he can put it away and swipes it three more times.

"What the hell?!"

"For yesterday," she retorts.

Zane weighs in. "I made a bird sound."

"Next time, send a text?!"

The cafeteria is buzzing since classes haven't started. I steer us to a tiny table by the window. My friends keep chatting but my knee bounces, my bare thighs rubbing together.

A flash of silver out the window grabs my attention. I'm out of my seat and breaking for the doors.

"Shay!" Megan calls, but I ignore her.

Jameson's Porsche turns into the parking lot as I bust out of the building, running down the steps to the front walk and dodging students on my way.

The car roars as it lunges. I beat him to his spot, the one next to Theo's, which is currently empty.

Jameson throws the Porsche in park, the bumper six inches from my knees. My heart is hammering with anticipation as he revs the engine. The sound is sinful. A roar that erupts from a purr.

"I'll bite," he calls out the lowered window. "What's Ghost Mode?"

"You said you wanted to be invisible, so that's how it starts," I say as I round to the passenger side and lean in, breathless with exhilaration and pride. "It strips everything down. Throttle response, suspension, traction control. Just raw speed."

Jameson's eyes drag down my body, lingering on my bare legs.

I almost regret the skirt—until his knuckles turn white on the steering wheel.

It's the smallest tell. For Jameson, it's everything.

Before he can respond, another engine roars. Theo pulls up in the best spot in his Lambo.

"Shay!" He's out of the car and crossing to us.

"Missed the fuck out of you this weekend." He loops an arm around my waist, bending me in a dramatic dip and brushing his lips over mine.

"You look insanely hot. How many flowers does a guy have to send to get your attention?" he murmurs against my mouth.

When I'm upright again, I glance past him to see Jameson out of the car, one of the girls from Test Track wrapped around him. She's practically climbing him and for once, he looks like he might be enjoying it.

My chest aches as if he physically stomped on my rib cage.

Not because of the girl, though when he slings an arm around her narrow hips I feel like I'm chewing glass. Because I spent the entire weekend working on this, enlisted my friends too, and there's not so much as an "I like it, Townie."

But Theo's already dragging me toward the doors, talking about some movie he watched on the weekend.

✥

WE'RE GOING AROUND the class discussing telemetry and aerodynamics. Normally I'm interested, but today, I can't bring myself to care.

It all feels pointless.

What if Megan's right and we don't matter? At all?

I lift a hand in the middle of Professor Vogel's remarks, and she trails off to call on me.

"Yes, Miss MacDonald."

"I want to work on the Challenger series car."

A hush quiets the class. Even Megan's staring as if I've lost it.

"There is no improving an F2 car. It's standard," Vogel says slowly.

"But the whole focus of this academy is preparing drivers for F1," I point out. "Everyone thinks the cars can't be customized. They can, within limits. We can give drivers a chance to tailor their cars and give engineers a chance to shine."

I've been circling the idea for a while, talking with Theo, with Megan, turning it over while I was working at the garage. But making the custom mode for the Porsche is what made it finally click.

A driver's car should feel like it's theirs.

"There are three races in this series. The first is a week away," Vogel reminds me.

"All the more reason." I shift forward in my seat, gripping the edge of my desk. "On the F1 grid, ARI is facing increased competition from Ignite and other teams. Whichever driver wins will be dropped into a pressure cooker. The stakes have never been higher."

Jameson's future and Theo's are on the line.

If you play your cards right, you could be on the same team.

Her eyes narrow. "So you work on one driver's setup and everyone else races standard gear?"

"No." This is the heart of the idea. "Every engineer could join a driver team, working on the cars and strategy in real time." I nod to Megan, who's wary but intrigued. If anyone deserves to work on these cars, it's her. She's smart and competitive and has had my back since day one.

"No driver will let you touch their car," Knox snorts. A few laughs go up.

I turn to look at Theo, expectant. This is what we talked about during our picnic. But there's no vote of confidence, no "maybe it could work." He doesn't even meet my eyes.

Every second of silence adds to my humiliation and despair. My nails dig into my palms, hard enough to draw blood.

"I'm sorry, Shay, but unless you have a driver to support this idea . . ."

I shut my eyes in frustration.

"I will."

My head snaps toward Jameson.

He coolly surveys the room, tapping his pen on his desk as if every individual in class is personally wasting his time.

"ARI has a history of developing drivers *and* engineers. There's no reason students can't work in a real racing situation under senior staff."

Hope fills my lungs. That spot between my ribs is glowing again, the possibility of showing what I can do closer than it's ever been.

"But given the stakes," he continues, "it's only fair the drivers pick their engineers and not the other way around."

"Since you're supporting this, did you have an engineer in mind?" Vogel's voice is far away. So's the rest of the class.

Jameson's gaze locks on me, carrying the same intensity it did when I was telling him about Ghost Mode.

When he speaks, it feels as if he's reached down my throat and grabbed me by the heart.

"I want her."

18

Shay

"NEED A HAND, New Girl?"

My breath collapses as I straighten from where I'm bent over a car at the ARI garage later that night.

"Theo."

He takes his time crossing to me, his jeans and a button-down rolled up at the elbows looking more rumpled than usual.

Keane's in the high security part of the garage on the other side of a locked door, but three other mechanics are working on their own vehicles. Each of them glances over to see the younger Ashford, two exchanging uncertain looks.

"I haven't been here in a long time." Theo scans the garage as he walks. "Probably since I was in karts. Dad used to let me come in on weekends."

"And you decided this was the time to come back?" Just my luck he'd stumble in here and blow my cover.

Since Dad and I struck our fragile truce about me attending the academy, he seems less suspicious of my after-hours activity.

Probably because he figured—understandably—that attending school was my only secret.

Theo runs a hand over the car I'm working on. "I was in the neighborhood and recognized your car. Made me curious. And I wanted to talk to you after Jamie picked you for his team."

"I would've been on your team, but you didn't go for my idea." I fold my arms, streaking grease across my skin.

He rubs a hand through his hair, embarrassed. "You could've given a guy a little notice."

"I did! That whole picnic we had, I was talking about this idea. Ring a bell?"

"I remember the part where you kissed me." His lips curve, and now I'm remembering how good they felt on mine.

"Pretty sure you kissed me."

"Either way, there were mouths, and intentions." He grins.

Having one Ashford on my brain was a lot. Two is impossible.

"Jameson didn't need any notice." It's probably unfair to say, but it's also true.

Theo doesn't seem offended. "Jamie has always wanted what's mine. At least, it feels that way."

Is it true Jameson's only interested in me because Theo is? The possibility shouldn't matter, but it does.

No, I decide. Jameson's too strategic for that. There's no way he would saddle himself with me given the stakes of the next three races if he didn't believe I could help him.

But a flicker of doubt lingers in my mind, one with sharp edges that slice at my pride.

"You want to tell me what you're doing here?" Theo's hard right drags me back.

I take a breath and explain all of it. How I've been covering my dad's shifts at the garage, that I kept it from him and everyone else I could.

"Keane and the guys went along with it, but it's not their fault," I finish. "He'll be back to work soon, which means I just need to hold it together for a few more weeks."

"I'm impressed," Theo says. "How the hell you managed to work night shifts and keep up in school is beyond me. And you're obviously doing a good job if the crew didn't out you."

Pride rises up, fighting with worry. "Please don't tell anyone. Especially not your father." He wouldn't think fondly of it, particularly from the girl who broke into his property.

Theo cups my face, thumbs stroking my cheeks. "I can keep it from my dad," he says at last.

Relief spreads through me.

"I like you," he goes on. "Even if I don't always pick up what you're putting down. Even if you're always two steps ahead of me."

I like him, too. But—

"Jamie know?" he asks.

I shake my head slowly.

"You want him to?"

Do I trust Jameson? The new possibilities swirling in my head have my guard up.

"He doesn't need to know," I decide.

19

SHAY: I have a condition.

JAMESON: You don't get conditions.

SHAY: Megan joins our team.

JAMESON: You're afraid you can't handle me alone?

SHAY: No. She's good and she deserves it.

SHAY: But also, your toxic ego is a lot for one person to manage.

JAMESON: Modesty looks terrible on me.

⁂

SHAY: Your tires will be trash in Austin.

JAMESON: Everyone's will be. Nature of the track.

SHAY: But what if you go higher tire pressure? Megan and I were reviewing the data. You'd have better straight-line speed.

JAMESON: And no grip. We'd be sliding all over.

SHAY: Not necessarily.

JAMESON: Yes, necessarily. It's called physics, Townie.

SHAY: Why did you choose me if you weren't going to even consider my ideas?

JAMESON: Couldn't stand to watch your sad face in class.

SHAY: UGHHHH.

JAMESON: Higher pressure would be unhinged. No one would try it.

SHAY: That's why you'll win.

JAMESON: It'd be twitchy as fuck.

SHAY: So don't twitch.

JAMESON: You think I'm that good?

SHAY: Don't let it go to your head.

JAMESON: Too late ☺

✤

JAMESON: I'll do it. If the modeling is solid we can run higher at Austin.

SHAY: YESSSSS!!! OMG. Megan will freak out.

JAMESON: But I need you on my side. Not Theo's.

SHAY: Okay . . .

JAMESON: Say it.

SHAY: I'm on your side.

JAMESON: Good.

SHAY: I'm running through the data again right now.

JAMESON: It's after midnight. Go to sleep.

SHAY: I want to be sure.

JAMESON: Townie. Get this through your pretty, stubborn head.

SHAY: ??

JAMESON: I won't let you lose.

20

CHALLENGER CHAMPIONSHIP
Race One

Shay

"ROAD TRIP!" MEGAN throws an arm around me and Raj as we meet in the boarding lounge at the Detroit airport. "What outfits did you bring?"

"Garage clothes. Going out clothes." Zane ticks off his fingers.

"I was talking to Shay." Megan rolls her eyes.

"Why? She only has one bag." Raj nods to me.

I've never been to Austin before, but in an hour, we'll be heading for the Circuit of the Americas, where the first leg of the Challenger Championship will be held. Seeing racing on TV is nothing like seeing it in person, and I'm buzzing with anticipation. This is the first chance for us, and the drivers, to show what we can do.

We turned in our final adjustments for the race car yesterday. It was both nerve-racking and exciting. Figuring out the tuning required studying Jameson's driving for way too many hours. The way he handles the car, how flawlessly he executes.

But the past week, what I keep coming back to isn't his driving, the way he upgraded my Fastback, or even how drawn I am to him.

It's his faith in me. No one other than my dad has ever believed in me like that.

Get this through your pretty, stubborn head.

I won't let you lose.

Those lines have been burned in my brain since I read them.

Before going to sleep, I typed out one more text.

SHAY: That comma was a mistake. Right?

I reached for the backspace button to delete it . . .

And accidentally sent it instead.

Shit.

I sound as if I'm fishing for compliments, or that I care way too much, both of which are weaknesses Jameson will exploit.

Dots appeared immediately. His response came through moments later.

JAMESON: I don't make mistakes.

I stared at the message window for way too long, my body on fire thinking of the library again, his hand covering mine, his body too close and yet not nearly close enough.

Megan's right. Feeling this way is a terrible idea. Even if I've come to understand and appreciate him more in the past couple of weeks, Jameson is still an asshole. An asshole who might be my ticket to a dream internship.

He's also Theo's brother.

I can't kick what Theo said. *Jamie has always wanted what's mine.*

"Look happier. We have a weekend away from school." Megan's voice breaks into my head.

"And we get to see the cars we've been working on this week. This is as much a test for us as for the drivers," Zane reminds us both.

Anticipation surges through me as the others catch up and we carry our things to the plane.

❖

MILES OF TRACK and garage and stands cover rolling hills right outside the city. The wide, flowing track corners are modeled after Silverstone in the UK and Suzuka in Japan.

I'm awestruck, first because everything is huge. Second, because as wild as the venue seems to me, this was my dad's life.

I text him a photo. **This is amazing.**

We make it in time to watch qualifying, which means half an hour of chaos while everyone tries to get the best lap times.

Race day tomorrow will be head-to-head action, but this is more intense, more technical. Less strategy and more flat-out speed.

There are still thousands of spectators. Everyone wants a front-row seat to watch ARI's newest driver.

"Damn." Megan whistles as Jameson lays down a great lap.

I watch every thrilling moment. He has fans in the stands, too. All the drivers do.

I'm noticing how the car responds to the track and the

conditions, but it's different than how the race will be. We're not running the higher tire pressure until then, when it will be the edge he needs.

And he'll definitely need it as Theo earns the best lap time.

I go to look for Jameson after but run into Theo in the garage first. His eyes meet mine and he grins as I make my way over.

"Congratulations!" I call. He ended up choosing Raj and Zane for his team, and I'm happy for all of them.

"Thanks." Theo sweeps me up in his arms and spins me around, making me laugh. "The lap was good, but I need more. Can I show you something?"

When I don't respond, he pulls some stats on his tablet and I skim them.

I need you on my side. Jameson's words come back and hesitation rises up. If I was working with Theo, I might suggest a few tweaks. But it doesn't feel right.

"Looks good," I say finally. "Drive your race and you'll be fine."

I go back to Jameson's car, but he's still not there.

SHAY: You drove great. You'll get it tomorrow.

While I'm waiting for his response, my phone rings.

"Dad!" I answer. "You wouldn't believe it here—"

"I just got a call from one of the guys at work. He was looking for you."

"Me? Why?" My heart thuds against my ribs.

"Apparently the person you arranged to cover your shift for the weekend forgot."

Shit. Shit, shit.

My brain scrambles to come up with a response, but surrounded by the buzzing of the track, it's like I'm trying to solve for a variable in a math problem I don't understand.

Dad doesn't wait for me.

"The paychecks haven't stopped coming because you're working my shift. Not because ARI signed off on my leave."

My stomach plummets. I've never heard him sound this remote. Not only disappointed, but hurt.

I've been careful since I started. Bree had my back if Dad called the diner, and I arranged for an excuse every time I went out. None of the guys would have knowingly betrayed me.

But none of that changes the fact that he knows, or that he's furious.

"It was temporary," I tell him. "You weren't ready to go back to work so soon after the surgery. They would have fired you." I clutch the phone tighter, pressing farther into the garage to try and find a quieter place.

"That's not your problem. You lied to me. I told you to keep your distance from ARI."

I flinch at his directness. He's the person I've always been closest to, whose approval I wanted more than anything. But as much as I shrink from his criticism, part of me rejects it.

"Everything is my problem," I say, my voice rising. A few heads turn this way, and I swallow and try to stay composed. "If it's your problem, it's mine. Just like my problems are yours. You've always said we're a family, even if we're a small one."

Especially if we're a small one.

Dad curses, and I hope to hell my words got to him.

"Listen to me, Shay. The Ashfords will make your problems worse, not fix them."

"Then why have you devoted your entire life to working there?"

I don't expect an answer, but I give him time anyway. Each breath is painful, my lungs tight and ineffective.

"If it's good enough for you, it's good enough for me," I say at last. "I'm your daughter."

"Your birth parents wouldn't have wanted—"

"They're not here," I bite out, because invoking dead people is a low fucking blow. "They're not here but we are, and we have to do the best we can."

21

Shay

I'M READING IN my room and trying to forget the fight with my dad. Even the '90s-pop playlist on the AirPods Theo got me can't make a dent in my mood.

You lied to me. I told you to keep your distance from ARI.

If I thought he was angry about school, this is worse. I meant to talk to him about it sooner. I got carried away with all the excitement of school and working on the car, but the thrill didn't solve my problems. It only made me forget them for a while.

Megan tried to get me to go to the impromptu party in another hotel room tonight but relented when she realized no amount of convincing would work.

My throat is full of emotion, hot tears behind my eyes that I won't let fall, when I hear the knock on the door.

Jameson.

He still hasn't responded to my text, but I want to believe it's him waiting outside. That he'll stare down at me with stormy blue eyes, snap out how annoyed he is that he didn't see me at the track today and that my ideas for the setup are in fact insane. And in some messed-up way, I'll feel better.

I pad across the floor in my bare feet and lean toward the peephole.

It's not Jameson on the other side.

"Wow. This is tragic," Theo says when I swing the door wide. He's dressed for the evening and with his signature smile, looking more roguishly handsome than anyone has a right to look in real life, while I'm wearing pajamas.

"I had a fight with my dad."

His eyes crinkle with sympathy. "I'm sorry. Come to the party," he insists. "You'll feel better."

"I can't. We both know you have to be the best-looking one in the room so . . ." I trail off and pat my messy topknot with one hand.

He snorts and brushes past me. The door swings shut behind him as he crosses to my bed, dropping onto it and picking up my books. "Well, if this is what you were doing to distract yourself, a party is definitely a better option."

I drop onto Megan's bed and pull my legs up. "You just hate the idea that not all of life's answers can be found in the bottom of a bottle of vodka."

"You're clearly not drinking good enough vodka." His grin is blinding, but Theo has this ability to make me feel instantly comfortable. It's his superpower.

"If you won't come to make yourself feel better, it'll make me feel better." His gaze searches my face. "Jamie's been AWOL all day."

His name has me instantly on alert. "You're worried?"

"Only that my father and brother are off colluding somewhere, getting his fire suit tailored for the F1 car next year." His smile slips a little.

The possibility hits me hard. What if Jameson is conspiring with his father to make all his Ashford dreams come true while Theo's here being honest with me?

I rub my chest with the heel of my hand.

"Or I could stay." Theo's voice edges into my brain. "We could hang out here. Find some way to keep ourselves occupied."

His eyes search mine. He's not pushing; he's asking.

As much as some part of me wants to take him up on it, to just forget everything that's going on, I know deep down I'd regret it.

I pivot. "You're right. Party it is. Let me get changed." I shift off the bed and cross to the closet to find some clothes.

When I glance back, Theo's reclined with his hands behind his head, his half-mast eyes trained on me.

"Yeah, you're going to need to turn around."

His exaggerated sigh has me laughing for the first time all day.

❖

THE PARTY IS upstairs in the penthouse, a mix of drivers and mechanics I haven't seen the likes of since Theo's birthday.

I grab a drink with Theo, downing the first shot with him. He hollers in delight as I grab a second.

"For the road," I say as I grab a third and head in search of Megan and my other friends.

I lose track of time, indulging in a whirlwind of dancing, more drinks, some games. I check my phone but there's nothing from my dad. Nothing from Jameson.

I'm spacing out when someone grabs my hand and drags me into a closet.

Theo.

Around us, the closet is full of coats. Music is muffled by the door.

"Sensory deprivation is very calming," Theo intones.

"So is not going to parties in the first place," I toss.

"I'm sorry about your dad," Theo murmurs. And whether it's this tiny hotel closet or the alcohol, I laugh.

"I'm sorry about yours," I say, and mean it.

He pulls me against him. His hands stroke my hair. I lean into his touch, enjoying the feeling of being held.

"My dad's probably kicking me out," I confess.

"Mine too, if I beat Jamie tomorrow." His lips tilt up.

I laugh.

"You make it look good," I tell him. "Being second."

He leans closer, his lashes lowering. "It's not so bad."

Awareness creeps over me. We're close, and it's Theo, the first person who was genuinely nice to me in this new world.

Sure, he's gorgeous. But right now, he's just the best guy I know.

The gap between us closes a millimeter at a time.

At the last minute, I turn, and his mouth grazes the corner of mine.

"You don't want to?" he murmurs.

"It's not that." I lean my forehead against his shoulder like an idiot.

I like Theo. He's hot and fun and funny and I genuinely care about him. I'm just not feeling it.

He sighs, the vibration through his chest rocking me, too. "It's okay. You've had a rough day."

I hug his arm with both of mine, holding on and pulling him closer even though I know it's not the kind of closeness he wants.

"Time to face reality again?" he murmurs.

"Your penthouse party is not real life, but yes."

He threads his hand through mine and gives it a squeeze.

We leave the closet, me still leaning into him.

I feel the attention before I see it. When I look up, there's a pair of blazing blue eyes fixed on us from the door.

Jameson.

He's wearing a jacket over a button-down, his clothes perfect but his expression wrecked.

My hair is a mess. My hand is threaded in Theo's.

I have no reason to feel guilty, but I do anyway.

He looks . . . betrayed.

Before I can react, he's gone.

22

Shay

"YOU GET ANY sleep?" Megan asks sympathetically the next morning.

I glance over at her from where I'm finishing brushing my teeth at the second sink.

She slides me over a jar of under-eye corrector from her impressive bag of makeup. "This is the good shit."

All night I'd been lying awake thinking of walking out of that closet with Theo, of Jameson's face when he saw us. Was it anger, or something worse?

We take the shuttles to the track. It's a gray day, but so far, the radar isn't showing rain.

The fans are out in full force, bearing signs repping their favorite drivers—it's mostly a sea of Ashford red but pops of other colors, too.

There are cameras everywhere. So much for this just being a qualifier event. It has the feel of the real thing. There's even a podium by the finish line for popping champagne.

The mechanics are in the pits making final adjustments to the cars.

"Miss MacDonald." An Ashford steward waves to me as Megan and I head to our car. "Mr. Ashford has asked that you not be involved this morning."

For a moment, I think he means Luca. When I realize which Mr. Ashford he's referring to, my teeth grind together. "Where is he?"

Megan's head swivels to me, startled. I stalk toward the changeroom.

"You can't go in—"

I barge inside to find half a dozen drivers in various states of dress.

"Shay?!"

"What the fuck, MacDonald?"

I ignore the cries from drivers and stalk around the lockers. In one corner I find Jameson, his broad back to me.

"You're really being that guy?" I demand. "You won't let me do my job."

"The one you were doing with Theo yesterday?" he says as he zips into his fire suit.

I throw up both hands. "You weren't here!"

But guilt edges in, because I did consider helping Theo.

"So I have to be here to earn your loyalty." Jameson's eyes meet mine, cold and accusing. This time, I've steeled myself for the betrayal. At least that would mean he cares, that I didn't imagine the moments of connection I felt with him these past weeks.

"Are we still talking about the car?" I ask under my breath.

There's a flicker of shock on his face.

Then he stalks past me toward the door.

❖

"NO MORE PARTIES before race days," Raj groans from his spot at the railing. He's wearing sunglasses and an Ashford Academy hat and holding his stomach.

Zane glances over. "You had one drink."

Raj pulls his hat down farther over his face.

On the track, Jameson gets into his car, adjusting his helmet.

The drivers start out of the pits in a procession.

"I'm worried," I tell Megan.

She doesn't ask about my love life this time. Her gaze is already on the track.

"Look how it twitches when he picks up the throttle."

I exhale. "You think the pressure is going to be too high."

Megan nods. "If he pushes, it'll bite him."

After the formation lap, Jameson lines up second, Theo first. My heart thuds against my ribs in anticipation of the start.

The starting lights hang over the grid—five red circles in a straight line.

One by one, they flare to life.

When I was a kid, I used to count them on my fingers, curled up on the couch beside my dad.

One.

Two.

Three.

Four.

Five.

The longest second in racing is the space between all five lights burning bright and everything going dark.

Go.

When the lights blink out at once, Jameson reacts faster. But Theo catches up by the time they get to the first corner.

"Theo's going to be quicker than yesterday," I breathe.

Megan's nails dig into my arm. "Jameson's coming back."

My heart is pounding because it's our car. Not because it's him.

Going into that first corner, I can see the tires twitch. Jameson hangs in too late.

Megan grips my arm. "If he lights up the rear tires again, he's done."

"I know." I'm already running down to the garage and Jameson's engineer. "You need to reduce the tire pressure when he comes in. He's not driving clean enough. If he lights up the back again, he'll lose control."

The engineer looks at me but finally nods.

It's neck and neck for the top four. I see one more case of oversteer in a corner and my heart is in my throat.

On the team radio, Jameson's lead engineer tells him to pit the next lap. "I recommend scaling back pressure for the rears for stability."

There's a pause. "No."

Jameson heads for the pits and all I can do is watch.

My heart is in my throat when he goes back out without making a single change to the car.

This isn't what I meant when I said we should take a risk. All of our projections were based on him driving perfectly, not on edge.

When I return to the railing, Megan's motionless beside me, eyes locked on the timing screen. "He could clean it up himself."

I look at her. "He has to be perfect."

I wait for him to make a mistake, holding my breath until spots appear behind my eyes.

But it never happens. He cleans up his corners. He drives as if we never fought this morning, as if he didn't walk in on me and Theo last night.

Cheers go up from the stands, the thousands of fans who came to see the future of F1 racing as Jameson flies past the checkered flag in first with seconds to spare.

"He won! *We* won!" Megan grips me as she jumps up and down, watching from the wall as champagne explodes and fans erupt.

Awe fills me. It's one thing to know you have a chance at being first, another to achieve it.

As Jameson's name and photo appear across the digital scoreboard, I'm giddy.

But I'm a little numb, too.

❖

THE ICE SCULPTURE is overkill.

When we were told about the gala after the first race, I wasn't expecting red carpets and spectacle. Still, it's the life-sized F1 car, expertly cut from a single block of ice and surrounded by roses on the dais, that puts it over the top.

"I want to drive it home," Raj says wistfully.

Zane snorts. "All the way from Austin? You'll freeze your balls off."

"It would be an improvement on the scooter," Megan decides.

The celebrations after the race are out of this world. The

drivers put it on the line today, and ARI corporate did their part tonight.

"Glad I brought a backup outfit." Megan nods to me. "It looks better on you anyway."

The black shift dress is slit high up one thigh. The shoes are black sparkly heels, and Megan found another classmate who lent them to us "for a good cause."

"No one cares what I wear," I insist, tugging down the skirt as a breeze blows through, making me shiver and long for a sweater.

"Incorrect," Theo says, descending. "We are all very grateful for this dress."

He pulls me into a hug, his chest hard and warm through the formal clothes.

"You did great," I say.

He makes a face. "Second."

"If you'd had another five laps, it would've been first."

Before he can respond, cameras descend. "Theo, what a drive right up to the flag. Tell us about it."

After a few minutes, the interviewer talking with him turns to me. "And who are you?" she asks.

"Ah. I work on Jameson's car. Megan and I do." I glance back to grab her, but she's talking to Zane.

The interviewer's expression brightens with interest. "Can you tell us about the adjustments you made?"

"Um. Well . . ." The spotlight makes me nervous. I'm looking past her, scanning the crowd without knowing what I'm looking for.

Until I see him.

Jameson.

On the other side of the room. Wearing a tux.

My world stops—my breath, my thoughts, the blood pumping through my body.

It's as if every atom of my being is required to process his mere existence. He's elegant, polished, and the most beautifully untouchable person I've ever seen.

Jameson looks around. Searching.

His gaze locks on me and that spot deep in my chest comes alive. It pulls at my ribs, hungry for all it can get.

Thud goes my heart.

"I didn't catch that?" the interviewer prompts.

I swallow. "The, ah. Tire pressure. We took a chance and went a little higher."

His attention drags down my body before returning to my face.

Thud, thud.

"Most teams don't mess with that." The interviewer's voice drifts through my ears, a dull echo.

Thud, thud, thud.

I blink, turning back to her. "Most teams don't have a driver like Jameson Ashford."

The interviewer looks like she wants to ask more but gets distracted by the sight of another driver and makes a beeline for him.

"You're going to be on TV!" Raj shouts, grabbing my arm. "You are basically famous."

"If you're not careful, you'll be famously basic." Zane narrows his eyes. "Next time if you don't want to answer a question, you can say 'no comment.'"

The truth is, it feels good to have gotten the win. It might be

Jameson's number on the car, but Megan and I made a real difference.

Then everyone's gazes shift past me, locking on something at my back.

I feel him before I turn to find Jameson standing behind me, his hair a mess of waves, his eyes nearly as black as his tux.

"That was a hell of a race," Zane says, looking at both me and Jameson. "No one else could pull that off."

"Are you staying?" Raj asks, hopeful. "We could get you a drink." He's already looking around for a waiter.

"No." Jameson turns back to me. "I came for a word."

His tone makes the hairs on my arms lift. "I'm off the clock."

"A *word*, Townie."

The others exchange a look. Theo opens his mouth to intervene, but I rest a hand on his sleeve.

"Go hang out with more adoring reporters," I tell him with a smile.

Theo looks as if he's going to protest but I shake my head. "I'll be back."

It's the reckless look in Jameson's eye that has me following him.

"What is this, Reign of Tyranny II: Revenge of the Hall Monitor?" I call after him.

"I don't know what you mean," he bites out.

"I mean you're being a dick." My most helpful tone doesn't blunt the words.

I remind myself that no matter how incredible he drove today, I'm angry. He disappeared yesterday after qualifying. Then showed up at the party and had the nerve to glare at me and Theo like his brother stole his favorite toy.

This morning, he told me I couldn't work on the car, the same one he publicly *claimed me* to work on. Then drove with calculated perfection, which only reminded me that when it comes down to it, nothing off the track matters.

Evidently, he's the only one allowed to rattle another person. When someone dares to do it to him, it's against the rules.

My heels click with every step until we reach the door to a concrete stairwell. It's open air at the ends, cut away to show off the sprawling city and lights below. In the distance, the racetrack nestles in the hills.

In the quieter space, I strike first.

"If you want to give me shit about the setup for your car, rethink that."

"Me?" Jameson looks around us at the stairwell, lit only by a sconce high on one wall. "You tried to change it mid-race."

"Because you couldn't handle it."

He's near enough I have to tilt my head up to meet his gaze.

"You were worried you'd look bad in front of the faculty handing out the internship." His face is cast in shadows.

"I was worried about *you*. I thought you might have been in your head after last night, but you weren't. After that pit stop, you drove so clean it's almost embarrassing."

A breeze has me wrapping my arms around myself. I'm feeling more vulnerable in the dark with him than I did in public with a camera in my face.

His square jaw works. "You thought that was clean."

"Yes!" I sputter. "Plus, you left after qualifying with no explanation and you didn't come back until late, and—"

"My dad was asked about the engineering students helping with the race," he interrupts. "Apparently, he rubber-stamped it last week but didn't realize the extent of it until now. He was furious, calling Vogel and threatening to pull the plug. It took most of the day to convince him not to."

"Oh." My mind is spinning. Shame fills my throat because I thought the worst of him. Again.

And he spent hours of one of the most important weekends of his life trying to keep me from being erased.

"Yeah, 'oh.'"

Jameson's mocking me, but it's hard to process when his hand catches mine. A line of heat traces straight down to my stomach.

Lower.

When his thumb presses into my palm, heat floods me. I sink my teeth into my lip.

He had a good reason for leaving. He saved my involvement in the race series, and all the other engineers' involvement, even though he had nothing to gain from it.

God, life was so much easier when he was just an asshole.

His gaze shifts down my body. I feel his attention on my breasts, my waist, my legs like a caress.

He's only touching my hand, but I swear I feel him everywhere.

"You really think that little of me, that I'd bring you to your first race and then bail?" When his eyes find mine again, his voice is softer.

I try to focus on what he's saying and not only the wanting vibrating through my entire body.

"No," I say honestly, because that would violate his own rules for himself. He might not give a shit about anyone else's, but he cares about those. "If you thought I was helping Theo, I wasn't—"

"Can't tell you how much I'd love to get through tonight without hearing you say my brother's name again."

His words are sharp, but there's no smugness in his expression.

"Too bad. Theo and I are friends." I realize the truth when I say it aloud.

"Friends." Jameson jumps on the word as he moves closer. It's unreal how quickly he eliminates the space between us. "And what are we?"

He looks wrecked. Like he's losing something he's wanted forever but never let himself claim.

My pulse kicks in my throat, my stomach doing that nervous excited thing it does when he's close enough our fighting feels like something else entirely.

"I think it's obvious."

His blue eyes are stormy, as if he's still on the track battling for a prize that's worth everything. His fingers thread through the hair at the nape of my neck. "Then fucking enlighten me."

Then he does the most disarming, horrifying thing of all.

He waits.

Everyone tells me what to want, what to do. Jameson simply ceases everything. As if the fastest person in the world decided I'm worth waiting forever for.

I say the only thing that feels right, the only one that captures the messy storm in my chest whenever he's nearby.

"Not friends."

His throat bobs. For a second, he looks as if he's going to let me go.

But something in him breaks. The hand in my hair forms a fist as he drags me up to him.

Then he's kissing me.

The universe splits in two—one reality where Jameson Ashford is kissing me, and one with every other possibility.

There's only one I want to live in.

His lips are as hard as the rest of him, but after weeks of barely there touches and stolen glances, it's the warmth of his mouth that's most overwhelming.

Desire courses through me, hot and sharp. My hands itch, and before I know it, they're exploring his chest, the hard muscles underneath.

My head tilts back as he angles me under him.

"Fuck. I've been trying so fucking hard not to do it." His words vibrate against my lips.

"What?" I manage.

He pulls back only a millimeter, his breath rough. "This."

He groans the syllable, claiming my mouth again like he's punishing me for his lack of restraint.

A breath shudders out of me—half disbelief, half surrender. Jameson's the most in-control person I know. Nothing makes him act without his permission.

Which is why this feels so surreal.

"The feeling," I pant against his mouth, "is not even a little mutual."

I press up on my toes and kiss him back. I'm delighting in the discovery that Jameson Ashford is reeling as hard as I am.

Possibly harder.

He reaches the hem of my dress, his fingers pressing into my bare skin.

I pull him off-balance and he follows me back against the wall. My shoulders bump the concrete, stealing my breath.

I'm mindless. The only thing that matters is skin and want and all the places we can't get close enough.

"This is a terrible idea, Townie."

He's desperate as his hands find my ass, then my thighs to hitch me up so I can wrap my legs around his hips.

"The worst," I agree.

He bites my lip, hard enough it hurts. We're back against the balcony rail now, his mouth traveling down my throat. He tugs the strap off my shoulder and resumes his path. It's scorching fire, that trail he's burning along my skin.

Whatever this is, it's more than envy or jealousy. He's the storm I craved, the one that tears through my life and leaves nowhere to hide.

A loud explosion makes me jump. I grip the collar of his shirt as red and gold streaks explode over the city beyond the balcony.

"You like fireworks?" he teases, breathless.

I glare but the effect is probably blunted by my greedy hands in his hair, my fingers under his shirt digging into the muscles of his back. "Everyone does."

Nothing could tear me away from this moment, but he turns me anyway, facing me toward the balcony.

His arm bands around my waist and his other hand slips under my dress. I'm pressed against him, my arm gripping his. I feel his hard body at my back, his breath near my ear.

It's like when we were on the motorcycle, only this time, I'm in front.

His touch skims up my thigh, inching inward. "This fucking dress."

"Useless. Can't even ride a bike in it," I manage.

"Not what I'm picturing you riding," he mutters, yanking it out of the way.

There's an entire world spread out in front of us, one I thought I wanted, but mine is reduced to his fingers when they brush between my legs. Pleasure shimmers through me.

My stomach trembles, my hips arching against him.

Jameson's teasing brushes turn into strokes where I'm already aching.

Then he presses a finger inside me.

He doesn't wait for me to adjust to him, he's already pumping in and out. Slow strokes that seem like they should soothe but all they do is make me wild.

Over my shoulder, Jameson's watching, his gaze hungry and out of focus.

He withdraws completely, and I'm about to protest when he returns with two fingers.

My breathing is shallow as he fills me, my body stretching to take him.

"If you knew how many times I've pictured this." His voice is a rasp. "How I'll look over and fucking wish I was inside you." Jameson's mouth comes back to mine, swallowing my needy sounds.

Another firework explodes in the sky, raining shimmering pink sparks that burn the backs of my eyes.

His thumb joins in, rubbing my clit as he presses inside. His rough breath keeps the time, the slow drag of friction punctuating each breath.

I arch against him, trying to absorb the sensation. I'm lost in pleasure, in him.

There's another crash. This time, I hear people crying out.

Probably on a balcony off the ballroom, celebrating the fireworks. Celebrating *him*.

Out there, they're cheering for one Jameson. The public one, the cool, restrained one.

In here, I'm learning about the real one.

"Fuck me back." Jameson's voice is a command.

My hips respond. I reach up, my fingers threading in his soft hair.

I can't stop. I couldn't if a hundred black-tie-clad guests barged through the door.

He groans and kisses me deeper, holding my concentration, his hand moving between my thighs.

Racing on track has nothing on this feeling. It's wanting and needing and having and somehow knowing it will never be enough.

Every stroke of his fingers winds me tighter. He's tuned into each moan and shiver.

I'm close.

I've never felt this powerful or powerless.

"More," I whisper.

Instead of speeding up, Jameson goes deeper, slower, more determined.

No.

I want to protest but I can't find the words.

From his rough breathing, I'm second-guessing the part where I thought he was in control.

Suddenly my body pulls tight, every part of me collapsing into a sparkling explosion of sensations.

My nails dig into his neck. I cry out, my sounds swallowed up by the oohs and aahs of the crowd nearby.

Jameson drags every ounce of sensation from me. I ride out the feeling, each ripple of pleasure somehow more consuming even as it fades in intensity.

I'm in trouble. My blissed-out body is a warning sign even before my head falls back against his chest, the muscles beneath still tense.

His lips press against my neck, and I feel the asshole smile.

"Told you I wouldn't let you lose."

The problem is, I'm starting to believe him.

23

Jameson

"FROM THE BEGINNING, my goal in building our headquarters here was to solidify F1's presence in the United States," Luca says as he tours a small group of prospective investors around the ARI offices with his sons in tow. "Forget showing up first, it's about who can keep going for years, decades, generations."

I'm distracted by dark hair passing a window, but it's not her. Not the girl whose voice I've been hearing in my head all week since the race, whose name I want to see on my phone every time it buzzes.

"Any update on who will race for ARI in a few months?" an investor asks, looking between me and Theo as if we're prize cattle.

Months.

That's the timeline for my future. The one I've been gunning for my entire life.

"That is still to be decided."

After the race last weekend, I'm in the lead. But we have two more contests, one in November and one the start of December.

That means two more opportunities for Theo, Knox, anyone to make their mark.

"Jamie pioneered an exceptional tire strategy last weekend that no one has executed before," Luca continues.

"Was this your idea?" another investor asks.

Luca smiles. "I can't take credit for *everything*."

They all laugh, but I hate that he's implying it was.

"It was a student's idea," I cut in. "And it flew in the face of everything we're advised to do. But we ran the simulations and decided it was worth the risk."

The investors exchange interested looks.

My father's eyes narrow, fists forming at his sides. "Since he's such a devoted spokesperson for Ashford Racing and its interests, Jameson has been undertaking a media tour this past week."

A wave of nausea rolls over me. My father reveres media, but this wasn't a reward.

"What of the rumors over Dekker's dismissal not being for cause?" another man asks.

"They're only rumors," my father says without hesitation. It's probably Ignite seeding gossip mid-season about our former driver's dismissal to cause havoc. But the man who spoke holds up his phone.

"I just received an alert that Dekker filed an official complaint, and the racing federation has opened an inquiry."

The hairs on my neck lift. This is news to me. From the way my father goes still, it's news to him, too. "No further comment." He recomposes himself, changing gears as smoothly as if he were in a car.

"We'll let you boys get back to training," Luca tells me and my brother before motioning the investors to follow him down the hall.

"Guess we're dismissed," Theo comments as we fall into step heading the other way.

"Think there's anything to this Dekker complaint?" he asks, his voice lower so we're not overheard by anyone in the offices flanking the hall.

"No doubt Ignite and other teams pressured the federation into opening an inquiry. Luca wouldn't have actually done what they're accusing him of."

"Because tanking his own car would be insane."

"It's an unnecessary risk."

Luca is strategic and aggressive, but he doesn't overreact. Pushing Dekker out this year so he can stage this spectacle would be reckless.

"With this press tour, he's really backing you publicly now," Theo comments.

"No, he's giving you an advantage."

It's been nearly impossible to train all week.

Which he knew when he assigned it to me. That was the price of keeping the student engineers involved, because he doesn't give something for nothing.

Still, there's the question of why he'd make things harder for me if he truly wants me to win the seat. If I didn't know better, I'd think he was trying to level the playing field. Our father loves an underdog story, but it's better if he's the author.

"Yes. Poor Jamie. Being the face of the company. However will you survive?" Theo asks as we continue down the hall. "Don't worry. I was more than happy to adopt your rogue engineer last weekend." He cuts me a look.

My brother's trying to get under my skin, and it's working. My mind drifts back to Shay.

"Nothing happened," I say.

"Between you?"

"No. Between you."

Theo's stunned silent.

The evening victory celebrations last Sunday were a mass of bright lights and stars, but Shay stood out in the midst of all of it.

When I spotted her across the room, wearing the fuck out of a dress and heels, I lost my words.

I wasn't ready to figure out what it meant but I had to be closer. When I got near her, she looked up at me like she couldn't decide if I was the good guy or the bad guy.

I didn't give a shit. I wanted to be the only guy.

What are we?

Not friends.

Her lips were soft but every other part of her was fire.

The way she met me stroke for stroke. I wanted to do so much more with her. I'd been wanting it for weeks.

With the press duties I've had the past week, classes have taken a back seat. Shay, Megan, and I haven't had a chance to focus on the next race. Hell, Shay and I haven't talked except for a couple of clipped *hi*'s.

But I stare at her when I see her down the hall. I've picked up my phone and started texting her more than once, only to delete whatever I wrote.

"You're into her." Theo's disbelieving voice brings me back. "Jamie Ashford, the person who puts driving ahead of every earthly desire, has it bad."

My brother likes picking scabs until they bleed, and I won't give him the satisfaction.

"Don't tell me you're calling dibs?" he prods.

"Maybe I am."

Theo's mouth works as we continue down the hall. He didn't expect me to say that. I didn't expect to say it myself.

"When was the last time you told me I couldn't have something?" he asks.

He's winding up for a mic drop and I'm not in the mood. I check my phone instead of responding.

"Never once. Certainly not a girl, not in all this time," he finishes.

I scan the hallway lined with offices, all the employees at ARI. The place I've wanted to take my whole life.

"Things change."

My brother's eyes widen, but he recovers quickly. Theo's adaptation skills are second to none. "You know she spent the whole weekend crying over a fight with her dad. You, go figure, were nowhere to be found."

My feverish memories fade. That's why she went to Theo. I kept her away from the car. Gave her shit. Made her life harder.

Theo was the one to comfort her. I should feel guilty, not jealous.

"You might be a fast driver, Jamie," he goes on. "But I know how to make a girl happy. And if you're thinking I'm going to concede, you're wrong."

Anger rises up. The kind I can normally manage, but he's not the only one on edge this week.

I round on him, shoving his shoulder hard enough he trips back toward the wall. "Your life is hard. I get it. I've done everything I can to make it better, and you know exactly what I mean." His eyes widen, but I continue. "You don't always have to make me the villain."

Theo's smile returns. Slow, and more assured than before.

"No." He brushes an invisible piece of lint off my shirt before meeting my eyes. "All I have to do is leave you to your own devices and you'll make yourself one."

24

Shay

"DAMN. YOU'RE FERAL." Megan sings her approval as I go to town on the villain on the screen.

"Is this not how you're supposed to play video games?" I grit my teeth.

"You've never played one?" Megan tosses me a surprised look from her seat on the couch next to me. "You really did grow up under the hood of a car."

I throw a chip at her, then keep mashing buttons like stubborn persistence will get me somewhere.

It's not working in any other part of my life.

In the week since the race, I've been crashing at Megan's in the two-bedroom apartment off campus she shares with Raj. I'm sleeping on an air mattress in her room, trying to act as if my life is normal and it's not eating me up that Dad and I have barely spoken since last weekend.

I tried calling him on our way home from the race, but he was so angry, insisting I leave the garage and drop out of school. The only time I saw him was when I went to the house to pick up some clothes.

He didn't look at me. Not once.

Almost like if he did, he'd say something he couldn't take back.

Keane told me Dad's insisting on returning to work, even though it's too soon.

But what's currently pulling most of my attention is Jameson.

The entire week following the race was torture. He wasn't in class, and the few times I saw him, he was trailed by media. He looked cool as ever.

I considered texting him but couldn't decide what to say.

Are you still thinking about it at least a hundred times a day like I am?

The next Monday, I was getting coffee at the cafeteria before class—my first one from The Junction was gone in a flash—when I felt tingles up my spine. I looked up to find Jameson watching me from the doorway.

"Hi." His hand brushed my arm when he joined me in line. My heart started to hammer.

"Hi. Didn't know you drank coffee."

"I don't." He bought mine without even asking.

I know how to act when he's provoking and derisive. This was . . . weirder. I needed some semblance of our old banter to feel like my world isn't off its axis.

"Bored with your adoring fans?" I asked Tuesday in Vogel's class after he ignored two objectively attractive girls trying to attach themselves to him in the hallway.

He unpacked his books, choosing a seat two down from mine in the same row—well outside of the ones the drivers normally occupy. "They're not going to help with my next race."

"So, it's my brain you like."

"Yeah, well, your mouth is annoying as hell." His gaze flicked down. "I can't stop thinking about it."

My retort died on my lips.

When Professor Vogel came in and started the class, I turned toward the front, my cheeks burning and my body throbbing.

Since we hooked up, I've gone from fantasies and daydreams to a 24/7 private steam reel I can't turn off.

If I was going to hook up with an Ashford, Theo would be the obvious choice. Evidently, I have the worst taste in guys, because all I see is his difficult, unyielding brother who shoved his way into my head and pushed all my buttons.

Wednesday, Jameson texts me and Megan to ask for a meeting in one of the garages on campus to start working on race strategy.

From the moment I walk in and our eyes lock, I'm trying to focus on the car and failing miserably.

We're going over the setup, his hip near mine.

"Here, let me," he murmurs when there's a long reach to fix something. His gaze lands on my elbow, as if he knows it's a strain.

"I've got it," I insist. I've survived the last sixteen years without Jameson Ashford's help, thank you very much.

"Stubborn." He reaches for the ratchet, but I hold on.

"Capable," I correct.

I should be worried about the wreckage of my life, but I can't because for the first time in over a week, Jameson and I are pressed against each other.

It's been way too long.

A breath shudders out. "About last week—"

"Yeah." He answers before I've finished.

"It was a bad idea."

He's standing behind me. His body lines up with mine through our clothes, and I'm feeling every inch of him.

"You think it was a mistake." His voice is quiet next to my ear.

"I didn't say mistake. I said it was a bad idea." The smell of motor oil fills the garage, but all I'm aware of his scent. Dark. Cool. Intoxicating.

"So you like bad ideas."

I twist to meet his gaze, my breasts brushing his chest. "How do you know?"

Jameson's gaze flicks down to my mouth, his dark lashes lowering over eyes that burn with intensity.

"Because you're thinking about doing it again right now."

His thumb slips under my shirt to rub torturous circles against my hip. A soft moan escapes my lips.

"You want me to zip-tie your driveshaft again, Ashford?" I manage, my eyes threatening to drift closed.

Jameson's lips ghost my neck where a few hairs escape my messy bun. "Don't make promises you won't keep."

Damn, he turns me on. I need his hand a little lower. His mouth too.

He's so close I can feel his breath. Just a couple of millimeters and—

"Guys! I have an idea . . ." Megan's voice comes from around the corner and we jump apart.

"What are you doing tonight?" Jameson asks an hour later at my locker near the garage as we're wrapping up. Class is over for the day, and so is our garage time.

His voice makes me want to say "you" like a bad joke.

"I have to cover a shift."

The disappointment in his eyes is so perfect I want to cry, but he regroups fast. "You're staying with Megan. She told me," he supplies at my look.

I nod. "And Raj."

I shuffle my books between the locker and my bag, and he shifts to rest his back against the metal.

"I could sneak in your window tonight."

He says it so casually I nearly drop my books.

The possibility sends a rush through me. The line of women who'd give everything to have Jameson Ashford text *U up?* is long enough to pave the streets of the Monaco Grand Prix.

"Sure thing, Edward Cullen. You'd get bludgeoned to death with a stiletto."

His lips twitch. "By Megan or Raj?"

"Megan. Raj would make you coffee and force you to hang out with him."

Still, my gaze drags down his body shamelessly. How anyone can be so beautiful is beyond me.

He hesitates, then keeps talking. "How're things with your dad?"

The question lands more heavily than he seems to expect. *Hello, hard right.*

"Are you pretending to care?"

Jameson looks offended. "I'm not pretending. Just figured that's why you moved out."

My gaze lingers on him as I finish packing my bag and shut my locker.

"We haven't talked since the race. He doesn't like me going to school here. He doesn't like me involved in the academy, or ARI. He thinks this world is destined to beat me down. All fragile male egos and that."

"No clue where he got that idea," Jameson deadpans, and my lips twitch.

When I start toward the back doors, he falls into step next to me. As we walk, I tell him how my dad took me in, how he's worked for ARI his entire career.

Campus is pretty busy still, and students and professors alike nod to him as we pass. If I figured we'd get weird looks, we don't. Probably because everyone knows we're working together.

If they knew what else we were doing, they might care more.

"You never told me you were covering for him." Jameson's voice brings me back.

My bag feels heavier suddenly, and I shift it on my shoulder. "I thought if you knew, you would tell your dad. I didn't figure Luca would look kindly on people going behind his back, even for a good cause."

"Why did you do it?"

"To take care of him after all he's done to take care of both of us."

"That's not it," he predicts. "Part of it, sure. But that's not the real reason."

I frown as he waits me out. "Maybe I wanted to prove myself, to show him I could fit into this world he's been trying to keep me out of."

His gaze sharpens, like I hit closer than I meant to. "The problem with always trying to be better is you never get to be good enough. Ask me how I know."

I blink up at him, surprised to hear those words from his mouth. Maybe it's one more thing we have in common.

We reach the back door and Jameson holds it for me.

"Where are you going?" I ask him, curious.

"Walking you to your car."

Oh. That's new.

We cross the street to reach the back parking lot, where the Mustang is one of a few dozen student vehicles.

"You told Theo about your dad," Jameson says. There's an implied question underneath, one I sense is about my motives, not my actions.

"He found out." I hear the edge in my own voice and hate that it's there. "Plus, I care about Theo. He was the first person to welcome me to Ashford. We have fun," I go on as I unlock the door and drop my bag inside.

"Fun." Jameson echoes the word as if it tastes terrible.

"You want me to drop you at *your* car?" I tease, straightening. I'm joking, and I'm not. I'm greedy for even a few more seconds with him before I head to The Junction to help Bree.

"I have a few more things to do at school first." He cocks his head as he steps closer, squinting into the sun. "Besides, I brought the Ducati."

Lust slams into me, leaves my knees weak. The thought of Jameson on that bike was hot enough when I couldn't stand him. Now, I can't even look at his mouth without picturing it on me.

"You keep stealing your brother's bike, he might lash out," I manage.

He hooks a finger in the waistband of my jeans, stepping his feet between mine and forcing my legs wide. He cups my neck, curved lips skimming the shell of my ear.

"Then I'll have to keep riding it until it's not his anymore."

25

Shay

THAT NIGHT I pull into the ARI garage to find my dad's truck already there.

I bang my head against the steering wheel when Keane knocks on my window.

"Got two MacDonalds for the price of one."

I look past Keane to see my dad watching from the door.

"You have a fifteen-minute break. One of you. Both of you." He waves a hand.

I drag my feet inside.

"Since when are you back?" I ask when I step into the garage. Dad's bent over a workbench, tightening a bolt that's already flush.

"This is my first shift. Keane said you've been doing a good job. You didn't need to do that."

"I wanted to." I hover near the door as if I might need to make a quick exit.

"You don't need to work this hard."

"It felt good," I admit.

The sounds of the garage fill my ears, a drone of machinery punctuated by metal on metal.

"Do you have any idea how it feels," he says, "to realize your kid took on your burdens without you even knowing?" He finally straightens, but instead of facing me, he reaches for a rag and turns away.

"It wasn't like that."

Except it kind of was. I think of my talk with Jameson.

"It wasn't only about your injury. I wanted to see if I could do it." I swallow, gesturing to the bays. "This has always been your thing. And I . . . I wanted to know if it could be mine, too."

I told myself I went to Ohio State to get the education that meant so much to my dad before opening a garage together. But really, it had been a safe place to be. Doing well meant staying on top of the work.

Here, it meant being willing to be uncomfortable and underestimated. To keep showing up anyway.

Dad's listening for the first time since our fight.

"Who's staying and who's going?" Keane demands, appearing in the doorway of the break room with his arms folded. His gaze flicks between us like he's bracing for shrapnel.

We stare each other down.

"I'm staying," Dad says at last. "Need anything?"

"No. Thanks."

I wait for him to tell me to come home. He doesn't.

We're on the verge of making up but I need to be honest. "I helped win the first race. And I'm going to help win the next one."

Dad's hand stills on the rag.

"I wish you wouldn't."

"Why not?"

"Because you'll get hurt and I won't be able to stop it." His clear eyes meet mine.

If there's a way to tell him he doesn't need to protect me—or that he can't—I wish I knew what it was.

Instead, I give him the sandwich I made for my shift. "Good luck, Dad."

I wait for him to respond. To say my name or to say anything really.

I leave anyway.

❖

"It's unacceptable. We're halfway through the semester and they won't even tell us how we're doing on the internship," Megan points out as we're emerging from our first class of the day.

"You want an ordered ranking?" I ask, shouldering my bag.

"Just a list of names, annotated," she decides. "'Zane—too preppy.'"

"'Megan—too jealous,'" he retorts.

"'Shay—fucking the drivers.'"

"Untrue," I counter.

Megan arches a brow. "I heard Jameson walked you to your car last night."

Yeah, and that's all he did. The lack of contact is driving me insane.

You keep stealing your brother's bike, he might lash out.

Then I'll have to keep riding it until it's not his anymore.

I can't stop replaying his words, but I'm here to win an internship and carve out a spot in this world.

The second race is just over a week away, and exams are looming, so we head to the library to study during our hour off.

We get settled around a table with our laptops and books. The place is overrun with engineers, all trying to absorb the impossibly comprehensive information covered by our classes.

"You really have to learn all that?" a voice murmurs by my ear.

I jump. "You need a bell."

Theo grins, dragging a chair next to mine and straddling it. "That takes all the fun out of sneaking up on people."

Megan lifts her phone and snaps a picture.

"What?" Theo asks.

"Documenting a rare sighting of a driver in the library."

Theo wads up a sheet of paper from the table and tosses it at her.

"Those were my notes!" Raj protests.

Theo ignores him and bends closer to me. "I haven't seen you since the race."

I twist the cap on my water bottle, noticing it's empty. "I know."

I push back from the table and stand, heading for the fountain on the wall tucked between two rows of stacks. He follows, leaning against the wall like he belongs there. "I thought we had something, New Girl."

The honesty in his voice throws me. "We did. *Do*. I just think we're better off as friends."

"Because you're allergic to distractions?"

"Because I'm kind of . . . in it with someone right now."

His smile falters. "If you're talking about Jamie, don't get sucked in by that brooding, self-sacrificing act. My brother isn't boyfriend material."

I fill my bottle and screw the cap back on. "I didn't know that's what I was looking for." I look him up and down. "Are you auditioning for the part?"

"For the right girl."

My chest tightens at the earnestness in his voice.

"I just don't want to see you get hurt," he adds.

My phone buzzes in my pocket. I glance down at it, careful not to tilt the screen too far toward Theo.

JAMESON: You look like you need a break.

My head snaps up.

I scan the library. No sign of him at any of the tables.

Then I see him.

Through the windows beyond the far side of the stacks. He's outside, his face just visible, but he's mostly hidden from the tables where everyone is studying.

"Tell me you'll think about it," Theo presses.

"I promise. Listen, I've got to go."

I pull him into a hug and he reluctantly lets me.

"If it helps, my dick is way bigger," he murmurs.

"Theo!" I shove him and he lifts both hands.

Hopefully, I've salvaged our friendship. Theo doesn't seem like a guy who'd let feelings over a girl keep him down for long.

When he heads back toward the tables, I cut between the stacks and cross the library, keeping my eyes down until I reach the window.

"What're you doing?" I demand.

Jameson leans closer. "Busting you out. You look bored."

"Convenient that I was bored talking with Theo."

"I didn't notice."

"Liar." I rest my elbows on the sill.

"You done here?" he asks mildly, as if he knows the answer.

Rain drips from the eaves outside, and I wrap my sweater tighter around me.

I make excuses to my friends, promising to be back in an hour, before I slip out the side door of the school.

Jameson's waiting by the road on his bike. I take a second to appreciate his graceful posture, the impatient tilt of his head. "Let's go."

Somewhere along the line, I started picturing my world with Jameson Ashford in it. At first, he was lurking at the edges. Lately, he's fully in frame. Consuming and unapologetic.

I put on a helmet and climb on behind him.

The speed is a drug. So is the feel of him, warm and hard and masculine in front of me. His hips between my thighs.

Rain streaks my sweater, beading on my skin, but I couldn't care less. He pulls off onto a shoulder with a view of the river and cuts the engine.

"This is my favorite spot," he says, dragging off his helmet. "I come here when I need to think. To forget about . . . everything I'm supposed to be thinking about."

I slide off the bike and walk toward the edge, admiring the serene setting. "You bring anyone here?"

"No."

The river roars below us, drowning out the world.

It hits extra hard that he brought me. When I turn back, Jameson is watching me, not the view. The expression on his face is wary—not like he's trying to shut me out, but like he's trying to decide if he can let me in.

I cross to him, standing close enough his knee brushes mine. "Did you bust me out because you planned it or you saw me talking to Theo?"

In an effortless move, he grabs me and sets me astride the bike, facing him. My thighs rest over his.

"Rest" is the wrong word. Every muscle in my body is tight, every inch of me wanting.

"Both."

His simple admission is a drug. I crave it, especially when I know how hard he works to keep his inner life private.

"And how much of this"—I gesture between us—"is because Theo wanted me first?"

Jameson's fingers thread in my hair, the strands tangled from the wind. "Who says he wanted you first?"

He takes his time as his mouth drags along my skin. I want to memorize him—his scent, his hands, the way he can shift from demanding to gentle in a heartbeat.

The rain has nearly stopped. There's only the occasional drop that cools my heated skin.

"The first time you rode on this bike with me," he says, pulling back an inch, "I couldn't think of anything else all week."

"Really." Forget aerodynamics, Jameson Ashford confessing how long I've been living rent free in his head is my new favorite subject.

"That and how you told me off. At my own damn house, no less. How'd you get so brave, Townie?"

I shift over him, trailing a finger across his shoulder, feeling the muscles jump underneath my touch. "You call it brave, I call it surviving. I've always had to look out for myself. My dad and I, we had to look out for each other."

He searches my face, tucking a strand of hair behind my ear. "I would've kept your secret."

The way he says it hits as hard as the words.

I usually have a response to everything, but now, I'm at a loss.

Jameson's lips tug up, and mine do, too.

If antagonizing him is a thrill, it's nothing compared with the high of being on the same page.

"What you did at that race, worrying about me," he goes on, "no one's ever done that. People like my name or what I can do for them. With you, it doesn't feel that way. It's never felt that way."

"Your name is inconvenient at best," I assure him.

He's holding my ribs, thumbs stroking just under my breasts. When he catches the underside on the next pass, a jolt of pleasure has me pressing closer.

I roll my hips, feeling the hard ridge of him between my thighs through our clothes.

He exhales a hiss of breath.

A car streaks by on the road. Neither of us looks up.

"I've had these dreams lately," he murmurs against my skin. "The party after the first race. The fireworks. What we could've done if we'd had more time."

"Wait. Don't tell me you wanted to get off, too?" I blink up at him with my most innocent expression.

Jameson mutters something I can't hear and drags me up to him.

When he kisses me, I'm already breathless. His fingers

tangle in my hair at my nape, dragging my head back as if he's finally had enough of our bullshit.

Maybe I have, too.

He cups my breasts through my shirt, my nipples hard from the cold and his touch. He twists one in his fingers, light at first. The sensation tugs through my entire body.

He grinds into me, and the friction sends delicious shivers down my thighs. I hiccup a breath. It's like being struck by lightning. Everything with him feels next level.

I want to see what color his eyes turn when he's crossing the finish line.

With a groan, he yanks my shirt down and latches onto my breast.

The rain soaked both of us but I'm not cold. His skin is hot under his wet shirt, my fingers greedy for every part I can reach.

"Easy," he murmurs.

Instead, I shift over him, getting an even better angle. It's tough with the layers of his pants and my jeans between us, but I'm up for the challenge.

"Fuck, Townie." His grunt is hoarse, a little desperate.

I don't let up. Not until Jameson goes tight under me, groaning into my neck.

When he pulls back, his expression is horrified.

"Did you just . . . ?" I swipe a finger across my lips.

He nods slowly, shifting on the bike.

My grin is unstoppable.

"Oh, you liked that, did you?" he tosses, every syllable laced with self-deprecation. "You're pretty fucking pleased with yourself."

"Delighted," I agree as I tug my shirt back in place. We

might have turned the side of the road into dry humping paradise, but we're basically still in public.

As much fun as I'm having, I can't kick the realization that I've never wanted someone like I want him. It's as if being with him changes me. Am I a different person when I'm with him, or do I just look different when I see myself through his eyes?

We're going down a path leading somewhere unknown, but I can't hear the warning bells. Not when he's right here. We're right here.

"Jameson."

His hands settle on my hips as he meets my gaze. "Yeah."

"Can I trust you?" I ask tentatively.

"I'd never put you at risk."

"Again."

He frowns, gaze searching mine.

"You'd never put me at risk *again*. Because there was that time you drove into me, which was a massively dickish meet-cute, by the way."

Jameson's eyes flicker. "Right."

A semitruck roars past. Its horn blares, its tires sending up a spray of water from the shoulder.

"That was absolutely the last time," he says, deadpan. I laugh.

My phone rings, and I briefly fantasize about throwing it into the river.

"Damn it. I promised Megan I'd study with her," I say under my breath.

His sigh is pure annoyance at the universe. "Guess I should get you back. We could stop and get you fresh clothes."

"Deal."

"I could come inside . . ." His thumbs press into my hip bones under my wet shirt, his mouth dropping to my collarbone.

I swear my toes curl. "You might not fail out of the academy if you have a bad test. But I definitely will."

I take a seat behind him again, feeling the thud of his heartbeat as we race back through the rain and wishing we had more time.

26

Jameson

JAMESON: I have a problem.

EDEN: You starting to believe that media bullshit you're spouting about the next race?

JAMESON: There's a girl.

EDEN: NO. Is this Theo? Did you steal Jamie's phone again?

JAMESON: Try again.

EDEN: Big brother, I'm happy for you. What's she like?

JAMESON: Stubborn. Smart. Exploits my limited weaknesses to a painful degree.

EDEN: Oooh, sounds promising.

JAMESON: It's not that big a deal.

EDEN: With you it is. Theo ties his heart to a rope and drags it behind his car. You guard yours like it's classified.

JAMESON: You're telling me to be careful.

EDEN: I'm telling you if she's worth it, you should let her in.

It's raining again.

For the second day straight, streaks of it paint the kitchen windows.

Normally I'd be irritated, because it means I'm skipping my track time. Instead, I'm replaying yesterday afternoon with Shay. Being relaxed doesn't come naturally to me like it does to Theo, but for Shay, I'm going to try.

It felt good to surprise her, stealing her away from the library like I could claim her. Better still, to take her down to the river, to a place that's only ever been mine.

"The second race is next weekend. How long did you train today?" Luca asks, taking in my jeans and T-shirt when he comes into the kitchen behind me.

"I didn't." I grab a protein drink from the fridge.

His jacket is perfectly pressed, the lines casually elegant. It's hard to picture him in a fire suit when the wool seems like his eternal uniform.

"You shouldn't be skipping workouts." He has a way of delivering the most neutral statement like a pointed critique.

"You shouldn't have assigned me extra PR duties." I pop the top on the drink and chug it.

Luca watches steadily until I'm finished. "Get it out of your system."

"What?" My head snaps up. I know exactly what he means.

"Whatever's distracting you. Get it out."

Pressure has amped up around my future, but that's not what's on my mind. It's not even that winning the seat feels less important than it did. More like something else had quietly taken first place when I wasn't looking.

Shay and I haven't deliberately kept it a secret, but downplaying spending extra time together made sense for both of us. All I know is that the more time I spend with her, the more I want to.

Touching her makes me feel grounded in a way I never have. And the worst part is it isn't even about getting off. It's her. The way she gets under my skin and stays there.

"This race could determine who sits in that second seat," Luca goes on. "If you do your job this weekend."

Because he's always counting. Always calculating.

Shay's words echo in my head about me being more than a PR stunt—being Luca's son, and him not treating me that way.

"Actually, you determine that," I hear myself respond. "Everyone knows you're calling the shots."

His nostrils flare. "Theo's already at the track. I never expected he'd be the one impressing me with his focus."

"Do us both a favor and stop using him to get to me for a single second."

I expect him to snap back. But instead, his voice softens.

"He gets to you because he's your natural competition. Not because of me. A lot goes into building a company like ARI. Even more goes into fighting to keep it. One day, you'll understand."

27

CHALLENGER CHAMPIONSHIP
Race Two

Shay

JAMESON: That's it. Only one Ashford is surviving the weekend.

SHAY: It can't be that bad.

JAMESON: I'm going to kill Theo. We have a four-hour drive and he's singing like it's karaoke night.

Nothing causes an uproar like the Ashford jet breaking down on the way to Miami. Thunderstorms in the area forced them to make an emergency landing at another airport ahead of the second Challenger race.

"Are they flying commercial?" Megan peers over the back of my lounge chair on the pool deck in her hot pink one-piece at the hotel. We got in an hour ago. Overhead, the clouds that wreaked havoc are clearing.

"Nope. Apparently, the drivers are all on a coach bus from

Orlando." I hold up the photo on my phone as evidence. Megan and Raj crack up.

This weekend is the second race that will determine ARI's new driver next year—and probably who will score an internship on the grid. We've been working on strategy for this race and have some plans for the long straights broken up by slow corners, but the biggest wildcard is the weather.

Since we're in South Florida, there's a good chance it'll be wet on track for at least part of the race. With tight walls and little runoff, there's almost no room for error.

Jameson and I have been texting all week and hanging out when we can steal time between classes and his ARI commitments. I figured I'd have more spare moments now that I'm not covering my dad's shifts, but between keeping up with school and working on the Challenger series, it doesn't feel that way.

Jameson's been jumping through hoops for his father doing extra PR for the company. I've been trying to keep up with classes while studying reams of data on the cars, the track, his driving.

This weekend, we might actually get a few minutes alone.

SHAY: If your strategy is pissing your brother off before the race, it's working.

Theo responds instantly.

THEO: Thanks for letting me know 😀

SHAY: Where are you staying?

I type back to Jameson.

Dots appear in my chat. Theo's window lights up with the name of a hotel.

It's the same place we're staying.

JAMESON: What are you wearing?

Heat tingles between my thighs.

"What's wrong?" Raj demands, probably clocking the change in my expression.

"The drivers are staying here."

"WHAT?!" Megan screeches.

I send a pic of the pool with my legs in it.

THEO: My room or yours? 😉

"Fuck!" I hurry to unsend it, but it's too late. *Wrong Ashford.*

JAMESON: You mean to send Theo a picture of your legs?

SHAY: I did not. As a concession, yours has tits too.

I take a new picture and send it.

JAMESON: I told the driver if we're not there soon, I'm taking over.

SHAY: Bring swimming shorts.

JAMESON: Too late. You'll have to take me without them.

Did he just send a devil emoji? Be still my heart.

There's a lot at stake this weekend. But first, there will be a riot if Jameson Ashford goes skinny-dipping in this Miami pool.

"I don't know how you do it," Megan muses over my shoulder.

"Do what?"

"Keep both Ashfords in line."

"I don't have to. Theo and I are friends. Jameson and I are . . . something else."

"So, Theo just backed off." She cocks her head.

"Why wouldn't he?"

We're still friends. I've done everything in my power to assure that.

"God, you're naive." She drops into her chair sideways to face me. "Let's recap. The second-fastest driver in school—possibly on the planet—has a thing for you. You decide you like his brother more, and he said, 'My mistake, yeah, Jameson can have first shot at you like he's had first shot at literally everything else'?"

I frown. "You say 'first shot' like there's going to be a second shot."

"Not the point. The point is, you're not the first thing both Ashford boys have wanted. You're the first thing Theo actually had a chance at winning."

❖

"WE'RE GOING TO change and go for a drink in town. Want to join?" Megan asks an hour later, nodding toward Zane and Raj, who are fighting over a lounger in the pool.

"I was going to wait for the drivers to get in."

Megan and I are staying on the first floor, which means we have patios facing the front of the building. I'm planning to head to our shared room to take a shower and wash the chlorine off me, because Jameson Ashford is on his way here and I have an entire hotel room to myself.

"Oh, I see how it is." Her grin widens.

"That's not it." Except it totally is.

Five minutes later, I'm stepping into the shower when I see it.

Big. Dark. Possibly fuzzy and definitely occupying the corner I was about to put my bare foot in.

"AHHH!" I wrap the towel around me and sprint out of the bathroom. "Megan!" I shout in case she's still here.

No answer.

I scramble for my phone and send off a text to my friend. She only left a few minutes ago. They could still be outside.

There's a knock on the patio door. I run to it and jerk it wide.

Jameson's there in a jacket and jeans, his hair messy from the wind. "What's wrong? I heard you scream."

He's all commanding intensity. Knowing he's on my side, it's oddly comforting.

"Shay? What is it?" Theo's right behind him.

I look between both Ashfords. A moment ago, I would have been thrilled for two saviors, but I'm realizing I'm standing here in a towel and they're not looking at one another.

"It's in there," I whisper, pointing toward the bathroom.

Jameson moves closer and inspects me for damage. While he does, Theo brushes past us into the hotel room.

"I've got this," Jameson calls after Theo.

"Do you?" Theo's already at the bathroom door.

I'm too edgy to roll my eyes as I follow them toward the light. When I get to the doorway, they're both standing staring at the corner of the shower.

"That's it." Jameson blinks.

"A spider?" Theo sounds underwhelmed. "You're scared of a spider."

"No one said scared." I fold my arms defensively.

Theo goes to the other room, returning a moment later with a shoe from the mat by the door.

"Don't kill it!" I protest, holding out a water glass from the counter. "Take it outside."

Before he can, Jameson grabs the glass from me and stalks over to the shower. In one smooth attempt, he catches it and traps it between a hand towel and upside-down glass.

He leads a strange parade of the three of us toward the patio.

There's a line of students along the walkway, watching the last of the drivers get off the bus.

I'm in a towel, flanked by Ashfords.

Great.

A pointed look from Jameson has them dispersing, but they're whispering.

"Thanks for the help. Both of you," I amend.

Theo's gaze flicks down my body. "You need anything else? Or is Jamie handling that too?"

Jameson starts to speak, but I hold up a hand.

"I'm fine, Theo. Thank you for the save." I force a smile.

He looks as if he wants to say something else, but only nods. He grabs a duffel bag by the door.

"Don't stay out too late," he says to his brother, and starts down toward the hotel lobby. I stare after him.

"What is it?" Jameson's voice brings me back.

I didn't expect this to be so rough on Theo.

"Nothing," I say finally.

I take him in, his probing expression, the tension in his body. Suddenly I'm not thinking of Theo.

"Come to think of it, I might need your help with something."

Heat flares in his eyes as he steps closer. "Say less."

He backs me toward the patio door. My hand slips down the door to the handle. It takes me three tries to push it wide enough for us to trip inside.

Jameson grabs me, keeps me from falling. Through one cracked eye, I glance at the corner of the room. It's dark and shadowy. Threatening.

"What's wrong?" Jameson asks as he feels me stiffen.

I don't answer.

His lips twitch. "Go have your shower. I'll do a sweep for eight-legged intruders."

Gratitude rises up that this time, he doesn't make fun of me. "Thanks."

I dart for the bathroom. As much as I want him, I can't keep my head on what we're doing. Plus, I need the shower.

"And don't leave," I call over my shoulder, clutching my towel with one hand.

He's already crouched in the corner, inspecting the crevice. "I won't."

I take a second to admire him before stepping into the bathroom, closing the door most of the way. The shower is modern, the kind that's level with the floor and doesn't have a bath, and hot water explodes from the showerhead when I turn it on.

As I drop the towel and step inside, pulling the glass sliding door after me, I still can't believe Jameson Ashford is in my room.

I stick my head under the spray, the warmth of the water feeling delicious on my body that's still cold from being outside in my towel.

The rising steam obscures part of the glass, but when I peer out, I can still see my face reflected in the mirror over the sink. The necklace around my neck.

I've never been the one with her future laid out in front of her like a bouquet of flowers to choose from. But somehow, I'm in a Miami hotel waiting to race a car I've worked on, Jameson Ashford playing white knight in my hotel room a few feet away.

Is this my life?

My dad's warnings come back at once—about the academy, about ARI. I'm sure he's just worried it's too much of a boys' club, or that I'll be disappointed when I fall short of attaining my dreams.

The knock on the door makes me jump.

"Yes?"

"All clear." Jameson's voice comes through the door.

"Okay." My throat is tight despite the humid air.

I rinse my hair, squeezing out the ends, and start to wash the rest of my body.

"You good?" He's still there. I can't see him, but I hear him at the inch-wide gap. "Townie?"

"Great. Fine." I say it in a rush.

Suddenly I'm overheating, and I reach for the glass door and slide it open.

Cool air floods in. I inhale gulps of it.

"They're calling for rain tomorrow." Jameson's words drift into my head.

"I'm not worried about the car. The drivers could be a problem though," I say. I'm staring at the mirror but seeing the track as I push a piece of wet hair behind my ear.

If they don't tone down the aggression and try to use the rain to outdo their rivals in wet conditions, losing could be the least of our concerns.

"I can handle a little water."

The bathroom door swings open. Jameson leans against the doorway, his eyes meeting mine in the mirror.

The heat flooding my body is back, but it's not from the steam or the water. His gaze moves all the way down to my toes. He's even slower on the way back up. For a man whose entire life is about speed, I've never seen him take so much time.

He lingers on my calves, my thighs, my waist, my breasts. Each part tingles under his gaze.

When his attention returns to my face, his expression is pure hunger.

I've always been a little self-conscious about my body, but the way he's staring, I feel beautiful. I swallow from anticipation and nerves. My finger traces my thigh of its own accord, because I need to touch something, to be touched.

"Um. The track will be wet." I swallow. Remembering I have a point to make that doesn't involve my tongue tracing the outline of his pecs is impossible.

Jameson steps toward me. "Wet," he echoes.

The next step brings him into the shower and forces me back. He reaches for the hem of his shirt, drags it over his head without breaking my gaze.

"Slippery." Somehow, I'm still speaking. "You'll lose grip."

His chest is hard planes and sharp angles, beautiful muscles and a small white line running across his pec. It only makes him more human, more real.

"Then I'll find something to hold on to."

Jameson grabs my hair and drags me against him.

He's hot and hard and consuming. His skin slides against mine under the spray and makes each touch slick.

He backs me against the tile, our bodies colliding.

His hands skim down to cup my breasts, squeezing just enough that I squirm. When I lean into him, making a little sound of pleasure, his lips follow.

He sucks my nipple into his mouth. Fire streaks straight through me.

All week, all month, I've wanted him. Our moment on the balcony after the first race was hot, but it was nowhere near enough.

When he switches to the other side, my fingers dig into his shoulders to keep my balance. Maybe my sanity.

"From the second you walked out in that towel, all I could think about were the things I want to do to you." His groan is swallowed up by the pounding water. The vibration of his lips on my skin says more than words anyway.

I shift against him, feeling his hard cock press against my stomach. In the mirror over the sink, I can see us, him bent over me.

Last time was him touching me. I want to touch him, to make him as unhinged as he's making me. I fumble with his jeans, the button and zipper causing me grief before he yanks them off his legs.

His clothes are forming a wet pile on the floor. It's so chaotic, I grin.

At least until his boxer briefs follow.

My breath stutters, my hand hesitating.

He's big. Thick and hard, and I never thought much about male anatomy being beautiful, but if there was a guy to change my mind on that, it would be this one.

Finally, I wrap my hand around him, rewarded by a hiss when I do. I slide my grip down over his length. It's easy enough thanks to the shower.

Watching the water streak down his abs, across my hand and him, is hypnotizing.

"Fuck," he growls. I lick my lips, suddenly wondering how good I can make him feel.

When I glance up, his hair is soaked too, hanging in his face until he reaches up to shove it away.

"Stop." Just when I'm starting to think he's going to let me find out, he tugs my hand away.

"You don't like it?"

"I do. But I've got plans for you." He turns off the shower before hitching me up so my legs are around his waist. He carries me out of the shower, not bothering to stop for a towel on the way out. Over his shoulder, I can still see his jeans and shorts in a wet pile on the bath mat.

"Of course you do," I mutter.

With his hands occupied holding me up, it's my turn to go on offense. My greedy mouth slides to his jaw, his neck. When I nip at the side of his throat, I'm rewarded with a low curse.

We get halfway into the bedroom before Jameson sets me on the dresser, the edge digging into my ass. His fingers dimple the skin of my thighs, tracing a path that leads between them and has my breath catching.

It's taking too long.

When he brushes where I ache, we both groan.

"You're soaked," he grits out.

"So are you." My fingers dig into his bicep, his skin still damp from our shower.

There's a light in the corner of the room and it's not doing him enough justice. He's gorgeous, every part of him.

"Shit." He pulls back. It's not the sexy curse from a moment ago, it's a "this is bad" curse.

"What's wrong?" I'm silently praying it's nothing, because if we have to stop, I might actually die.

"My condoms are in my room. With my brother," he says meaningfully.

I blink with comprehension. Going down to Theo's room right now is a bad idea.

I shift out from under him to grab a condom from my bag. It falls out along with a wrench.

"I always keep condoms with my wrench set," I say at his raised eyebrow.

"Always?" he challenges, but his eyes dance.

"Lately," I admit. "In case."

"In case of who?"

"You," I breathe.

I'm a little embarrassed but the look on his face wipes it away.

He takes the packet from me and tears into it, rolling it on without breaking my gaze.

"In case we were just working and lost control and I had to fuck you right that second?" Jameson leans in, his mouth hot against the shell of my ear.

"Maybe."

His words are a drug. It's like every single part of Jameson Ashford is purpose-built to turn me on, to wreck every one of my protests.

"Smart girl." He angles me so I'm brushing the head of him. Then he's pressing inside, one inch at a time. Gravity and angles are pulling me down on his cock.

We're doing this. I'm not sure I believe it.

The expression on his face says maybe he can't either.

God, the feel of him. The stretch, the fullness.

Finally, he's all the way in.

I can't move. Can barely breathe.

"Fuck, Townie." His forehead presses against mine.

The edge of the dresser is going to leave a permanent line in my ass. He lifts me and carries me over to the bed, never breaking our connection.

He tugs down the duvet and sets me on the edge of the mattress—way more comfortable than the dresser—and follows me down until my back is pressed to the sheets.

Jameson starts to move, shallow at first. Then deeper.

"That's it. So good." He pins my right hand up by my head. My other hand digs into his back.

It's like racing on the back of his bike.

It's a million times better.

He's chasing me, I'm urging him on, the only competition is our own unhinged need. His strokes are getting more intense, his breathing rougher. When he trails a finger down my stomach to between my legs, brushing my clit, I buck against him.

He rubs circles that mimic the rhythm of my hips.

The relief I'm craving is impossibly close. "Don't stop."

He doesn't but he does change the angle, rocking into me so he hits me in entirely new ways. A few more strokes and my core pulls tight, pleasure destroying me with its blinding intensity.

His eyes are wide and wild, his dark lashes spiked from the shower.

Then he goes still too. His jaw clenches, his abs flex. Every part of him focused on me. Us.

It's beautiful, watching him fall apart.

When he tugs me down on top of him on the bed, we're a mess from the shower and our sweat. I study the patterns on the ceiling. "That was . . ."

"Overdue," he finishes.

My lips curve as I lean my head against his shoulder. "Yeah?"

"That's been on my mind way too long. Couldn't get you out of my head. Didn't help that you were everywhere I looked, and the drivers wouldn't shut up about it. Knox's had a thing for you since day one."

I press up on one hand to look down at Jameson, my mouth forming an O. "You mean I could be in Knox's bed right now?" I start to shift off the bed.

"Not funny." He grabs my wrist and drags me back.

I land on my stomach on top of him. The chain around my neck pools on his chest.

"It was my mom's," I offer when he lifts the ring, turning it so he can read what's inside.

He frowns. "You really don't remember the crash?"

I shake my head as I think of how they died. "My dad doesn't talk about it. Whoever was in the other car fled the scene, so there's not much to know."

Jameson turns the ring carefully to read what's inside. "'Through the fire.'"

"It was supposed to be a testament to their love. Doesn't seem like it worked."

"Sure it did. It saved you." His gaze meets mine.

Did he hear my heart crack open? The entire world must have.

The feelings in my chest are suddenly way too intense. It's one thing to hook up with Jameson, another entirely to feel as if he could make my heart stop beating with a glance or a word. I flop onto my back, feigning casual as I tuck my head into his shoulder.

"What would you have done if you hadn't gotten into the academy?" Jameson's voice rumbles through his chest.

I'm grateful to have the question to focus on. "Go back to Ohio State, get my degree. After graduation, I was planning to open a garage with my dad. One where we didn't have to report to anyone besides ourselves. He could retire and be comfortable."

"And then what? When your dad was comfortable, what was your dream?"

The hotel lights move beyond the curtains. "I don't know. I figured if I got that far, I'd already won."

He's quiet a minute.

"What did you want to be before you wanted to be a driver?" I ask.

"I never thought about anything else," he says. "Figured if I gave myself a safety, I'd give myself an out."

"Life doesn't always go to plan."

"Then you need a better plan."

"That simple, huh?" I admire his conviction. Still, it's easier to have conviction when you've grown up surrounded by opportunities.

"I didn't plan on you," he says.

His lips brush my temple, and I blink in surprise at the sweetness of the gesture. My fingers curl around his forearm before I can stop them.

"Mmm. You trying to get in my pants again?"

"I'm still in them." I can feel his smile against my skin.

He threads his fingers through mine. It's unsettling how in the dark with the sheets pressed against my skin, we're just two people. It doesn't matter where either of us came from. What we're capable of.

I'm not cold but I have the sudden urge to pull the duvet over my body. To remember that my heart has been beating fine for the last twenty years without syncing up with his.

"So if you always have a plan, was it your bold plan to run me over with the Turbo on the first day of school?"

His shoulder tenses under my head. "No."

"You never apologized," I say absently. It's one thing I still can't square with everything I've learned about him. "Now would be the ideal time," I suggest.

His thumb stills. "I can't."

There's an edge in his voice, and frustration rises up in me to match.

"What do you mean, you can't?"

I push up to a seated position and fold my arms, feeling the scars in my skin. The ones that will probably be there forever thanks to another person's carelessness, the actions they can never take back.

"You're too much of an Ashford to admit you fucked up?"

He leans back on his hands, watching me with those cool eyes. "It's not healthy being obsessed with the past. Trust me."

His reaction only fires me up. The entire week I've been wanting to be closer to him. Trying to let myself be vulnerable.

But he won't accept any real responsibility.

I thought we had more in common despite him being born with everything, but it's not true. The realization echoes hollowly in my chest.

"So you're above accountability because you have money and power," I decide. "The thing about being a good person is you have to do it even when it's not convenient."

The words are too sharp, but I can't take them back.

He flinches. "You said pain wasn't a contest," he reminds me. "You only mean that when you're winning?"

I jump up and rummage in my bag for a T-shirt, yanking it over my head.

"Townie."

I ignore him.

"Shay—"

"You should probably turn in," I say when I face back to Jameson. "Big day tomorrow. For me, too."

Disbelief etches on his handsome face. "You're serious."

"I'll walk you out."

I hear Jameson curse under his breath. But he gets up and goes to the bathroom to collect his clothes. If he's uncomfortable wearing the half-soaked jeans, he doesn't let on when he emerges and follows me to the door.

"Night." He bends to brush his lips across mine, but at the last moment I turn, letting them graze the corner of my mouth.

"Night."

I let the door swing shut behind him, squeezing my eyes shut and resting my back against it.

It's a full minute before I hear his footsteps recede.

28

Jameson

MIAMI IS ON fire.

The track is packed with fans who've come to watch the next generation of talent.

Since Luca's announcement of the race, I've been focusing in, doubling down on my workouts and logging extra sim time. I review the intel and video of all my competition. Even my brother.

But I know him like I know myself. He's not going to surprise me.

"You look extra grumpy," Theo comments when he finds me in the dressing room before the race. "Especially for a man who could clinch the most coveted seat in racing today."

I look up from my phone, where I'm scrolling through timing data. "It's nothing."

The life of a driver has a ton of ups and downs. Most recently, a big fucking "up" in the form of last night in Shay's room, followed by a "down" when she basically escorted me to the door.

The chaos of our flight and bus ride culminating in new

sleeping arrangements was irritating, but the moment I saw her in that towel, I forgot all of it.

Memories keep playing in my mind—how slick she felt in the shower. The way she gasped when I drew her down onto me. How her eyes, dark and hungry, got a little bigger every time I stroked into her.

I can't remember a time before I wanted her, and having her come apart under me, around me . . .

In a messed-up way, we fit.

It's inconvenient at the best of times, but I can't escape it.

I meant it when I said she wasn't part of the plan. I can handle racing flat out on the track, but share a smile with her and I'm spinning off my axis. Talking about our dreams feels like losing control.

Last night when we were lying in bed, her lips still swollen from mine and her neck still damp with sweat, she pushed me away.

You never apologized.

I wanted to say the right words that would fix it. I couldn't.

"By nothing you mean Shay."

I glance over. Theo's leaning against one of the lockers, arms crossed.

If he's feeling gleeful that there's friction between me and the girl he wants, he's doing a remarkably capable job of hiding it. He's still my brother, still the person I share the deepest connection with.

"She's angry." I zip up my fire suit.

His smile slips a little. "It means she cares."

"She cares about you too." I mean it as a consolation. Shay

defended him from day one, not realizing how much that same tendency is part of me.

It doesn't have the desired effect.

"I don't want to be the 'also,' Jamie." His eyes color, his voice taking on an impatient edge as I grab my helmet and start for the door. He falls into step beside me. "I'm a good fucking driver, also. I'm Luca Ashford's son, also. I'm worth something, also."

"I've always had your back. Every time you deserved it—"

"And a few I didn't," he supplies. "Because that's what you're thinking. I'm a fuckup."

I want to argue with him but it's not a lie. Not entirely.

"Theo. If I win today—"

"Don't say it." He nods toward the hospitality area, where the Batak board is mounted near the wall. "One more for old time's sake?"

I take the first turn.

Fifty-seven.

"Not bad," my brother says when I'm done.

Then it's his turn.

"Sixty-five," the lights blink.

I stare back at them.

It's a high number. A near-impossible number.

"I've been practicing," he supplies. "While you've been busy being Jameson Ashford, running our father's and the family legacy, getting your boxers in a bunch over a girl, I've been trying something new."

No shit.

I always thought we could both get what we want. If I was a

good son, a good brother, that we could all live happily ever after. Or at least our fucked version of it.

Now I'm not so sure.

"I'm going after this, Jamie," he says with an edge I've never heard. "You've pulled punches in the past. Don't this time. Because I'm not going to."

29

Shay

"HERE WE GO!" Raj rubs his hands together with anticipation.

My friends and classmates line the fence at the pit wall.

The crowd filling the seats around the track is amped for a spectacle, plenty of Ashford Racing flags and gear proudly displayed, along with some other teams.

I watch Jameson get in the cockpit on the monitors—he's frustrated.

Last night with Jameson was like a fever dream. I'm still shivering twelve hours later, still thinking about how good it felt just to feel. His body. His intensity. His knowing what I wanted even if the words were slow to come.

Except . . .

When I pushed him, he dug in his heels.

It's a reminder that attraction is one thing and real connection is something else. This is why cars are so much easier than people, why trusting is a mistake.

I shouldn't have been so quick to forgive the way he ran into me the first day of class, how cold and ruthless he was after. Would he ever give a shit about people like my dad and me if it wasn't for the way we were pushed together at school, the fact that our paths crossed, forcing him to pay attention to me?

My fingers clench on the railing as the cars line up in order. Theo and Jameson are side by side on the front row, Theo a few inches behind.

Luca's rules kept it simple: Finish order of the last race sets the next grid. No extra qualifying, no reset.

Theo's pulling on his helmet, adjusting his position in the car as the mechanics take off his tire covers. Radar says the rain we anticipated might hold off. If that's true, the dry tires will hold up and be fast and safe.

If it's not . . .

I send up a prayer as the drivers take a formation lap. I watch from the monitors in the garage until they return to the start.

Megan squeezes my hand. When she got back last night and found me curled up in bed, the covers pulled around my ears as I stared holes in the wall, she cursed.

"Let me guess. Jameson?"

I didn't answer.

"I will end him . . ."

I grabbed her arm before she could make it to the door. "I'm fine," I said. "Let's put on a movie, okay? No cars."

This weekend is about more than me and the messiness of my love life, especially as the three of us are supposed to be a team. But I felt her worried gaze for the rest of the night.

Now, I rip my attention from her and back to the red lights counting upward. The dreams of every person on this track, everyone here in the garages, ride on the cars and drivers out on the grid.

One.

Two.

Three.

Four.

Five.

Lights out.

Engines roar as the dozen cars lunge forward. Theo has a better start, but Jameson's right behind him.

They go into the first turn, a steep one and out of sight.

On the huge screen, Jameson hangs on Theo's tail. The third and fourth cars are tucked neatly behind, stalking them.

"It looks good," Megan says.

It's Jameson's impeccable driving plus the tweaks we made to the setup to suit him. Theo's no slouch either, enjoying the rare lead and putting in impressive corners.

In a lap, Jameson's almost in a position to pass Theo.

"He's catching up," I breathe.

Jameson sets up to pass, but Theo covers the inside.

My hand squeezes Megan's. Raj and Zane are behind us.

"Come on," I say.

"Don't count out Knox," Raj warns.

Another few laps and I feel the first drop on my face.

Megan lifts her palm, testing. We exchange a look.

"Fuck," I swear, my stomach plummeting as more drops find my skin. "Rain's starting."

"Who's coming in for tires first?" Raj asks.

"Jameson and Theo are both staying out."

Jameson ducks past Theo in an incredible move. My heart is galloping in my chest.

Theo takes it back.

My gaze flicks to the screens. "They have to pit," I say. Different tires will give them enough grip to keep fighting.

"They're not."

I'm not thinking about our argument. I'm thinking about how slippery the road is, how good Jameson is, how even the best driver in the world might defy physics but he can't rewrite it entirely.

I'm remembering Jameson's eyes, the urgency in them.

I won't let you lose.

"It's raining harder."

"Back off," I mutter to Jameson. "Get your tires and come back at him after."

They're neck and neck down the backstretch.

Jameson tries again, this time a riskier move. But Theo attacks aggressively.

Neither of them backs out.

"They have to brake." Megan's voice is a tight whisper.

"Jameson will," I say with more confidence than I feel.

Everything slows down.

Who says he wanted you first?

Theo's front wing clips Jameson and time stops.

Knox is just behind and catches Jameson's rear wing, sending the car spinning toward the wall.

My heart is in my stomach as the chassis spins, hurtling toward the barriers at the side of the track. Barriers are designed to stop cars. They're not comfortable. Not at two hundred mph.

The front of Jameson's car catches the wall and rips in half.

It's raining but not hard enough. Oxygen catches, combusts, and flames engulf the chassis, licking at metal and paint.

In the time it takes me to draw a breath, there's no sign of the driver.

I scream his name so hard it hurts.

30

Shay

"CAN YOU GO any faster?" I demand of the cab driver on the way to the hospital.

It takes way too long to get there. Every traffic light is agony. The constant guilt I lived with for weeks when I was lying to my dad is nothing compared to the hollow pit that appeared in my stomach the moment Jameson's car hit the barrier.

"I need to see Jameson. Ashford," I add at the nurse's station when I finally arrive. She looks me up and down, ready to shoo me away. I dig into my damp shirt and flash my ARI badge and her expression wavers a little.

"Take a seat."

No. But I can hardly bowl her over, so I do and watch her head into a private room to confer with a doctor.

Today was supposed to be a triumph on the track, a chance for him to clinch the ARI seat and for me to prove my skills. Instead, I'm missing the rest of the race and bouncing my knee in a cramped plastic chair in a room with fluorescent lights, curtained bays, and wristbands.

Impatience and desperation take over. I look both ways

down the hall. There are staff at one end, passing back and forth. The nurse from before is busy a couple of rooms down.

I duck inside Jameson's room. My feet squeak on the floor as I cross to the metal bed.

Jameson looks pale against the white sheets, his face bruised and eyes shut. His hair is plastered against his skin. My breath sticks in my chest, heavy and painful. The antiseptic smell fills my nostrils, the beeping of the monitor invasive and insistent.

"You know, the first time I saw Theo, I thought he looked like an angel and you looked like the devil."

He doesn't answer.

"Not that I'm advocating for you to walk toward the light. You'd probably go to hell. And I bet it's humid as fuck there and your hair will be a mess all the time and you'd hate that."

I trail off and shift on my feet. I hate hospitals. The people here make amazing things happen, like they did for my dad when he needed his surgery, or me for that matter. But you don't typically come here unless you need those things. Which means somewhere along the line, something has gone wrong.

Jameson's hands are limp. I reach for one, threading my fingers through his like he did with mine at the hotel.

I'm regretting last night. It's not that I forgive him for what he did, or for refusing to apologize. It's not even that I forgive myself for trusting him.

It's that this is the first moment I can remember where I'm strong and he's weak, and it doesn't feel nearly as good as I thought it would.

"You were off to a good start," I chide. "You could have won the next corner. Now they've red-flagged the race. Theo will probably win by default."

My fingers brush his knuckles, more for my benefit than his. "Why the hell didn't you try again the next corner?" I know it's unfair. I know the rain and the wall and the physics of it. But grief isn't reasonable.

And maybe some part of me wanted him to push.

I'm still praying his eyes will blink open and he'll give me shit in his most insufferable tone. The only answer is the slow beep of machines, the deadly calm of Jameson's utter stillness.

"If this is because you promised you wouldn't let me lose, you shouldn't be so literal."

I think of our car feud, our study sessions in the library, making out on the back of his bike. He's shown me he cares: gifting me my dream upgrade for the Fastback; protecting opportunities for me and my friends, even when it cost him; keeping quiet about my dad once I told him; being concerned enough to ask how I was in the fallout.

He had my back when I needed him. Who has his?

My hand presses against my chest, over the bump from my ring.

It saved you.

I hesitate before I reach up to unfasten the necklace and slide it off. It falls into loops of chain in my hand. I press it into Jameson's, folding his fingers around it.

Then the nurse is here, pulling a cart of supplies into the room.

"How did you get in here?" she demands.

Another presence fills the room before I can answer. Luca Ashford stands in the doorway like he owns the building.

His gaze goes to Jameson. Then to me.

"I know you. You were at my house." His voice is flat. "She doesn't belong here."

My hand tightens around Jameson's. "I'm not leaving."

Luca's mouth barely moves when he speaks. "You don't get a vote."

"You did this," I say. "You built a rivalry and told them it was a family."

"Shay." Theo's voice breaks in, raw and breathless as he pushes past his father. "I got here as fast as I could." He's still wearing his fire suit, his face plastered with rain and sweat.

His eyes go to Jameson and he turns white. "Is he—"

"I don't know."

The nurse raises her voice. "Everyone who isn't immediate family needs to leave."

I let go of Jameson's hand slowly. Putting space between us hurts.

"Theo." I pause halfway to the door. "Look out for him, or I swear—"

"He'll never forgive me?" He swallows.

"I won't."

31

Jameson

I CAN'T LIFT my arm without seeing stars.

Three days ago, I could take a corner flat out at two hundred miles an hour. Now, I can't pull a fire suit over my head without help.

"Luca still wants footage of both?" The photographer whispers to the assistant.

"That's what he said."

Driving with an injury, particularly a collarbone fracture, is going to suck, but I'm in a sling for the next few weeks. At least I'm supposed to be, though my record for that has been dismal so far—I've already ditched the sling today for media.

The assistant continues talking to the photographer. "Luca loves a dramatic ending."

"We have pistols. Ten yards at dawn," Theo calls as he enters the gym.

They bow their heads as he drops his bag near me.

"Eden sent flowers to the house. Obscenely huge. Probably on Dad's credit card."

"She called too."

Our sister was worried enough to forgo our usual text conversation and leave ten messages the moment she found out about the accident. From the amount of her on my voicemail, she must have missed the equivalent of a week of senior-year classes at her Swiss private school.

We're doing shoots for ARI press, in the gym dressed in fire suits to promote the upcoming season. I've been involved in PR since I was four, but this is the first time I've done it with a broken bone.

He snakes a hand toward my shoulder, and I reach across with my good one to slap it away.

"Dad's pissed. That's going to be hard for his favorite son to drive with. You really fucked yourself this time, Jamie."

"I did? You're the one who made me spin out." I grab a water and twist it open, crossing to the window to stare out. "Heard you got the win, even with the ten-second penalty."

"Made up enough points to tie us going into the final race," he says lightly.

Luca couldn't have designed it any better. I don't need to go online to know ARI talk is blowing up, that the F1 news cycle will be hijacked for the better part of a week by my crash and its implications.

The photographers are checking lighting and setting up again, deciding exactly what props they want in the background. It'll all wind up getting photoshopped out anyway.

"Dad would be proud."

Theo grimaces. "You're angry."

"I didn't expect my little brother to try to kill me."

He sighs. "I didn't mean to. I wanted something that was mine for once." He lifts a hanger off the rack and inspects the jacket, making a face.

"I didn't realize how hard you'd fight for it."

"The seat or Shay?" Theo shrugs into the jacket, turning to look at the sleeves in the mirror.

I think of the last time we were together, the night before the race when she pushed me away. I've never wanted to let someone in who does nothing but create havoc in my life. Somehow, she dug her way under my skin, left an ache like my collarbone that I can't get out of my head.

"Both." I frown.

When Theo pressed me in the race, the logical thing to do would have been to back off.

I couldn't.

Not because of pride, or even competitiveness, but because I needed to prove I wouldn't back down this time. Until the car started to spin out and I wasn't thinking about the outcome.

All I could think of was her.

"I tried to stay away." My words sound distant. "For weeks, I held back. A hundred moments when I wanted—"

"That doesn't make me feel better." Theo groans, and it's pain and frustration rolled into one. It's always been my job to fix his problems for him. But I can't this time.

"She was at the hospital," he says at last, and my head snaps up at his words. "She left you this. I didn't want Dad to find it." He holds out Shay's necklace.

I take it, staring at the ring, the inscription.

Doesn't seem like it worked.

Sure it did. It saved you.

She was trying to protect me. I don't know how she feels, but I have to believe it's something.

"She wanted me to apologize for hitting her the first day of the semester. She thinks I'm an asshole." My hand closes around the ring. "Maybe she's right."

Theo shoves both hands in his pockets with a curse. "I can't fix your collarbone. But I can tell her the truth."

I stare at him, suspicion turning into disbelief when he continues.

"I'll tell her it was me who drove into her with the Porsche."

32

THEO: We need to talk.

SHAY: I'm kind of mad at you right now.

THEO: This won't help.

33

Shay

THE GARAGE AT the Ashford mansion is quiet except for the speaker in the corner playing "The Hills." Moody bass under the vocal track, low enough it seeps into the concrete.

Behind the Porsche and the Lambo, tucked in the back corner under lights, there's one person working.

Jameson's wearing jeans and a tank streaked with grease. I expected to see him in a sling, but there's nothing. He's bent over a car that's low and wide, with a long hood and a sharp nose.

"Nice Stingray," I say to break the silence. The body is fiberglass, with the faint ripple old Corvettes get that makes them classic, not perfect.

"I've been rebuilding it for a couple of years."

I circle it, eyeing up the chassis, peering past him at the engine. "It's a '70."

"'69."

He looks like a European guy. This car . . . isn't.

"Where'd you find it?"

"A guy in town needed to unload it. A friend of a friend

who'd run into some money problems. I probably paid twice what it was worth, but it seemed like the least I could do."

It's another reminder that in public, he's rich and entitled. In private, he's a different person.

"Why did you let me believe it was you driving the Porsche?" My voice echoes in the garage.

Jameson swipes grease onto a towel without looking up. "Theo had a demerit on his license for careless driving after my mom left. Taking the blame could've ruined his career. He didn't deserve that."

"So instead it had to be you."

He rethreads a bolt, focused and steady. "It wasn't a big deal."

"It is a huge fucking deal, Jameson." I take a step closer. "Just because you decided it would be better if everyone thought it was you instead of Theo doesn't make it okay."

He straightens to grab a different wrench.

"Were you ever going to tell me?" I ask.

"I wanted to. But it wasn't about what I wanted."

I step between him and the car. He grabs me and physically moves me out of the way.

I reach past him, slam the hood shut, then plant my ass on it.

Jameson's stare turns lethal.

Try ignoring me now.

"You made me hate you."

"I tried." His eyes shine down at me. "Didn't work how I expected."

Jameson didn't hit me. Theo did. Everyone's best friend, Theo.

It's breaking my brain. I'm questioning every conversation, every judgment. He was protecting his family. Which doesn't stop his lie from hurting like hell.

"Do you know how much I hated you for that? How much I hated *myself* for wanting you, even though . . ." I swallow.

"You lie when it's convenient," he retorts.

"I did what I had to."

"So did I."

We stare one another down, neither of us willing to concede.

He takes me in for the first time, my white tank top and jeans, the sweater I grabbed on my way out the door. After talking with Theo, I didn't stop to check my appearance.

One moment he's standing over me. The next he's following me down onto the hood of the car, my shoulders pressing into the fiberglass.

"How do you think your father feels when you lie to him?" His breath mingles with mine.

"Okay, ouch." He's not trying to be cruel, and that's the worst part.

His eyes soften. "Theo was always my little brother. I didn't realize until later how much it mattered that my mother wasn't his. She tried to treat him like he was but couldn't unsee our father's cheating. And Luca . . . ignored Theo.

"Until Theo took an interest in racing. That's when Luca realized he could use Theo to get to me. To make me better."

"It didn't work," I say, quieter. "You protected your brother."

"I swore I wouldn't treat him like that." His voice cracks slightly. "His whole life, he was an afterthought for everyone who was supposed to love him. Including me."

I'm shaking my head.

"Until you," he goes on. "He wanted you and I would have been the best brother in the world not to come between you."

This stupid family, this entire legacy. Falling for Jameson Ashford is a dangerous game.

"I have a say in who I'm with," I inform him. "You don't get to decide whether to 'give me' to your brother. Do you ever think about what I want?"

Jameson takes my face in both his hands, his eyes wide and clear. "All the fucking time."

Fuck.

Right when I think I can keep some distance between us, he tears down every wall I've built. Makes me want to give him all of me, the rough parts, the ugly ones, the ones I'm not proud of.

I fist a hand against his chest and he winces.

"Does it hurt?" I ask, perversely satisfied.

"Yeah."

"Good." I huff out a breath.

His eyes flash a warning. I ignore it.

"This thing between us, it's messy. Maybe I even like that, because it feels real. But . . ." I swallow hard, reminding myself to be brave. "It's not only the games and the arguing. It's something else."

Jameson fists a hand on the hood, like he's fighting with himself. "I know."

His throat bobs, his eyes searching. The expression on his face makes my ribs ache.

"I stopped studying with you because I couldn't look at you without wanting you."

His lips brush mine, once.

"I asked you to work on my car because you're so fucking good even you don't see it."

Again.

"I want to be near you. To talk to you, touch you, whatever I can get."

His heart thuds under my hand.

"Driving fast I can handle. You?"

His eyes burn as he leans in.

"You make me out of control."

His mouth claims mine.

Honestly, it does. *He* does.

He's the driver everyone worships. Heir to the biggest sports legacy on the planet, with more than anyone can imagine resting on his strong shoulders.

Jameson is warm and hard, and I want to touch every inch of him, to reassure myself that he's okay. I need the image of him in that hospital bed to be a distant memory.

I kiss him like I know it's not. My hand finds the ring on the chain around his neck. *It saved me again.* Because if he'd been hurt, or worse, that would have ruined me.

"You scared the shit out of me," I confess against his mouth.

"I'm sorry." His voice is low and raw.

So he can *apologize.*

The cool fiberglass under my shoulder blades makes me shiver, or maybe it's the heat from his body and mouth.

"I don't forgive you." My fingers thread in his hair as I arch under him, kissing him back.

I thought I could still back away from him, that I had an escape hatch. But after the hospital, I know I can't. He matters too much. The way I feel when I'm with him matters too much.

My thoughts melt away when his hand strokes under my shirt. Even with only one fully functioning arm, he's undeniable.

"That's too bad," he says on a groan, his thumb brushing the curve of my breast.

Kissing him isn't enough. I need to see every inch of him to assure myself he's the same person he was before the crash.

I yank at his shirt impatiently. He strips it over his head, his awkward shrug and sharp hiss of breath the only indication it's painful.

The pattern of bruises has my eyes widening but he's already reaching for the hem of my shirt. The next second it's gone. My grip on his neck tightens and I press my breasts against his chest, needing to be closer.

"I thought about you," he murmurs. "When I hit the barrier, my first thought was of you."

Our last time was fueled by need and desperation. This feels different.

Jameson unfastens my jeans and tugs them and my underwear down my hips.

"Forgive me yet?"

I shake my head. "Still no."

He levers over me, tracing a path across my stomach and down my thighs.

Whatever advantage I had, I feel it slipping away under his ruinous blue gaze filled with intent.

He yanks my legs wide. My breath catches.

I've pictured Jameson Ashford between my thighs. This time, it's not a dream.

His mouth lowers to my body, far too slowly.

The first brush of his lips on my inner thigh makes me gasp.

The next is higher, closer to where I need him, and it's chased with a graze of teeth.

The garage is cold. I'm on fire.

"Jameson . . ."

He licks a slow path up my slit where I'm already aching. Pleasure streaks through me, has me arching against his mouth.

"What about now." His voice rumbles against my skin.

My hands fist against the hood of the car, nails scraping the topcoat. "Not yet." It's a whispered plea. My fingers tugging on his hair are a command.

He growls as if he wants to argue. Or maybe he approves of me sending him back to his work.

He's focused, and having every ounce of that intensity on me is mind blowing. He slips a finger inside, working it in slow, rhythmic motion with his wicked mouth.

Almost.

When he groans, I realize I've said it out loud.

He builds the tension, handling me as if I'm the only thing he wants to drive. Then presses two fingers inside me so deep my toes curl. I'm practically purring.

I ride his hand and his mouth until the need overwhelms me with pleasure. Every muscle in me pulls tight, sharp.

He doesn't stop. He sucks on my skin, the pressure of his mouth and the stretch of his fingers sending me over the edge.

Everything goes bright. My eyes are shut but I'm blinded by hot white light.

Pleasure ripples through me, so much I'm not sure my body can take it. He stays with me, holding me, chasing me until the last of the shocks fade and I can breathe.

It's not enough.

I drag him up to me by the hair. His pupils are blown, huge and dark with desire. I need him, all of him.

My legs wrap around his hips. "I'm on the pill."

He traps my chin in his fingers, like he needs to believe what I'm saying. "I've been tested. But—"

"I trust you." I do, I realize.

His expression fills with gratitude and something more.

His hand threads through mine, pins it over my head, his thumb tracing circles in my palm.

I hear the zip of his jeans, and a moment later, he presses inside. I choke on the sensations of him over me, in me.

He keeps going, his hair tickling my face. My throat tightens as I arch to take all of him. I want him to crawl inside me, to see where I live, to know my dark sides.

"Fuck, you feel so good," he mumbles against my throat.

The hood of the car is hard against my bare back. When he hitches me up, it sticks to my skin, tugging and stinging.

Jameson's so deep in me that his groan rumbles through my body. Our sweat mingles as his nose grazes mine. His lips brush my throat as he strokes inside over and over.

Nothing has ever felt as intense, as consuming, as this. Having Jameson Ashford, the man who has everything, want this as much as I do makes it matter even more. I meet him every stroke, hitting his rhythm and changing it, making it into one that's only ours.

His eyes are indigo, warm with hunger and something more, and a million miles deep. If I'm drowning, I'm beyond being saved.

The lights flicker, as if the garage can't handle what we're doing.

You and me both.

His hand slips between us, between my thighs. I buck against him, every part of me pulling tighter.

"Oh my God," I pant.

Jameson's breathless and gorgeous and triumphant. "Say it again." His lips fuse to my damp throat.

When I come, my entire body shaking, he holds me like I'm all he needs. Everything up to this point lit the match, and his confessions set fire to me.

He breaks too, his muscles bunching under my hands, his hips flexed and jaw tight.

I feel every bit as wrecked. He rolls us over so I'm on top, my damp face pressed to his chest.

I'm not sure what this is, but if it ever stops?

I might not survive.

34

Shay

"TABLE EIGHT IS taking forever," Bree whispers, glancing over the pass-through at the four truckers.

I stack clean plates on the counter. "They're enjoying their meal."

"They've been enjoying it for two hours."

I grab a fresh pot of coffee and run it over to them. "Top-up?"

They nod and I pour each before heading back to the pass, a bounce in my step.

"Are you whistling?" Bree demands.

"No." I pause. "Maybe."

The Junction is busy for the evening, which is why I offered to pitch in when Bree texted after another server called in sick. Nothing can kill my good mood as I pile dishes to send back to the kitchen, swaying my hips to the music.

"Did Mr. Fix-It ask you out yet?" I call to my friend.

"Not exactly. But he's stopped by twice to see if I need anything."

I stop what I'm doing and spin to face her, grabbing her face between my hands. "Bree. He likes you. Even I know this."

Her eyes narrow. "What is up with you? Wait, don't tell me. Your dad apologized?"

"Nope."

"You won the internship?"

"Nope."

The bell dings over the door.

"Then—"

"She got railed by an Ashford." Megan's voice comes from the kitchen doorway. "Coffee?" She presses both hands together, pleading.

Bree gasps. "You've been holding out on me. Which one?" She puts out two mugs. "Theo." She points to one. "Jameson."

I roll my eyes and grab a third mug, pouring coffee into all of them.

When Megan started showing up at The Junction, there were territorial vibes. Then Bree fed her blueberry pie, Megan showed her some K-pop moves, and the hostilities dropped.

"Is it both? Preferably at the same time?"

"No." Though it's not the worst visual . . .

"Jameson's been trailing her like a brooding puppy all month," Megan fills in as she takes a mug and practically chugs it.

"He was almost dead after the race last weekend." Megan shoots me a look. "To be clear, I would have killed him. Not the crash in Miami."

"Got it." Bree nods.

"But from your face, I'm guessing he did some prime groveling?"

My fingers slip on the salt and pepper shakers. "I think I have a rash on my back."

Their eyes widen.

"From the hood of his car," I add quickly.

"Damn. Way to go, Jamie." Bree lifts her brows.

Each sexy, sweaty second has been replaying in my head nonstop in the day since. Last night, after I got back to Megan's. As I lay in bed. When he texted me to say good night.

I do trust him—though he lied, I get why. And as hard as it is to let him in, to ask him to care about me beyond just what I can do for his car, the alternative is worse.

I used to think Theo's attention was like being warmed by the sun. Jameson's is like being watched by the moon and a thousand stars, each a silent, unflinching witness.

Everything he told me about his family echoed in my head. Growing up, I imagined having more family would make life better. From Jameson's experience, it doesn't. His father's control, his mother's desperation, all of it must have felt oppressive for a boy coming up in a world of expectations and scrutiny.

I can't pretend to understand why he feels so responsible for Theo, but I respect his devotion. I also told him if he lies to me again, I'll cut his balls off.

Bree sighs. "I told you big brother was endgame."

"No one said endgame." My cheeks burn. I can't tell if it's from the coffee or the fact that part of me wants that.

"So what now?" Bree asks.

Megan reaches for her steaming mug. "There are three weeks until the final race of the Challenger series. Plus the F1 season is wrapping up soon and ARI's—"

"Two points behind in the team standings," Bree finishes. "I'm guessing Luca Ashford is chewing glass right now."

"And there's still no update on the investigation into

Dekker's dismissal." Megan sips her coffee. "Are you coming out in public? Or is this a secret tryst?"

"I don't know. It's not anyone's business."

"But Jameson is everyone's business."

She's not wrong, but I don't have an answer. There are too many ways this can still go, and none of them feel safe enough to examine.

The bell over the door rings and my dad comes in with Keane. Even though I haven't moved home, seeing him at his work shook something loose. Our stubborn standoff cracked, left room for . . . I'm not sure what.

I start to wave but they don't even look over. They're in an intense conversation, leaning over the table in a corner booth.

". . . Luca called. Said he wanted to talk about Shay." Dad's voice is hushed. I inch closer to try and hear.

"About the crash?"

"No. Something else."

I cross to them. My dad spots me first.

"This is about Jameson, isn't it?" I start.

He and Keane look at each other. "What about Jameson?" Dad asks slowly.

There's a noise behind us. Bree knocked over a coffeepot. She flashes an innocent smile. "Keane? How about I get you some eggs? On the house."

"Huh?"

"Only catch is you've got to come up here to eat them." She points at the counter.

Keane catches on and clears his throat. "Oh. Right." He shifts himself out of the booth and I take his seat across from my dad.

"Shay, I know we haven't always seen eye to eye lately, but this is important. Tell me you didn't do anything to put yourself on Luca Ashford's radar." His jaw tightens. "I've seen what happens when he takes an interest."

"Megan and I gave Jameson an audacious tire strategy for the first race of the Challenger series."

"That's all?"

I reach for Keane's untouched coffee, turning it in my hands. "I might have wandered into the garage at the Ashford estate one weekend."

"Shay . . ."

"It was a joke. But he might be more upset that I chewed him out at the hospital in Miami after the last race."

"You did what?!" Dad's horrified. I'm genuinely worried his eyes might pop out of his face.

When I list out all my infractions, I can see how I might not be on Luca's good side.

"I couldn't help it," I say. "He plays his sons off one another. If you saw how he tries to manipulate them, you'd be upset, too."

"The Ashfords hardly need a defender."

I think of Jameson lying pale in the hospital bed. "Against him, they do." I let that sink in. "I bet Jameson and Theo would have been a lot less screwed up if they had a father like you."

Dad's expression softens. "You're saying that to get back on my good side."

I lean over the table. "Is it working?"

He shakes his head, but there's a glint in his eyes.

"I'm sorry I lied to you," I say. "I realize now how shitty that feels, being lied to by someone you love. Even if it was for the right reasons."

"I know. I'm trying to protect you the best way I can. I'm proud of you. You get that, right?"

The backs of my eyes burn as I nod. "Sure."

He pauses. "Why were you with Jamie Ashford in the hospital?"

I shift in the booth. "That's a conversation for another day."

"No, I think it's today," he says. "Bree, can we get some more coffee? We might be here a minute."

"Dad . . ."

"I mean it."

Of all the things I was hoping to avoid talking about with my dad this year, falling for the heir to the Ashford dynasty wasn't on my list.

"He's smart," I say, trying to sound measured. "Capable. Dedicated."

"Bree?" Dad calls again without breaking my gaze. "Is that what all those fan posts on the internet about Jameson Ashford are about? His—what was it—dedication?"

I can feel myself turn red.

"No, it is not," my friend chirps as she tops us up. "Judges would accept: fine body, baddest blue eyes, or aura personified."

"What does that even mean, Bree?"

"It's undefinable. You just know it when you see it."

"Okay, okay!" I groan. "The point is, I like him."

Suddenly I'm thinking of Jameson's handsome face, and the reckless, bold way I feel when I'm with him. How I'm more myself but also someone better when I'm around him.

"Probably more than like him," I admit.

Maybe it shows on my face because my dad huffs out a breath.

"You going to ask if he likes me?" I cross my arms.

"No. He'd be an idiot not to." Dad's gruff loyalty has me feeling lighter. "It's been a long time since I saw those boys—they were probably still in karts. Memory serves, Theo was wild and Jameson was terrifying, but neither of them was out of their mind."

It's strange to think of my dad knowing them. I guess it's not so odd since he worked on the grid for ARI all those years.

"What did Luca want?" I ask.

He takes a long sip of his coffee, setting it down with care. "Nothing to worry about. You've taken care of me enough lately. My turn to take care of you."

I smile, but my hands twist together under the table.

Dad can say it's nothing.

But I've learned this year that when men say "nothing," it's usually a warning.

35

Shay

JAMESON: What are you doing tomorrow night?

SHAY: Fixing Bree's car.

JAMESON: That's no way to spend the weekend. I'm taking you out.

It's a week since I moved back into my dad's house after our talk at the diner, but I'm still unnerved by what he said.

What did Luca want?

Nothing to worry about.

But even when I brought it up again, he insisted everything was fine.

So when Jameson's texts land, it's a welcome distraction.

Except that he refuses to answer any questions besides providing the address, which turns out to be the airport.

Jameson meeting me on the tarmac in jeans and a peacoat pulled high around his neck doesn't do anything to dispel my nerves, or curiosity.

"Where exactly are we going?" I call over the wind.

He takes the duffel bag off my shoulder. "Vegas."

I get virtually nothing more out of him on the three-hour private plane ride.

"Luca offered you the jet to take me out?" I ask from my seat across from him. Because there's no way his father volunteered his resources for this.

"ARI has business this weekend too. But that's not why we're going," he adds at the look on my face. "We've been so focused on school and this race series, and I wanted to focus on you for a second."

I glance at my phone. "Well, Megan just texted and threatened us both not to talk strategy without her."

He laughs. "Tell her it's a deal. That is not what I want to do with you tonight."

I shiver with anticipation as he goes to retrieve a big rectangular box from the back of the plane and sets it on my lap.

"Is it a designer pizza?" I guess.

His lips twitch. "Open it."

Inside, there's a dress and shoes and jewelry. The dress fabric is a silky dark burgundy, slipping against my fingers when I lift it from the box. "Wow."

"Do you like it?"

"It's beautiful. I've never worn anything like this."

"You don't have to." He backpedals so fast I get whiplash. "You look good in anything."

It's cute seeing Jameson uncertain, even about something as simple as clothing.

"Is this what it's like to date Jameson Ashford?" I ask.

"I don't know. You tell me." A ghost of a smile lifts his lips.

Surprise has me frowning. "You've never taken a girl on a date."

"Not in any way that mattered."

He hasn't done this either. That makes me feel better.

"Well, I should at least try the dress on," I decide.

The dress fits perfectly. Thin straps, long with a slit up one side, silk that skims my curves. There's an attendant who helps with my hair and makeup. By the time the plane lands, Jameson's in a suit. For a guy who does his best work on the track, he looks unbelievably sexy in formal wear.

Somehow, I'm more nervous than I was before. It's one thing to be in this messy relationship with Jameson, another to have him take me out on an official date.

A fancy, out-of-my-depth date.

But soon we're being whisked away by a limo to a car dealership. The entire ride over I'm aware of the feel of the silk fabric on my skin. I barely have time to drool over the showroom of exotics before the owner is shaking Jameson's hand and murmuring in hushed tones.

Jameson considers, then shakes his head. He nods toward the front of the showroom. The owner passes him a key fob with both hands.

"Ferrari SF90," I say as I follow Jameson into the showroom.

"The closest thing to a race car while being street legal," he confirms, rounding to open the passenger door for me.

That tracks. "And we're going where, exactly?"

"Dinner at the Bellagio."

My stomach growls, this time with hunger. It's already dark and we're heading toward the Strip, which I've only seen on TV. It rises up out of the desert like a neon midway.

It's awe-inspiring and a little terrifying how easily the world opens for him.

I'm still staring out the window when Jameson gets a call.

"Yes. No. I told you, I'm in Vegas, I can't . . ." He hangs up on a grunt.

"What's wrong?"

"There's an F1 event tonight at the Wynn. Luca wants me to stop by."

Disappointment fills me at the idea of Luca interrupting our date, but this is Jameson's father. The family company. "Of course."

"It would only be for a few minutes." He hesitates. "Will you go with me?"

I blink at him. The fact that he wants me at his side has me nervous in a different way.

I can't pretend to be his engineer. Not wearing this dress, this jewelry.

"Yes," I decide.

The tension on his face relaxes as I reach for his hand and he squeezes back. We stay like that, fingers linked, the entire way to the venue.

"Why does he want you there?" I ask as we head up to the ballroom in a blur of lights and glitter and beautiful people.

"Something about instilling confidencc despite this baseless Dekker claim."

"You're sure it's baseless." I want to believe him, and Jameson glances over. "I just mean it was weird how his performance dipped right after the summer break without any huge changes to the car."

"Teams don't sacrifice performance for no reason. My

father and the rest of ARI leadership don't agree on everything, but they all want to win." He says it as if he's thought about it.

When we get inside, Luca notices immediately. His eyes fill with satisfaction until he spots me.

"I'll make the rounds," Jameson murmurs in my ear. "I'll be right back."

I lift a glass of champagne off a waiter's tray, mostly to give my hands something to do.

I'm hoping to stay tucked into a corner. My plan works for all of thirty seconds.

"I almost didn't recognize you, Shay *MacDonald*." Luca appears beside me. "That is your name," he goes on when I don't answer.

"It is." I stare out at the crowd of well-dressed businesspeople and racing personalities. "But I was nervous the first time we met."

"Appropriate, since you were trespassing on my property. Did you know your father used to be one of our mechanics?" he continues without waiting for a response.

"He still is."

It feels like we're playing a game, only I don't know the rules.

"Of course. How are you finding the academy? I understand you've made quite the impression."

"It's challenging. Different than college."

"Understandable. And now you want to work on the grid to be close to my son?"

The hairs on my neck stand up.

This isn't like playing a game with Jameson, who pushes you because he wants to see you at your best.

This is a trap closing. I can feel it.

"I cheered for you," I hear myself say. "I grew up watching you on TV, with my dad. I was proud that he worked for you. I couldn't look away."

Luca's eyes glaze, as if he's fascinated but not sure where I'm headed.

Maybe I'm not sure, either.

"I'd love to work with Jameson. He's incredible."

"He's an Ashford."

I take a long sip of my drink. "He's more than that."

Luca frowns.

"She can be close to me no matter what her job is." Jameson materializes behind us. "Or mine for that matter."

"Jameson, there are other stakeholders to meet—"

"I'm off the clock." He reaches for my hand, squeezes it. I squeeze back.

"Let's get out of here," he murmurs in my ear.

"Yes, please. But I think I've had enough of fancy rooms and waiters for now."

"Understood." He considers as we head for the doors. "We can get takeout."

Somehow, he gets the restaurant to pack everything up to go. We head off the Strip, and a few minutes later we're pulling off the road to a private facility.

"Speed Vegas," I read off the sign.

Tonight, the commercial track is stripped down and quiet—floodlights humming, empty grandstands looming, the asphalt still warm from the day.

Jameson drives straight onto the infield and parks.

We sit on the hood of the Ferrari, eating our dinner and

staring up at the sky. After the pressure of the hotel party, this feels like the world has been lifted off us.

"What's the first car you ever worked on outside of your garage?" he asks.

My shoulders relax as I bite into the best steak I've ever tasted.

"My friend Bree's older brother's. Bree and I go way back. When we were kids I had trouble fitting in. But when I could fix something using my head and my hands, it felt right."

"I bet it made you lots of friends."

"Not exactly. In high school, this guy who used to torment me got a flat in the middle of nowhere. I was driving by, so I fixed it. He was embarrassed enough that a girl saved his ass that he lied and said he did it. But honestly, I didn't mind. Having expertise was something nobody could take away from me."

Jameson reaches for his drink, considering. "I wish I could say I was as generous as you. I tried to share my, ah—expertise, though in hindsight, it was probably more like I told the other kids what to do."

My lips twitch as I picture Jameson as a kid, informing the others of how they should drive and tune their cars. "That's very self-aware of you."

"Right?" He grins. "I stopped trying when I realized the other drivers would undercut me anyway. One year racing karts, I let myself get distracted and lost in the final points. Luca was pissed, but more than that, I saw how fast it could all be taken away. And through the entire offseason I realized that without racing, I'm nobody."

The smile fades. I've never met someone who goes from

happy to serious so fast, as if being too happy for too long is dangerous.

"That's not true, Jameson."

He takes another bite, chewing and swallowing before he responds. "I like that you think so. And that you said so."

The softness in his voice makes my heart expand. I'm remembering my words from earlier to Luca as we finish our meal and Jameson packs the remainder back into the bag.

"Ready?"

"For what?"

He waves a hand to our surroundings. "We're at the track, Townie. I didn't bring you here for the view."

Jameson presses the keys into my hand and disbelief floods my system.

He's serious?

"You said you'd never let me drive," I remind him.

"You're right, forget it," he bluffs.

But I'm off the hood and adjusting the driver's seat. My face hurts from the smile stretching my cheeks.

"Shit." I can't drive with stilettos, but Jameson's already retrieving a cardboard box from the trunk.

"Rental shoes?" I guess.

"These are new. I ordered them for you."

I want to kiss him, so I lean in and do it. He's warm and solid.

Every part of him feels right. Feels *mine*.

But I also want to drive the fucking car.

We start on slow laps, going over braking points, the lines, the apexes. If I expected him to be anything but an exceptional teacher, I was wrong.

It's nervy but I trust him and the car. He fixes my hands and seat.

On a straight, I floor it.

It's exhilarating. I've gone fast before, but never like this. I feel totally free, not because of the speed but because I'm the one in control.

I laugh, breathless. For a few perfect seconds there's no academy, no fallout waiting back home.

When I glance over at Jameson, he's watching me.

Not the track, not the car. Me.

Speed isn't Jameson's obsession. It's his love language.

And right now, he's sharing it with me.

"I'm actually good at this," I crow after a new fast lap.

"Not bad." He leans an arm along the back of my seat.

"And in a dress, no less."

"I noticed." His gaze drops down my body. Jameson's smug grin makes me want to hit him. And other things.

"There's a hotel suite waiting for us. We should probably head there. In case we need to check for spiders."

We start to drive back to the Strip, when a row of cars, hoods popped, catches my eye. I buzz down the window and heavy bass music streams in.

"They're drag racing," I say, leaning out. "Pull over!"

Jameson hesitates but parks, drawing more than a few admiring looks for the Ferrari.

I shift in front of Jameson when we both get out, unbuttoning the collar of his shirt. Then the cuffs, rolling them up around his arms.

"Am I approved?" he drawls.

"Yes." I'm way overdressed, but past caring.

The hoods are all up and we walk down the street, admiring cars and feeling buzzed. We're just two people who love cars.

A woman with bright pink hair is commenting to another racer. "Ugh, she's spinning off the line every time. I don't know what's wrong."

I'm already scanning the engine bay first, then the stance of the car. The nose sits high, the rear squatting hard even at idle.

My eyes flick to the back wheel well.

There it is.

The rear shock adjusters are cranked soft. Way too soft.

"Rear damping's the problem," I say. "You're dumping weight instead of planting it."

"What?" a guy standing near her scoffs.

"You're unloading the tires off the line," I continue, already crouching.

"Who the fuck are you?" the guy asks me.

Jameson steps between us. "Someone who knows what she's doing."

The confidence in his voice is addictive.

The woman turns it over, my implied offer to help. She's definitely clocked who Jameson is, though I get that it's random to have a stranger in a silk dress weigh in on your drag racing setup.

"What does it hurt?" I prompt. "You're already not winning."

Finally, she nods.

I reach into the wheel well, fingers searching for the adjuster.

This is way harder without a hair elastic. I try to sweep the hair out of my face, but it keeps falling down.

Jameson captures my hair in his hands and twists it around his fist. My eyes meet his over the car, and heat floods me.

I'm imagining him holding my hair back in a very different way.

My heart hammers in my ears while I finish the adjustment.

Click. Click.

"Try that." I straighten, looking around for somewhere to wipe my hands.

Jameson holds out an arm, the sleeve of his dress shirt already rolled to his elbow.

No way.

He's always perfectly put together. But he steels himself, unflinching as I brush off my hands on his cuff.

We head to the start line to watch the race.

The pink-haired racer is fastest from the jump. I can't tell if she'll win, but at least now she's got a chance.

"Nice work, Townie," Jameson murmurs next to my ear.

"What if someone else needs my help?" I protest as he starts to drag me back toward the Ferrari.

"Too bad. Tonight, you're mine."

36

Jameson

THE ENTIRE WAY back to the hotel, I sneak looks at Shay from the driver's seat. I'm on a fucking high. It's like the first year-end championship I ever won—the thrill of victory, feeling invincible.

This date didn't go to plan, but she handled the ARI imposition and my father. At Speed Vegas, she impressed the hell out of me. Even though it was her first time on the track, she absorbed all of it.

Watching Shay help that racer with her car . . . the sight of her in that dress, her hair falling over her determined face, made me feral.

I'm not sure I've ever been as turned on in my fucking life.

We pull up to the Bellagio, and I hand the Ferrari over to the valet.

"At the risk of sounding ungrateful for what's probably a very expensive dress, these might be my favorite part of the outfit." In the elevator, Shay holds up her racing shoes in one hand.

My lips curve. "I'd be disappointed if they weren't."

The elevator doors open to our suite, which occupies an entire floor.

We get inside and she sets the shoes on the foyer table next to a huge spray of fresh flowers.

She reaches for a piece of her hair, her fingers coming away black from touching the ends. "Oops."

"What's a night without a little motor oil?"

"After all your efforts to keep me clean." Her eyes dance as she steps closer. "It didn't affect you that you had to hold my hair up?"

Those are the wrong words.

"It affected the hell out of me."

Our breath mingles. I'm scared of how right it feels. As if everything else has been wrong.

"Thanks for supporting me back there. It meant a lot that you told that guy to fuck off."

"I'm a big fan of your work."

"My work?" she echoes. She's a goddess in that dress, a siren sent to make me lose my mind.

"I also love the way your ear curves right here." My finger brushes her skin, and she lets out a little hum of pleasure. "The way you stare me down when I say something I shouldn't." Her lips part as she looks up at me through thick lashes. "The way . . ."

I trail off, surprised, as she drops to her knees.

"Keep talking." Her hands go to my belt and trousers.

It feels like I've been hard the entire night but even if I wasn't, the sight of her determined face, her curtain of hair shining in the moon through the window, her kneeling in front of me, would have done it.

My head swims as she pulls me out.

"If this is a thank-you for the track lesson," I murmur, "should've taken you there a long time ago."

"More like I had so much fun driving I figured I'd do it again."

Her tongue darts out to lick the underside of my cock.

The moment she wraps her mouth around me, my vision narrows. It feels like the world has slowed down. For a speed junkie, it's oddly hypnotic.

My fingers fist in her hair. I'm trying not to lose it. "Townie . . ."

"You're a good teacher." Her lips vibrate against the head of my cock, and pleasure shoots down my spine. "But I think I can handle it from here."

I'm tormented by the sight of her. The exquisite feel of her mouth. She slides down my cock, and I groan.

Holy fuck.

I've pictured this so many times. The fantasies never did it justice.

"I suppose I could take some basic feedback. Faster. Slower. That sort of thing."

I swallow hard as she licks along the underside of my dick. Her tongue feels like fire.

"And of course, approval is always welcome."

"Got it." My molars grind together.

Shay's beautiful. I'll admit what I couldn't early on because my attraction to her felt like the first warning I was approaching a cliff I wasn't prepared for. But seeing her tonight, and like this, it's overloading my circuits.

"How am I doing?" Her eyes flick to mine, and there's arousal there, but eagerness, too.

I take her chin in my hand, my thumb brushing her lower lip. "So fucking good."

I could come all over her face this second. I hope she appreciates it's taking everything in me not to.

When she shifts forward, swallowing me all the way to the back of her throat, I could actually die.

I know she doesn't let her guard down easily. But the way she was tonight—going toe-to-toe with my father, how she can be tough in one moment and soft in the next—is a goddamned gift. I'm not sure I'm worth it.

But I want to be.

My fingers work in her hair. "Shit. Slow down."

I try to pull her back, but she makes a sound of protest.

Then I'm pumping between her lips. I can't stop.

"Fuck. You feel so fucking good."

I reach for the ties at the back of her dress, unfastening them. It comes loose and tumbles down, catching on her breasts but I can see the tops over her lace bra.

Now it's worse, because her tits bounce every time she moves and I'm completely losing it.

"Townie. *Fuck*. Shay . . ." I don't even know what I'm saying, but she's humming around me. I'm not even conscious as I thrust into her, my cock hitting the back of her throat.

Heat barrels through me, my muscles contracting.

She sucks, her cheeks hollowing out, and I come, hard and violent. I'm shaking as I finish.

When I force my eyes open, she's watching me through those thick lashes again, licking off her lips.

"Well?"

"You're too good at that."

Her smile widens.

"I'm not done with you," I growl softly. "Give me one minute."

She shifts to standing, a triumphant expression on her face. "I'm going to change."

Shay takes off her shoes, then starts for the bedroom. My hand circles her wrist before she can. "I said *one minute*."

I drag her back and set her on the table, bracing my hands in front of me. I don't want her out of my sight for a second.

I try to steady my heart rate, to gather myself.

The seconds tick away and she watches me, fascinated.

Her fingers find my shirt, unfastening the top button.

One.

My abs tense, my heart hammering dully against my ribs. There are a million taunts I could toss her way. Neither of us speaks as she undoes another.

Two.

Who is this version of me that's desperate for something other than the future I've been building? The one I've bled for, sacrificed for? It's like spending your entire life trying to breathe only to realize oxygen isn't as important anymore.

I'm drowning in her. Just silently suffocating.

Three.

It's like the countdown of a race, the lights blinking on before we go tearing off the start line.

Four.

Her fingers trace my scar through my shirt from memory. I brush her arm. We've both been impacted by the world. Both done what we had to in order to survive. Maybe all of it brought us here.

Five.

When my shirt hangs open, she angles her face up at me, smug.

"Well, that's one—"

I cut off her words with my mouth.

37

Jameson

"TOO FUCKING SLOW!" Knox calls.

Across the room, the bartender carrying the full tray of pints toward our booth scurries between the tables.

A few of us are grabbing a drink after evening workouts. My session was seriously compromised thanks to the busted collarbone, but no one said it out loud.

The downside of never having been in a wreck is I'm not used to navigating injuries. I'm short on not only patience but rehab skills.

"I could still beat you both," Knox's saying to me and Theo. "While you're taking each other out at the front, I'll sneak right by. I could rename ARI. Change the team colors—"

"The prize is a seat in the car, not the CEO job." Theo laughs.

"First the car, next the company."

I nod at the bartender who brought my beer, sliding him a nice tip for dealing with my boisterous friend.

"You can pry it from Luca's cold, dead hands," I say, lifting my glass to my lips with my good arm.

But Knox's comments remind me the third and final race is

less than two weeks away. The real question is whether I can compete seriously in the final Challenger series race. I'll have to.

"You want to leapfrog both of us, your engineers better come up with a Hail Mary," Theo's saying to Knox.

"You mean they need to put wings on his car," Mateo says, shaking his head.

Knox flips him off. "If only we all had engineers who would fix our tire pressure and suck our dicks when they're done."

He reaches for his beer. I reach for his neck.

In less than a second, I'm across the booth and holding his throat with my good hand.

"You want to stay friends when I win my first world championship, you'll say a hell of a lot less about Shay from here on out."

Eyes are on us, but I don't care. Knox wheezes, incredulous. "You're not serious."

I squeeze.

I've tolerated his antics for too long. Not anymore. Not when he's directing them at Shay.

"Your expressed opinions will be limited to polite applause when she wins, breathes, or so much as deigns to look in your direction." I adjust my grip, because this might set my healing back, but I need him to fucking hear me. "Understood?"

Hollers from the other guys go up as I let him go. Even Theo's brows are at his hairline.

"That feel good?" my brother asks, leaning over.

"Physically, no. Emotionally, yes." I take my seat and shake out my hand.

"You could've told me you're in love with her." Theo's low words have my head snapping toward him.

"I didn't say that."

My brother glances toward Knox, who's rubbing his neck and cursing. "Yeah, you did."

His words have spots appearing behind my eyes, and it's not from the pain in my sternum.

Since the crash, Shay and I have been inseparable. There are no guarantees in life, but Miami was a stark reminder of what really matters.

Giving up that lie about the first day of school was a weight off my chest.

For weeks now, I catch myself thinking about her smile. The way she cares about her friends, and her father. How she looks when she's concentrating on a problem, as if every obstacle in this world is just a puzzle she's going to enjoy wrestling with.

Last weekend in Vegas we spent more time in bed than out of it. Talking. Touching. Falling asleep with her curled into my side and waking up with her hair in my face.

We flew home like nothing fundamental had shifted.

Except everything had.

It made me realize I could be more than the heir my father wants and the brother Theo deserves.

Fuck, maybe I am in love with her.

Every time she looks at me, I'm more reckless. Every time I touch her, it's harder to imagine being without her.

It's terrifying.

I don't know how to make it stop.

I'm not sure I want to.

My phone buzzes. Unknown number. I don't normally answer, but I need a second to get my head on straight.

"Hello."

"Jameson, it's Dekker. My lawyers advised against this, but I didn't know where else to turn."

The voice of ARI's second driver has me out of the booth and heading for the hallway, the others protesting.

"Keep talking."

"When my contract got canceled, I knew something was wrong. Hell, I knew before then. ARI tried to say I didn't perform, but the truth is the setup wasn't the same across the cars."

"That's not possible."

There's no way the team would do that. My father wouldn't tank one of his cars. A season is worth too much.

"It's not only possible, it happened. That's why the federation launched their investigation. But they're having trouble finding the evidence."

Because there is none. I bite my tongue.

"Why trust me?"

"I figured that with a busted collarbone you could be rethinking your career path, too. A few weeks and you'll be as much of an outsider as I am."

His words sink in. He thinks I'll lose. While I've pointedly ignored looking at the betting line, I've heard it swung massively after my crash.

Theo scored points. I scored a weakness.

Still, these rumors surrounding Dekker's firing have been circling and I'm beyond trusting they'll go away on their own—or that Luca will deal with them. But maybe I can do something about this.

I click off and head back to the booth. "I have to go," I announce.

Theo follows me out to the hall. "If this is about Knox, he's a prick. He's always been a prick."

"That's not it." I start to make something up but stop. Protecting my brother hasn't always been as productive as I thought.

"Dekker called me. He swears the rumors are true."

"You think he's right?" Theo's voice is wary.

"I want to see it for myself."

I wait for Theo to laugh. Whatever I think my brother will say after I drop that on him, it's not what comes.

"I know where to look."

Theo drives. At ARI headquarters, I go to swipe us in, but Theo shakes his head and waves to the security guard instead. He chats the man up, and we're waved through without having to scan our IDs.

"Who the fuck are you?" I mutter as he disengages from the conversation with a laugh.

"You'd be amazed what a charming smile gets you access to. Of course, you wouldn't know because you've never tried being charming."

His dig has me snorting as I follow him down the hall. A few turns later and we're in the records area. It's rows of computers plus some old-school files.

"What exactly are we looking for?" he asks.

"Inconsistencies," I decide. "Something that isn't wrong but is . . . off."

Not that I know what that looks like. It could be correspondence between ARI team members. Testing results for Dekker's car.

This could be impossible.

"It won't be in the files since it's new." Theo says it under his breath, as if he's talking to himself.

"So, we log in." I take a seat at the computer, and he pulls up a chair next to me.

We both stare at the screen, the initial adrenaline wearing off as we take in the blinking cursor asking for our credentials.

"You know Dad's password?"

"No. But I know Vogel's." She has photos of her Great Dane all over her desk.

I type in his name and a second later, we're in.

We go through the records, looking for evidence that there was a material difference between the cars.

I wish Shay was here. The thought sneaks up, but I brush it away almost as fast. As much as it would help to have her eyes and brain on this, this is the last thing I want to drag her into.

I want to prove Dekker wrong. And maybe prove that I've been right to stand by my father, despite everything. He might be an asshole, but he wouldn't sabotage his own company.

"There's nothing here," I say two hours later, rubbing a hand over my face. We've searched through reams of files, enough data and emails to make our eyes cross.

Theo sighs. "Is there a bathroom on this floor? I shouldn't have had a beer before this."

"Go. I'll finish this file and be right there."

I pull up more of the car setup details side by side for the first race after the break. There are expected variances, accounting for driver preference and the like.

Except . . .

Braking is fresh in my mind after the last race, and that's why I spot it.

The brake setup is different across the cars. Not hugely, not enough that anyone would call it out, but enough to cause overheating relative to the first car. Enough to cost a few tenths of a second every lap.

It would be attributed to Dekker's driving. His engineers would tell him he needs to be less aggressive, to better manage the car.

But it wasn't his fault.

The team did it. They tanked their own driver, and I have the evidence in my hands.

I take photos of the pages on the screen.

"Jamie. You find something?"

I look up at Theo in the doorway.

He's eager, ready to follow my lead. My little brother, always looking up to me. He has his own future. One I don't want to ruin.

"No."

I log off and follow him out.

38

Shay

"WITH ONE RACE left in the F1 season, ARI is still fighting for first place," Vogel says, clicking to a slide of the São Paulo circuit. "Which makes this weekend decisive."

Rumors are still swirling about ARI's dismissal of Dekker, and gossip has reached a fever pitch about their next driver with Jameson sporting a broken collarbone, and him and Theo neck and neck heading into the final race.

ARI's reserve driver has done an adequate job of filling in, though he's not as comfortable with the car as Dekker was, so the team slipped another spot in the standings.

This weekend determines which team wins—meaning significant money and status for next year. No one really remembers who finishes second.

The past few days, Jameson's been quiet. I assume it's the injury. Or the race. Or both.

I know he's trying to get in the best possible shape for his final drive, but even his texts seem shorter than usual.

"It is also my pleasure to announce the finalists for the

internship," Vogel says. The drivers' side of class is sparse this week, with those in the Challenger series getting a pass if they're prepping.

But those of us who remain are invested. An excited buzz fills the room, and Megan, Zane, Raj, and I exchange a look.

"Once again, this is based on your coursework, but also your impacts on the Challenger Championship for those who have participated."

She reads off three names, then Megan's.

My friend's eyes go round. I'm already hugging her startled frame when I hear my name.

"Fuck yes!" she shouts into my hair. "You deserve it."

"Thanks. So do you."

It's not a win yet, but the fact that we're in the top five across candidates is exhilarating.

Raj and Zane look disappointed, but Raj manages a smile.

Vogel's not done. "The finalists are being flown to São Paulo for race weekend to see the F1 grid firsthand."

Our jaws drop in unison. It's a chance to get a glimpse of our potential future. As much as the Challenger series has been a stand-in, this is the real thing.

"How long do you think the ARI investigation will go on?" I ask Megan as we grab lunch in the cafeteria.

"It depends. But it would be weird for it to continue beyond next weekend if it impacts the final standings."

We take our food to our seats, and I pick at my plate.

I want this internship more than ever. Not because I need to stay at ARI for my entire life, but because it's one way to guarantee I'm in this industry.

My gaze drags to the window, where a crowd is forming by the front doors. A limo with the plates ASHFRD1 is pulled up at the curb in a strict no parking zone. The driver walks to the back and opens the door and I see two long, slim legs emerge wearing dangerously high heels.

Their owner slides out, elegant and self-assured. Her hair is set in bouncy blond waves. I'd guess she's our age or a little younger.

She tucks an impractically tiny bag under her arm, then strides up the walkway to the front of the building, her coat flying behind her.

Raj's chair scrapes back. "She can't be here."

He's already out of his seat with excitement, the internship news forgotten.

"What is going on?" I whisper.

We pull up in the foyer, where the girl has too, arms folded as she sweeps the room with her eyes.

"God, this place hasn't changed a bit. Would it kill them to add some decor that's not trophies and ARI red?"

Her gaze lands on me. There's a familiar intensity about it, but before I can place it, she speaks.

"You must be her."

"Do I know you?" I respond.

Her laughter tinkles through the foyer as she crosses to me. "I'm Eden. I had to meet the girl my brother lost his mind over."

It clicks. The limo plates. Her familiar expression. How she walked in like she owned the place.

It's because she does.

She's an Ashford.

❖

"I DIDN'T KNOW they had a sister," I say after we invite her back to our cafeteria table.

The possibility of Luca having more children never occurred to me. I've never seen her mentioned in the media, and neither Theo nor Jameson ever said anything.

Eden smiles as she takes the seat next to mine. "I usually avoid making an appearance until the holidays." She leans in confidingly and winks. "But you're dating Jamie, so I came to make sure he wasn't making a huge mistake."

From her expression, I wonder if she's joking.

I'm surprised Jameson told her about me. He doesn't offer up things that matter lightly.

"Townie." Jameson's voice has me turning.

My heart speeds up at the sight of him, especially after being deprived the past few days. Wearing a button-down and jeans, his hair falling across his handsome face, he's still breathtakingly gorgeous. Especially when all of his attention is on me.

"I heard you're a finalist," he says.

"And I'm glad to see you're alive," I tease.

"Barely." He stops behind me, bending to brush his lips over my neck. "But my condition is improving as we speak."

I'm swooning from the feel of his mouth on my skin when loud laughter fills the cafeteria.

We both look up to see Eden's eyes gleam. "My friends said I should have just called, but this was definitely worth coming in person for."

"Hi, Eden."

"Jamie!" She bounces out of her chair and throws her arms around Jameson. He hugs her back.

She pulls away to scan her brother from head to toe, frowning. "It looked bad."

"I'm okay. I promise." He stares her down, but with an expression that's full of calm and patience.

It takes me a second to recognize what's happening.

Eden's visit wasn't about me. She came home to check on him.

My chest aches at the realization that he does have someone who looks out for him, even if it's from halfway around the world.

A bell sounds, alerting us to the top of the hour.

"We have to go to class." I rise, and Jameson reaches for my book bag.

"To be continued. Jamie, get us a dinner reservation," Eden instructs.

"We don't have time for dinner out tonight, Eden." Despite his words, there's genuine regret in his tone.

She frowns. "But I came all this way to see you. The last time you came to see me, things weren't the best." There's a tiny crack in her polished facade. "Now I wanted to see my brothers and cheer them up heading into the biggest race of their lives. Is that so bad?"

Jameson hesitates. "We're going to São Paulo."

He says it as if it means something more. Megan and I exchange a wary look, and our uncertainty is confirmed when Eden claps her hands together in delight.

"Perfect! There's always room for one more on the jet."

39

Shay

"WE SHOULD HAVE become guests of ARI a long time ago," Megan vows as we land on the tarmac in São Paulo. It's hot and sunny even in November.

If I wasn't sure how mesmerizing it is to be part of the spectacle of F1, I'm getting it now. After we drop our belongings at the hotel, we head directly to the track. The atmosphere is electric—the fumes on the grid, the heat and sweat and purpose. The fashion of the spectators, the commentators, the executives. Today is for qualifying, and it feels as if an entire city, an entire country, came out to be entertained.

The season has come down to this final race. ARI is in second by a hair, but the big story is how fast Ignite has closed in for third. For a new team, they have no business doing this well.

I've been so caught up in my life at the academy and the fight for next year's seat, the stakes for the actual team have been more remote.

Not anymore. There are billions of dollars of engineering on display. The fastest cars, the most cunning strategists, the most elite drivers are here to compete.

The guys are already standing over the cars in the ARI garage. Theo's in chinos, a T-shirt, and designer sneakers. Jameson's wearing a sand-colored jacket and matching tailored pants, his crisp white collared shirt open underneath. I take a moment to ogle as he crosses to us, tugging his aviators off his face. "Hi."

"Hey."

His gaze flicks down my outfit, lingering on my legs. "You look beautiful."

"Thanks. Megan helped me pick this out." My dress is green and flowy, a sleeveless design that ends high on my thighs. I vetoed the spiky heels she suggested in favor of wedge sandals. "You look good, too."

There are cameras on us, around us. But whatever seemed to have been distracting him lately isn't bugging him today.

Jameson bends down to brush his lips over my cheek. "I'm sorry I got pulled away on the plane."

"Eden kept us company. Why didn't you tell me you and Theo have a sister?"

"I guess I'm as protective about her as she is of me. Plus, with Eden, you kind of need to experience her firsthand."

We both glance over to see her gesturing wildly, a tiny bag shaped like a cupcake around her shoulder.

Cameras crowd us. I resist the urge to duck my face as they click everywhere.

"Jameson, what's your take on the allegations against the ARI team for contract tampering and other infringements?"

He tenses. He was probably looking forward to a day off from the media. "I trust that everything is being resolved to the satisfaction of all parties."

The answer rolls off his lips. It's so lawyer coded, even for

Jameson, that it sounds less like an answer than a shield. But he's already grabbed my hand and is tugging me after him.

Watching qualifying together is a total rush. All twenty cars in a tightly choreographed sequence, each vying for the fastest possible lap to determine the final start grid for the next day. Ignite steals the front spot from ARI and Navarro, who line up second. Dekker's temporary replacement is in fifth.

That night, we all go out. Ten of us, with a couple of security guards in case things get rowdy. We end up at a low-lit club tucked between concrete buildings, with pulsing bass and bodies pressed close.

Eden drags me and Megan out to the dance floor. "He keeps looking for you," Eden shouts into my ear. "Jamie, I mean."

I follow her glance. His lips curve when his gaze meets mine, and my heart gives a little kick.

A while later, Eden and I emerge from the stalls in the bathroom at the same time.

"You came back for him," I say. "You were worried after the crash, and that's why you came back."

She laughs as she dries her hands. "Jamie's good at taking care of business. He's terrible at taking care of himself." The music vibrates through the door as she meets my gaze. "Theo told me you gave Daddy shit about Jamie at the hospital in Miami. Was he exaggerating?"

I wince. "They probably heard me all the way back in Michigan."

Her smile widens, like she sees something she's been searching for.

"Damn," she says softly. "I was not prepared to like you this much. Come on." She loops my arm in hers and leads the way back outside. I'm still not sure what to make of her, but she loves her brothers. I can get behind that.

I drag Eden and Megan back out to the floor, and Jameson even joins us after a few songs. Eventually, I catch myself yawning and check my phone. It's two a.m., and between my academy and work responsibilities, I'm not used to staying up until the morning hours.

Jameson notices. "It's late. Let's go," he says in my ear.

I'm grateful when he grabs my hand and tugs me toward the door. The others follow and the group of us stumble back out onto the street, the hairs on my neck curling from sweat and my face tired from laughing.

Theo mumbles, an arm around Megan and another around me. Jameson comes up behind us, raising his eyebrow at Theo's arm though he doesn't press it.

"Can't believe we're finalists." Megan grins at me, her expression blissful and buzzed. "I'm so happy you're here. Never thought I'd actually want someone else to win as much as I want to."

Warmth fills me as I reach across Theo to grab her hand. "Me too."

"If one of us makes it, I see more flats in our future. These fucking shoes." She kicks the pavement lightly in her strappy heels, wincing.

I glance down at my more sensible wedges. "Switch me."

"Really? I love you."

We trade and I walk back in the highest heels ever, soaking in the jokes and laughter swirling around us.

I don't even mind the blisters.

Once we get back to the hotel, we drop Theo off at his room. I wave goodnight to Megan and Eden and the others, trading questions about what we're wearing and last-minute race predictions.

I'm still smiling when Jameson pushes the door to the next room wide to let me in, the moonlight from the balcony streaming in. "Welcome to the penthouse."

"You're drunk," I accuse. Before tonight I've never noticed him have more than one drink.

"Only a little," he corrects.

Before us, the city is sprawled out in the dark, all glittering lights dancing in the warm breeze. Now, I'm thinking of the first time we hooked up, the fireworks over the city and Jameson filling my senses.

This is the first moment we've had alone in a while. There's always somewhere to be, something that needs doing, something to worry about.

"You seem distracted," I notice.

He frowns. "Race weekend's always chaos," he says. "Even when you're not driving."

I'm not sure that's all of it. I get the sense he's not telling me something but can't put my finger on what.

I open my mouth to ask, but before I can come up with the words, he fills the silence.

"How'd you like being on the grid?" Jameson leans on the railing next to me.

"It was beautiful."

"You fit in."

A laugh bubbles up. "Hanging out at Jameson Ashford's side? Next year, you'll be winning on the biggest stage. You might care less about your cheering section then."

"Impossible. When I told you I wouldn't let you lose, there was one thing I didn't expect."

"A running commentary on your driving choices?"

"No." He turns toward me, reaching for a piece of hair that's fallen in my face and tucking it behind my ear. "Now that I know how it feels to win with you, I don't want to do it any other way."

My chest expands.

A few months ago, I couldn't see myself fitting in at Ashford Academy. Now I have friends who want me to succeed and the heir to ARI—who happens to be incredibly talented, sexy, and caring—is telling me he wants us to achieve our dreams together.

A yawn chooses the most fucking awful moment to hit me, and I try to hide it with the back of my hand.

Jameson's lips curve. "You should sleep. I'll tuck you in."

"I'm fine," I protest.

He's already heading past me toward the bedroom.

"Where are you going?" I call over my shoulder. I turn and lift my hair, waiting for him to return.

After a moment, his hands brush my neck as he reaches for the zipper on my dress. "This how you want to be tucked in?"

"The only way," I agree.

He slides the zipper down. The fabric of my dress pools at my feet. He turns me, then grabs my knee and hitches it up around his hip.

"You're still thinking about racing, aren't you?" he murmurs as his lips skim my throat.

"Mmm. Telemetry and tire deg and braking zones."

His fingers slip between my thighs to press inside me. I'm so wet he slides right in.

"Right now?"

"Yes," I lie. "Friction and drag."

"I see." He pulls both fingers back toward me in a way that has me curling up to him. "It's fucked up how much I like that."

I laugh, grabbing on to him to keep from falling when my knees give out. "That's what turns you on."

"Pretty much." His thumb finds my clit, rubbing slow circles in time with his fingers pumping in and out.

Somehow, it's better every time with him.

"You don't have to be quiet."

I exhale shakily. "Because Theo's in the room next door?"

His teeth flash white in the dark.

"You're beyond redemption, Ashford," I whisper.

His lips brush mine, his eyes soft shadows. "Try anyway."

40

Shay

THE NEXT MORNING, the flags are flying in São Paulo.

It's a bright sunny day for a race. It feels as if the gods have blessed this as the final outing of the year.

I woke up in Jameson's room early, the expensive sheets soft under my skin and the curtains blowing in the breeze. He was asleep beside me, his dark lashes resting on his cheeks.

He'd told me he had trouble sleeping. He looked pretty peaceful to me as I traced a finger along his jaw. "You're cute when you're sleeping," I murmured when his eyes blinked lazily open.

"You're cute all the time." He rolled me onto my back and, despite my meager protests that we were going to be late, proceeded to show me exactly what that did to him.

I reluctantly went back to my own room, where I showered and put on a linen dress and heels before meeting Megan and Eden out at the front of the hotel.

As we make our way in a limo heading to the track, the media notifications are blowing up.

"Results are in: ARI is cleared of all wrongdoing," Megan reads off her phone. "You have thoughts on this?" She prompts the single Ashford in the car.

"Nope." Eden only smiles as she looks out the window.

The track is packed full of fans, tens of thousands crowding the area where it will take place. Like yesterday, the seating is full, plus spectators watching from the hills lining the track, well behind safety barriers.

It's an atmosphere of celebration in the garage. The race that will determine the team of the year is still to be won, but the tension has eased a degree.

Megan, the other finalists, and I get introduced to the ARI team. It's a big crew, and a little overwhelming. I repeat the introductions in my head.

Jameson and Theo are already trackside wearing headsets. Jameson catches sight of me and his eyes turn warm and knowing.

He waves me over. "Check it out." He pulls his headset off one ear and offers it to me. Instantly the team radio is there, talking about last-minute prep. Excitement pounds through my veins.

"This will be you next year," I remind him during a break in the conversation. "You ready for it?"

"Yes," he says seriously, tugging me against him.

"I like the confidence."

"It's not only that. More like I've thought about it so much it feels inevitable. Like I've already lived it so many times in my head."

Pride surges through me. I can't wait to watch Jameson drive. It's nerve-racking and dangerous but also thrilling. After everything he's done, he deserves this. Maybe he was born into that, but he's also worked his ass off and sacrificed.

"I better go," I decide, tugging out of his grasp. "I'm going to watch final prep in the paddock." I can catch the last steps before the cars set off.

"I'll start in the garage and grab a bite to eat. Somehow, I'm starving." Jameson's voice is rough, and my stomach flips at the thought of what we were doing this morning that made him so hungry.

"I can grab you something before I leave," I promise, heading to the team catering area. Food at the academy is decent but this is next level. Everything from pastries to eggs to full farmer's breakfast. Carafes of freshly brewed coffee, piping hot.

I grab coffees for me, Megan, and Eden and mash them into a quad tray. Then I start to pile food onto a plate. Eggs, bacon, pancakes. A sandwich for Jameson. When I knock a container of jam on the floor, I drop to my knees to collect it.

"It was dismissed. It can't come up again."

"There's no reason it would."

Voices near the doorway have me stilling.

"We dodged a bullet. No more mistakes, especially today."

That voice.

I've heard it on television. In person.

The hairs on my neck lift.

"Is someone here?"

I plaster myself against the floor, trying to make myself smaller. I don't know what will happen if I'm caught, but it won't be good.

The voices disappear down the hall. I sneak back out, my heart pounding the entire time.

"You okay?" Jameson's voice cuts through my haze when I get back to the garage.

I nod, then realize why he's looking so oddly at me. "They were out of breakfast sandwiches."

"Coffee too." His gaze drops to my empty hands clasped in front of me.

"Oh. Yeah." I nod stiltedly even though the half dozen carafes dance in my mind. "I have to go."

He starts to say something more, but I practically sprint toward the grid. I watch the jewel-toned cars dotting the asphalt. What I overheard replays in my mind, an unwanted soundtrack on what's otherwise a glorious day.

Luca materializes next to me, leaning on the rail at the side of the paddock.

Most students and ARI employees would probably wish to stand this close to him, but my palms are sweating.

"I was wrong about you," he starts. "At first, I thought you were a nuisance. But you've shown me you were meant to be here."

I turn and blink at him in disbelief.

In Vegas, he wanted me gone. Now he looks conciliatory.

"You don't mean that." There's a tremor under my voice that betrays me.

As much as he makes me uncomfortable, I *want* him to mean it. Everything would be easier if he did.

"There's no denying my son's feelings for you. The question is whether you're loyal."

Loyal. It's a good attribute, but it doesn't feel good right now.

The hope I felt crumbles into ash.

It was Luca's voice I overheard in the garage. His I overheard talking about not making more mistakes.

He did fire Dekker, he did arrange to sabotage the second ARI car, and now he wants my silence. In return, he won't be an obstacle.

My fingers flex on the railing as the cars come back from their formation lap and prepare to start the race.

One red light.

Two.

"This is bigger than you," Luca intones softly, persuasively.

Three.

"Hundreds of people are involved. Some are people you care very much about. People I know you don't want to hurt."

Just like there are people who'd kill to know about this. Ignite, for one.

"So tell me, Shay MacDonald."

Four.

"Are you loyal?"

Jameson's words from last night come back. I'm in this now. It's his future, not only mine. My stomach drops.

Five.

"Think quickly," Luca urges.

The starting lights go out.

41

Shay

THE RUMBLING IN my stomach isn't hunger. Even though I'm half asleep on the plane, my fingers, my toes, even my nose vibrate.

"You okay?" Theo brushes a piece of hair out of my face. "You were twitching."

I blink my eyes open to find the younger Ashford perched in the seat opposite me. The jet is at cruising altitude on the way home from São Paulo. I'm curled up in my seat with a blanket tucked around my legs.

ARI took the driver's title. Ignite took the team championship.

Luca got what mattered most to him.

It still wasn't enough.

I'm still replaying the conversation with Luca even as the hours bleed into one another. If you can call it a conversation.

He made me an offer. A bribe, really—delivered in that cool, expectant tone of someone used to the world falling in line.

I blink, realizing Theo's still waiting for me to respond. "Sorry, I might have drifted off."

"Sleep is good." He nods to an empty glass and grabs a

bottle of water from a side shelf, holding it out. "But you need to hydrate at altitude." I take the water from him.

Ashford Racing was willing to lose placings and millions of dollars to put Luca's son in the seat and make it look legit. It's another glimpse of Luca's hand and the lengths he's willing to go in order to have his way.

"I can't believe that's going to be one of you on the grid in a few months," I say, setting the champagne flute on the side table and uncapping the water.

Theo spreads his hands. "Welcome to my life."

"How do you deal with it?" I ask on impulse. "The circus, the roller coaster."

"You can't change it," he says kindly. "You have to decide if you can live with it. If you can find ways to be yourself despite the circumstances."

Jameson appears over Theo's shoulder. "You're in my seat."

Theo winks at me. "This is my plan. I just need to get there first and refuse to leave."

I start to laugh. Theo joins in.

Jameson drops into the seat next to mine. "I found a better one."

He lifts the armrest and nods his chin at me. I curl into him, getting comfortable with my head against his shoulder.

My eyes drift closed on one last thought. Luca's manipulating me. He's also responsible for these two humans I'm grateful to have in my life. And I don't know where that leaves us.

BY THE TIME I get home, I still haven't figured it out.

"What if someone made you an offer but it came with strings attached?" I ask Dad over bacon strips and coffee at The Junction the next morning.

Even indoors, he's wearing the ARI championship ball cap I brought him from São Paulo.

"Trouble with strings is you can rarely see what's on the other end. Who's really pulling them, and what it'll cost you."

My coffee mug warms both my hands, but I'm still cold on the inside. "If you had a chance to work on the grid again, would you take it?"

He turns it over, then shakes his head. "My time there is over."

"But if it wasn't for the accident, if it wasn't for me, you'd still be there," I point out.

His expression is troubled. He takes a bite of his pancakes, chasing it with a swig of OJ.

"A lot of things would have been different, Shay." His gaze drops to my elbow, the scar there. "When you went in for surgery after the crash, you were so brave. The entire time you healed and through your rehab, you were the best patient. It keeps me up at night that the person who did it never faced the consequences."

I'm shaking my head before he finishes. "But you couldn't do anything about that."

Dad sighs.

I reach across the table to snag a piece of bacon off his plate. I haven't finished mine, so it's more about lightening the mood.

"I wish your parents were still here," Dad says after a moment. "But then I wouldn't have you."

Finally, he smiles.

42

Shay

A WEEK LATER, I still can't find the right way to talk to Jameson about the ARI scandal. It really doesn't seem like a text.

Hey miss your face. PS your dad tanked the F1 season. XOXO

Plus, he and Theo have both been on the road, and the final race to determine who claims the open ARI seat next year is this weekend. It's going to change not one of their futures, but both.

Megan and I have been putting our heads together for any insight that could give Jameson an advantage for this race and track.

"This is some party," Bree comments dryly, stepping inside the sim lab and looking around.

The room is smaller than most of the classrooms and full of racing sims and old cabinets. Students camp out here when the library is full or they need a space to decompress.

Exams feel less important than everything else going on, but I've heard the combination of written and applied evaluations are grueling. So, I've had my nose buried in textbooks and manuals for the past few days. I even fell asleep on a book last night. When I woke up, Dad was pulling it out from under my face and tucking a blanket around me.

"You bring snacks?" Megan calls.

Bree crosses to Megan with a bakery box and pulls the top back.

She groans. "I haven't had a carb in hours."

"The horror."

Raj is across the room next, Zane on his heels. "You're a goddess," Raj declares.

I go to see what they're looking at and find half a dozen chocolate cupcakes in a box. I lift one out and take the chocolate piece off the top, popping it into my mouth and letting its decadent sweetness dissolve on my tongue.

"Is it actually worth it?" Bree prompts. "You look like you haven't had a shower in days. All to get a contact high off some fast cars."

"Yes," we all chorus.

Before this semester, I never appreciated how much different it would be to go through the experience with other people. Not just classmates but friends.

But it's not only for the cars. It's for us. For the feeling that we're all working on a dream together. That no matter where our lives take us, we'll all have these moments to look back on.

"My cousin thinks he can get me into his F1 team," Zane announces. "After grad, I mean."

"Wow. That's huge." Raj's eyes are round.

"You upset you weren't short-listed for the ARI internship?" Megan asks.

Zane folds his arms. "I've been thinking about that since

you went to São Paulo. After school, I want to go somewhere where I can control what happens. It would be easier with a smaller team, less pressure."

"That's really mature of you, Zane." Megan's voice has an unusual amount of respect in it. "What about you?" She nods to Raj.

"Oh. I've already started talking to professors at U of M about putting in an application for graduate school after next year." He shrugs sheepishly. "I'm not sure I want to spend my life on the grid."

"Megan?" I prompt.

My friend frowns, tucking her hair behind her ear. "I want this internship. I want to prove I didn't make a mistake."

Her longing echoes in my chest. At the start of the semester, all I wanted was to get what I needed from the academy and get out. From the moment I started believing I could be part of this world, really part of it, it made me want more.

Except, after last weekend, maybe there is a price I can't pay. I suddenly feel cold.

"What are you going to do on your break?" Bree asks.

We exchange looks.

"I'm going on vacation with my family," Raj says. "It's still hard being away from them for a semester at a time."

"We'll have two weeks of bliss. No early-morning classes, no Vogel, no grease under our fingernails," Megan adds.

"Snowball fights. Baking. Reality TV marathons on Netflix."

The door clicks but I don't notice until there's a familiar voice.

"That sounds wholesome."

Jameson.

His eyes find mine and there's that ripple of awareness, the tug of more every time I see him. I want to run to him and throw myself into his arms.

"Do you get at least one day of skiing in the Alps or whatever you rich folks do? Or is that ruled out in your contract?" Bree asks.

"It's allowed as long as we're in sponsor-approved gear," Jameson says.

"Was that a joke?" Raj asks Megan.

"Yes, Raj, that was a joke," Jameson answers. "Got a second?" he asks me.

"As long as you're more entertaining than aerodynamics." I shift off the simulator, taking my books and the cupcake with me.

He's wearing jeans and a button-down, looking perfectly pressed despite too many hours of traveling. His face is lean planes and hard angles, the same ones that used to make me want to fight or run.

"How's studying?"

The rest of the room's pretending not to watch.

"Delicious." I swipe a chunk of icing and lick it off my finger.

Jameson's attention lingers on my mouth. "I, uh. Wanted to ask you about something."

"Come on." I set the cupcake, still in its wrapper, on a sim and tug him outside and down the hall.

A handful of students drifts through the building. Everyone has their own shit going on, but ours feels bigger. Jameson pulls me into a closet where we won't be overheard.

"You've been holding back since the last race," he says after tugging the door shut and flicking on an overhead light.

The space is barely big enough for the two of us. The walls are lined with cleaning supplies, and there's a low desk that bumps the back of my legs.

I tip my face back to take him in. "Okay, Mr. Traveling-the-World."

He frowns. "I know I haven't been the most available. If I pushed you too hard with what I did or said in São Paulo—"

"You didn't." I take a breath and steel myself.

"So, what's the problem?"

He steps closer and cups my cheek with one hand. He's near enough I can smell him, and I want to bury my face in his shirt and forget everything outside this closet.

My throat tightens, the knot lodged in it reminding me that I can't. "I overheard a conversation."

His nostrils flare as I fill him in on Luca talking about ARI cheating, leaving out the part about his dad telling me not to say anything. It feels as if I'd be putting even more pressure on him.

When I'm finished, Jameson presses his fingers into his temples. "Let me get this right. You overheard my father and another employee admit that ARI tanked Dekker's car on purpose. And you didn't tell me."

"There were other things on your mind. I know it's a shock . . ." I trail off at the distinctly unshocked expression on his face. "Wait. You knew."

He grimaces. "I suspected something," he says carefully. "Before São Paulo. I didn't want it confirmed. It'll sink ARI if it gets out, shred the company's reputation."

Anger rises up. "Luca should have thought of that first. What about the team, all the engineers and mechanics who worked their asses off to build the best possible car?"

He exhales heavily. “I get it, Shay. I do. But ARI is bigger than my father. It’s the only place I’ve ever felt like I belong. And if this gets out, it’ll be a scandal too big even for our company. I have to believe there’s something worth saving.”

My heart skips at the desperation in his words. “You could drive for another team?”

He’s already shaking his head. “ARI is all I’ve wanted. All I’ve prepared for.”

I’m frustrated he sees it that way. Under the collar of his shirt, the chain I gave him glints. My fingers brush the metal I’ve always treasured before shifting up to his face. He’s warm and real and present.

“The past doesn’t matter as much as the future,” I say. “I learned that from you. I hope you’re ready to live by it.”

43

Jameson

SHAY'S WORDS ARE still echoing in my ears when I go down to the gym late that night.

I grew up wanting to be part of ARI, but I didn't understand it. Now, I'm seeing its flaws run deeper than I knew.

But there's a chance it can be better.

I'm supposed to be at the academy the next morning, but what I have to say won't wait. That's why I go straight to ARI headquarters instead, take the hall to my father's office, and push on his door.

He's inside in a meeting with half a dozen execs who all look up in surprise.

"We need to talk," I announce.

"I have room in my schedule this afternoon, Jameson—"

"Now."

The suits clear out at Luca's pointed look.

"I know what happened with Dekker," I say, barely waiting for the door to close before I start.

Luca's eyes narrow. "How?"

"It doesn't matter. I want to know why."

My father paces behind his desk. I wonder if he's always been uncomfortable with stillness. "Dekker isn't an Ashford. I want my blood in that car."

"Badly enough to compromise everyone in ARI to make it happen?"

He points to photos and trophies on the wall. "This company, this entire town, thrived because of me. I was a driver, Jameson. But I had a vision for myself, my heirs. If you wait for things to happen, they never will."

"Then it's only nepotism."

If the words sound hollow, that's exactly how I feel. Theo's worst nightmare might have been losing his family, but mine is this—winning when I don't deserve it, especially when I'm forced to confront the casualties.

It's one thing to race for the seat, another to know it was made available in the first place through back dealing and sabotage.

"Nothing is 'only.' There's always *and*. A winning season is skill *and* luck. A winning driver is talent *and* opportunity. Even when the stars align, the world can conspire against you to keep you from your destiny.

"Like this girl you're infatuated with. She will keep you from your fate."

"She *is* my fate." I say it without thinking.

He laughs. "She isn't. You'll see that soon enough. You think you're worldly, son, but you've lived a very short and sheltered life. The things I've done before you were old enough to step in a kart."

His voice lifts the hairs on my neck. "I don't believe you."

Luca rounds his desk, closing the distance between us.

Proximity with my father never felt like intimacy. More like control.

"Sixteen years ago, we were in a competitive season, defending our title. Everyone wanted to bring us down. We ended up winning a world championship, but it could have gone very differently thanks to one particular crash."

I scan my memory, reels of film and recaps and stats.

"There was no crash that season." I'm confident.

"It wasn't on the track. It was late one night, not far from here. The weather turned bad. An ARI employee was at the wheel on one side. On the other, a husband and wife, and their child in the back seat."

My chest squeezes, my ribs knitting together.

"The employee walked away from the scene," he goes on. "In the second vehicle, only the child survived. A girl. Five or six, with minor injuries."

He's staring at me like he did when I was young and taking too long to catch on to a game. I was smart, but he was always two steps ahead.

"Does any of this ring a bell?" he prompts.

"Why should it?" I shove my hands in my pockets, irritated.

"It was kept out of the public eye. That employee was protected. But it was necessary—that kind of attention would have been extremely damaging."

My fingers close around the ring and chain.

It clicks, then. How was I so stupid.

"Four." I can barely form the word.

"Excuse me?"

Bile rises up my throat. "She was four. And they weren't

minor injuries." I think of the plate and screws. A lifetime without her family. "What happened to the other driver?"

"Nothing. The driver was a key employee of this company. Like you aspire to be."

I'm struggling to focus on the facts. Nausea rips through me, denial hot on its heels.

"And he was at fault," I say.

"It's too easy to assign blame, Jameson. The public sees a trophy and confetti, an instant of celebration, and believe victory comes in a moment. The truth is that it takes years, decades, to build that foundation. All of it can be ripped away in a heartbeat."

The denial is fading, leaving horror in its place.

Shay didn't know the truth of how her parents died—only that someone wiped their hands clean of it. She spent her entire life questioning, guessing, longing, wishing. She grew up with nothing, all so I could grow up with *everything.*

White spots dance behind my eyes as another wave of nausea rolls through me, followed by the sledgehammer of guilt.

My father stole everything from her. To preserve this company, this legacy.

His.

Mine.

How can we make this better when it's built on a lie? How can I look her in the eyes and tell her I care when my dad ruined her life?

I tried to believe I could change this company, that I could change it with her.

Now I know there's no fucking way.

44

Shay

THERE'S NOWHERE BETTER to be alone with your thoughts than a garage. The focus, the repetition, the physicality.

I'm bent over an engine, socket wrench in hand, when Keane comes by.

"Surprised to see you here tonight." He wipes his hands on a rag in his belt.

"Dad wasn't feeling well, so I offered to fill in."

Keane shakes his head. "He's lucky to have you. I don't know anyone else who could've done school and everything else."

I straighten, rolling my shoulders. "The first half of the semester, I was running on fumes." That and guilt, but I don't say that part.

"Doing great things takes a big effort. You need to be a little tireless, a little insane." He jerks his chin toward the other end of the garage. "Let me show you something." Keane walks toward the restricted part of the garage and swipes a key card. The door unlocks with a soft beep.

I follow him into the second part of the building.

Inside is the F1 car for next year, crouched low like a wildcat ready to spring. Millions of dollars of engineering. Exposed carbon and relentless efficiency, ready to wreak havoc on the track.

"One person looks at this, he sees metal and parts. What do you see?"

I step closer and run a hand over the smooth bodywork, my breath catching.

Freedom, I would have said last summer.

"Possibility," I say instead.

Keane nods. "Why do people push themselves that hard? For me, it's doing things together we can't do ourselves." He taps his chest. "I can't build this car. But we—" He gestures back toward the bays. "We can build something faster than the wind. And for me, that's the point of it all."

"Pummeling nature into submission with technology and engineering?" I ask.

He laughs. "Doing something that's never been done before with people who're just crazy enough to think we can."

My body thrums with his words. The spark deep in my chest flares, but this time it's not only the possibility of winning.

Maybe Keane's right. There's more to this than any one person.

Luca can't make ARI, and he can't break it, either.

After my shift, I drive the Mustang across town in the dark to the Ashfords' complex. It's nearly midnight, but when I texted Jameson, he answered right away.

I hit the buzzer and realize it's the first time I've asked to get in.

The gates swing wide.

Beyond, the driveway is illuminated by lanterns. I pull to a stop outside the garage.

"Can't sleep?" I ask when I step inside.

Jameson's bent over the Stingray, his shoulders straining against the black T-shirt.

He rounds the car, going to the workbench to rifle through the drawers. "I need to be better tomorrow. Better than I ever have been."

"You will be." I cross to him, put my hand on his arm. "You're Jameson Ashford. No one drives like you."

"It's the only thing I'm good for."

He pulls away and turns his back to me.

Alarm bells sound in my head. He's cool and remote in a way he hasn't been with me, not for months.

"That's not true," I say, needing him to hear it. "You're a good brother. A good friend. You're good for me."

"Am I?" Jameson's laughing, but his face says he doesn't think it's funny.

"You know you are. I wouldn't be here if it wasn't for you."

His expression twists and a flicker of the person I've come to know is visible through the cracks. "This place is wrong, Townie. I never saw how wrong because I didn't want to."

He returns to his work. Once more, I'm on the outside, looking in at him.

"You can win this," I insist. "And you can make ARI anything you want."

Jameson's eyes flick toward me. "That assumes there's a company that deserves to exist."

A few days ago, we were talking about our future. Now it sounds like he's saying we'll never have one.

I wish he would yell. I know what to do with his fire. I can't handle his defeat.

"What happened? This isn't you. This isn't us."

"We're not the same. You have nothing here," he says. "No future. No security. No family to fall back on."

Every word lands hard in my chest. The feelings churning inside are overwhelming, an inescapable tide of wrongness.

"I told you once that if you stayed," he continues, "you'd wind up with Ashford tire tracks up your back."

My chin lifts, defiant. "And I stayed anyway."

Jameson knows how to score a point off an enemy, but I don't know how we ended up on opposite sides.

"You need to leave." He says it like if he pushes hard enough, I'll actually go.

"Leave what?"

"ARI. The academy. All of it."

Hurt and betrayal twist together, a dark pit in my stomach.

I never expected these words from him. Not now, not after everything we've been through. But I'm staring at the person who helped me believe I could belong here, and I don't recognize him.

"You don't get to decide what I need."

"Someone has to."

The deliberate cruelty doesn't hurt as much as the casual dismissal. I forgave him for lying before because it was about fear. This feels different. This is about control.

"You sound like your father." I whisper the words.

Jameson starts, his eyes clearing as if he's seeing me for the first time tonight. "I'm not him."

"No? Because right now, I can't tell the difference."

I spin on my heel. The first time I left this garage, I'd sabotaged his car and was running on adrenaline and fear.

This time, it's heartbreak that fuels me.

45

CHALLENGER CHAMPIONSHIP
Race Three

Jameson

"JAMESON! HAVE YOU processed that the next few hours will change your future? Do you still think you can beat Theo given your injury? How do you feel about your chances today?"

The reporters are a throng of phones and lights, pressing question after question as if they expect me to divine my future in convenient soundbites.

It's the final test in the Challenger Championship at the Mid-Ohio Sports Car Course.

The circuit is the nearest one to Ashford HQ and the academy, so all of the company's employees and stakeholders are in attendance. The track itself is compact, tricky, and unforgiving.

It's all I've wanted my entire life. Driving the fastest cars in the world. Racing the best. But suddenly it feels empty. I told myself the hole inside my chest would be filled once I got the seat. That was before I learned exactly what we've allowed to happen in the name of success, achievement.

I always needed to prove myself.

Why was I born first? Why am I more deserving than Theo? Why do we both have the name, but I get all the perks?

Now, it feels as if I have to demonstrate there's something good to come out of ARI, and out of my family. I can't make all of the suffering—Shay's, Dekker's, who knows how many others'—worthwhile. But I can do everything in my power to try.

Pre-race media ends and the morning is a blur. There's the tension of race day, the banners in the crowds, the cameras capturing footage to broadcast around the world.

After a month of supposed healing, my body still hurts. But I can't afford weakness. The stakes are too high for anything less than all I have to give.

Theo and I run into each other coming out of the changing room.

"Shay's not coming," he says.

My head snaps up. "Since when?"

He adjusts the collar of his fire suit, fastening the snap at the neck. "You tell me."

My brother's eyes are calmer than usual. Instead of the amused irreverence that normally lives there, I see genuine disappointment.

Theo grew up. Part of me's satisfied to see it, but I hate that it's me he's disappointed in. All those years I tried to be what he needed, and I failed him anyway.

"You better hope Megan didn't fuck up your car." He glances over toward the engineer across the garage. Her glower when she spots me answers whether she knows about Shay.

I'm still using the setup they advised on.

Even given what I said, deep down I figured she'd be here

today. She deserves to be, and it's one more thing I've taken from her.

I've been haunted by our last conversation. Of course I shouldn't have expected her to go down easy. But the way she fought for me, fought for us . . .

I thought I'd buried the hurt, but it snakes out a tentacle and stings deep in my chest.

Shay worked her ass off for this moment, and I told her to go. I said horrible things in the name of showing her exactly how little she has in the world, thanks to me and the company that bears my family name.

The speakers crackle to life, and both our attention lifts to the podium at the head of the VIP area of the track.

Our father fills the podium. He's in his element, as much as he can be outside of a car.

"This day will decide our future as a company, and an industry. Nothing will stand in the way of Ashford Racing."

There's a grim edge to his voice, a finality and satisfaction that used to be comforting, but now is unsettling. What he's not saying is that one person could still get in the way of ARI's future.

One person.

Luca's eyes meet mine.

My father might be ruthless and demanding, but if there's one thing my father isn't, it's careless. He'd rather go scorched earth than leave loose ends.

Shay's a loose end.

The thought sticks in my mind as he keeps talking. She knows about Dekker. That the car was purposely sabotaged. That my father ordered it.

Does Luca know she heard it? Even if he does, he wouldn't do anything so reckless. He's arrogant, not stupid.

Still, cold ripples down my spine as I think of what I've learned about my father recently—the way he pushed Dekker out of a job, manipulating an entire company and probably costing ARI the team championship. That covered up Shay's parents' deaths neatly for sixteen years because the thought of it messing with his life, with his plans, was inconceivable.

Once you see what someone's capable of, you can't unsee it.

I scan the crowd of fans, all of them eager for the contest that's about to begin. The next two hours will determine whose number goes on the ARI car next year, who they'll get signed photos of, who they'll gossip about on social media.

I've already handed my phone off to an admin for safekeeping, but now, I demand it back. I hit Shay's contact.

The line rings once. Twice.

"This is Shay . . ."

Voicemail.

I rack my brain to remember whose shift she was on. Then search a mobile version of the ARI employee records.

A moment later, the phone is ringing again.

"Hello?" Shay's dad answers.

"It's Jamie Ashford." My words come out in a rush. "I'm looking for Shay."

I can hear him bristle. "She's not home."

Relief edges in, but it's short-lived. "I need to speak with her but she's not answering her phone."

"As I understand it, all you need to do today is win a race."

I pace next to my car. They're waving for me to get in, but I turn my back on them.

Shay's dad takes a breath. "I know how important it is for you to be in the right mindset for this race, which is why I don't say this lightly. You should've known better." Guilt rises up, a familiar companion with sharp new teeth. "I can only imagine the upbringing you've had with Luca, but that's why you should know. She might act tough, but she has a soft heart and you drove right over it."

His words are a gut punch.

"I'm not going to argue. That's not why I'm calling. I learned that my father was involved the night Shay's parents died. He covered up the accident for an Ashford employee to save the company's reputation, and I think he might be willing to do it again."

Worry has my words blurring together, the paranoid ramblings of a desperate man.

I expect him to question my story or say he doesn't believe me. Instead, there's silence on the line for so long I think he's hung up.

When he finally speaks . . .

It's fucking chilling.

"Your father didn't cover up one of his employees killing Shay's parents. Luca was the driver."

46

Jameson

I'M COMING OUT of my skin as Theo and I line up at the start line.

The track lights slice through the darkness. In the bleachers, there's a dull buzz from the crowd, excited fans holding up signs I don't try to read. They know they're witnessing history. This is what the passing of a torch looks like.

I look over and meet my brother's eyes.

This is it. What we've been waiting for all our lives. It's our chance to fulfill the destiny we were born and raised for.

None of it feels right.

The first red light blinks on.

One.

Memories flash across my brain.

Me and Theo racing as kids.

Me wanting my father's approval.

Two.

My mother's sad looks, the way she argued with my father until she gave up.

The way I came to understand this was my legacy, my responsibility.

Three.

Shay getting up in front of the Porsche, shaken and furious.

Her working on my car at my side, clever and resourceful.

Four.

Her lying next to me at the hotel in São Paulo, talking about our futures.

The way I feel when I'm around her, alive and hopeful and a better person than I've ever thought I could be.

Five.

It's one thing to try and persuade someone to stay quiet. Actually taking steps to shut them up is a bigger risk with rippling consequences.

But Shay has leverage over my father, more than even she knows.

He wouldn't hurt her. Except he already has.

What if.

What if.

The lights go out.

I accelerate like I've practiced a million times.

The car leaps under me. In my peripheral vision, Theo does the same.

The roar of the crowd fills the night. Fuel fills my nostrils, the cold air scorching my throat.

Competitiveness takes over as we gun it toward the first corner. I brake where I need to, Theo's more aggressive and gets there first by braking late.

I have a chance coming out to gain the lead, but I miscalculate and we're neck and neck again.

Pull it together.

The next corner, I do. I get there first, Theo has to back out.

The rest of the field is behind us, close enough I need to keep tabs on them too. If I let Theo past, I've got every other car to contend with. In theory, Knox could still steal a win.

But deep down I know it's about me and Theo.

It's always been us.

It's a sequence, back and forth.

The curves are hypnotic. I'm pulling ahead, and every part of me that's trained for this moment overrides my emotions.

I can win. I know it.

Suddenly, I'm thinking about being on the Ducati with Shay.

Luca would never give her a chance to tell someone. Not now, or next season.

What would my father do to keep her quiet?

What *wouldn't* he do?

I look up at the screen and see him, triumphant.

What if.

What if.

My disorientation turns to fear. My hands tighten on the wheel as I switch gears—not on the car but mentally.

If I quit now, this is over. My career and future. Everything I've worked for my entire life.

If she's not okay, I won't have a future.

The realization slams into me.

I might not be the kind of man who deserves her, but I can

be the man who cares enough to do the right thing. Whether or not I can have her, I can get out from under my father's expectations and rules, the lying and the control. I thought if I played along, eventually it would be worth it.

It never will be. It's not worth this. Not worth *her.*

The turn barrels up at me, the car flying along the straight. There's the exit to the pit lane, where the ARI team would be startled but able to take the car from me. I could hand it off to them, but there would be questions. They'd stop me or slow me down.

Instead, I eye up a service alley.

I brake early, reversing to make my way. The car downshifts to a stop, tossing gravel in the parking lot.

Back on the track, Theo's racing himself. Fans are still watching me from the stands, looking between the track and where I've gone. No one knows how to respond because they have no idea what I'm doing.

The loudspeaker system is crackling, imploring fans to stay in their seats. Whatever they say after that, I tune out.

I'm working to climb out of the car, throwing off my neck brace when my feet hit solid ground. There's a team bike illuminated by the overhead lights, and I cross to it in a few loping strides.

A voice stops me when I reach for the handle. "Jameson."

I spin to see my father running out of the service road, his hair and eyes wild.

"Get back in the car. We'll do a restart. Say you had a moment of insanity. Three months from now, you'll be driving every track you'd ever dreamed. This will all be in the past."

I pull off my helmet as he says the words some part of me

longs to hear. I can still have what I want. I can pretend these last few months were nothing but a blip in the radar.

I reach into my pocket for the ring she gave me. It's cool and smooth, tiny but significant, and undeniable in its ability to endure.

"The cover-up wasn't for some faceless Ashford employee. It was you who hit her parents' car. You killed them."

He blinks. "It makes no difference."

"It makes every difference," I spit out. "Tell me she's fine."

"The girl?"

"Say it," I repeat. My jaw is locked, my fists clenched.

He exhales. "She's fine."

His confidence always reassured me. Even when I didn't agree with his methods, I trusted him to be strategic. Predictable in his ego and vanity.

"Swear it."

His eyes widen as he crosses to me, gravel crunching under his shoes. He's studying me as if he's not quite sure who he's dealing with. Like maybe I'm not the son he raised.

"I swear."

He reaches for my shoulder, grabbing it and shaking as if he can instill his faith in me. Dull pain shoots across my chest from the pressure.

The man I once idolized might be a hero to millions, but he's not to me. We're not the same. I can be better than him, not on the track but where it matters even more.

"I don't believe you."

My father's face explodes in fury. "Jameson . . ."

I'm already yanking my helmet back on and getting onto the bike, the keys in it.

"You can't leave. Everything you are is here. Everything you've built, everything I gave you."

I kick it in gear and tear off into the night, gripping the ring between my palm and the handle hard enough to leave a mark.

47

Shay

"YOU SHOULDN'T HAVE come."

I'm not swayed by Bree's ominous words from the passenger seat. "That's not true. I love looking at dresses." I pack as much enthusiasm into my voice as humanly possible.

"And bags?" she challenges.

"Especially bags."

It's a half-hour drive on back roads to the mall where I promised to help Bree shop for her date with the guy from The Junction. My romantic life might be going up in flames, but I can help my friend.

Bree shakes her head and rests an arm on the windowsill of the Mustang. "He's an asshole. Whatever he said to you, I'm going to rip him a new one."

Emotions rise up my throat. "Don't waste your effort."

I shouldn't have let myself get caught up. Not in Jameson, or his world. Everyone warned me off it from the start. When it came down to it, he thought I was nothing. We were nothing.

On the radio, Phoebe Bridgers starts to croon about emotional motion sickness. I turn it up until the ache dulls.

Despite my efforts to push him from my mind, the time on the clock reminds me that the final race has started.

I didn't need the reminder. I think of him every time I get in my car.

The feud was supposed to be about winning. Piece by piece, he left his mark on the Fastback. When I wasn't looking, this place that was mine for so long became his, too.

Someday, I'll watch Jameson on TV. Maybe I'll even go to the grid where I can see him in person. If I wait long enough, I will have forgotten how it feels to have his beautiful smile pointed my way. The way his body tightens under my hands. How soft his voice gets when we're alone.

"You're going to be okay," Bree says. Her hand closes around mine on the steering wheel, her eyes bright with concern.

"For sure." I swallow hard. "Where's Trevor taking you on this date?"

"A concert. That way if we have nothing to talk about, we can just dance and nod."

My lips twitch. "Judging from the way you've both been flirting for the last two months, I doubt that'll be a problem."

There's a turn in the road ahead. I brake early in case the pavement is slippery. Though the temperatures outside are dropping, there shouldn't be ice.

The car responds by wavering under me.

Weird.

Bree doesn't notice. "I should have brought the shoes I want to wear with me."

I'm listening, but part of my brain is still on the road.

We're climbing a big hill that disappears into blackness. I ease off before we hit the top. We crest the hill and I realize exactly how big the drop-off is on the other side. The Mustang starts down the hill, and I press on the brake.

We're not slowing.

I can't stop.

The realization hits me.

"What's happening?" Bree's voice rises at the end. She knows something's wrong but still trusts that I've got it under control.

God, I wish I did.

"Come on," I implore the car, trying again even though I know it won't help. "Come on."

Panic starts to rise in my throat as we descend the hill. I'm picturing exactly how bad this could go.

Think, Townie. I hear Jameson in my head.

We're alone. There's no other traffic. That's good. We won't collide with anyone. I size up the angles at the bottom of the hill and downshift hard. The engine roars and my back wheels shudder.

It's not enough.

The emergency brake. I reach for it, pull it on slow. Then a truck appears, coming the other way.

Shit.

I have to steer for the runoff.

"SHAY!" Bree's terrified voice lifts above the sound of the car.

"It's going to be okay." I grab for her, trying to keep her secure.

The truck flies past us, disappearing up over the rise. Relief seeps in.

Until we hit the barrier.

My lungs explode, the air punched out of them. Every rational thought goes out the window.

This is what it was like for them.

It's so hot.

The heat is what I feel before I black out.

48

Jameson

I'VE NEVER BEEN paralyzed. But the moment I spot the Fastback upside down in the ditch, I can't move.

Flames lick up from the engine bay, smoke creeping into the cabin.

"Shay!" I holler.

The bike skids to a stop a few meters from the wreck. I leap off it and rip off my helmet, reaching the car in a few frantic steps.

There's a person on the other side. I'm there in a flash, and it takes less time to realize it's not her.

"Bree."

The woman, who's coughing, points back to the car. I don't wait another second. I've never been so grateful for my fire suit. I try to get the driver's door open. Fail.

Because the car's vintage, there are no airbags. I break into the window, my chest screaming. I ignore the pain and reach for her seat belt, working it free.

Burning. Every instinct in me says to get the fuck out of there, but all I care about is what's inside the crackling furnace of the car.

I should have gotten here faster. Shay's dad told me where she was headed, and I floored it the entire way.

Shay's eyes are closed, her face scratched and banged up.

I have to get her out.

Nothing else matters. Not the fact that my father did this, though I swear to God if she gets through this, I'll kill him.

If she doesn't . . . I don't know what I'll do.

There's no time to call for help. Sweat drips down my face as I work her out of the vehicle.

She could have all kinds of injuries. I shouldn't move her, but the fire grows, and we can't be here if it erupts.

I'm trying to keep my hands steady and avoid wrenching my healing collarbone out of joint.

But I have to get her to safety.

Finally, the seat belt gives way.

I lift her in my arms as carefully as I can, relying mostly on one side. Her head lolls against my chest. She must feel my heart hammering.

Unless she's . . .

I get her away from the car and set her on a hill clear of the wreck, my hand supporting her head. Then check for a pulse.

She's breathing.

Thank fuck.

"Shay. It's me."

No response.

I search her body for injuries. Her leg is at a bad angle, but I'm worried about things like internal bleeding. The classic Mustang scores points for cool, but the lack of safety features makes me hate it.

"Jameson?" Bree croaks from behind me.

She's not moving fast, either. Fuck.

"I'm calling an ambulance." I fumble for my phone and make the call, watching Bree for signs of distress. Shay would want me to make sure her friend is okay.

"What hurts?" I ask Bree when I'm on hold for an operator.

She points to her knee, which looks pretty scraped. Possibly from getting out of the car. Better to keep her from making it worse if there is a serious injury.

"Can you keep still until the ambulance gets here?"

She nods in understanding and reclines on the ground. When I'm satisfied she's not in imminent danger, I turn back to Shay.

The operator comes on the line and I tell her about the accident, snapping out our location.

When I hang up, I feel Shay's pulse slow under my fingers.

"Oh no. No, don't do anything stupid," I warn.

I'm here and I've got her. But what if it's not enough?

I hold her in my arms, feeling the weight of her. My gaze falls to her elbow, the pins that seem normal now.

No. She's been through so much already. She's tough. Too tough to let my father bring her down.

"Come on, Townie," I try. "I said I wouldn't let you lose. This would be a terrible time to make a liar out of me."

No response.

"Wake up, baby. Don't let him win." My desperation deepens. "No, fuck him. Do it for *me*."

There's a smudge on her cheek and I brush it with my thumb. The dirt doesn't come off.

"All the things I said, I didn't mean them." The words run together in a desperate voice I don't recognize. "You're it, okay? You're everything."

Now I'm thinking of her in a sweater and jeans and headphones the first day of school when I looked out the windshield of the Turbo.

I grabbed the wheel, but it was too late. My heart stopped at the impact.

I started to get out to check on her, but I caught Theo's frozen expression. He needed me.

The next second he was moving, and I was, too. I was afraid I'd lose my brother.

When she stood up and looked at me with those eyes, I felt it in my soul. I didn't know why then, but I do now.

"I need you more than I've ever needed anything, and that's why I tried to send you away. Because as much as I need you here . . . I need you to exist even more."

I swallow, thinking of the ring she gave me.

"Come on, Shay," I whisper. "Through the fucking fire."

49

Shay

MY SKIN AND my lungs burn.

I'm on something hard and bumpy. If this is a bed, it's the worst mattress in the world.

"Bree," I manage, but my lungs are weak. All I can think about is my friend, the one I'm responsible for, who was beside me tonight. Bree, whose brave voice trembled when she realized I couldn't stop the car.

When the answer comes, it's not Bree speaking.

"She's okay."

And so am I because Jameson Ashford is holding me. It's his voice in my ear.

I must have hit my head. It hurts, but more than that, he's saying the most beautiful, un-Jameson things. The pain is overwhelming but I'm straining to make out the words.

Then, he's gone and I'm being put on a stretcher.

No, I try to say, but my throat won't work.

There are more words but they're not the ones I want. I don't recognize the voices now, issuing calm commands like "breathe" and "don't move."

"Jameson." I croak it.

His hand finds mine and relief has my muscles sagging again.

Paramedics are carrying me but he's right there every step.

He's supposed to be driving.

Confusion fills my mind. There was a big race. One that mattered.

They tell me they're putting me in the ambulance. My fingers tighten on Jameson's. "Come with me."

I'm straining to hear his answer right up until everything goes black.

50

Shay

"YOU CAN'T COVER her losses."

"Watch me."

"You're making a faction! That's against the rules."

In the darkness, voices bounce around me. Megan, Zane, Raj. I'm sore everywhere, but the pain feels less important than the familiar tones, the calm that takes root deep inside knowing I'm surrounded by friends.

I might be disoriented but for once, I'm not alone.

"Ever heard of house rules?"

"We're not in a house."

The fourth voice has my eyes blinking open. The hospital suite is huge, bigger than any room I've seen, with seating for my friends. They're opposite the bed, playing some kind of card game.

My gaze lands on Bree, curled up in the nearest chair. Relief washes over me.

"You're okay!"

She grabs my hand like she did before the crash. "Just some

bruising. Got me out of a shift at The Junction, but I'll be fine in a few days."

The wreck feels as if it just happened, but some time must have passed. I have so many questions, but my brain is so foggy I can't verbalize one.

I squint against the brightness as Megan gets up to adjust the blinds of my hospital room.

"I'm jealous. You've barely been out of school one day, and the academy has already offered to defer your exams."

So today is Tuesday. That was a question I had—how long I've been here.

"Your dad went home to shower and rest, and only because we made him. We said we'd stay with you," Bree informs me.

Good. A second question answered. It feels like progress.

Before I can try to think of another, a nurse clears her throat from the doorway. "I'm glad you're awake. You were lucky to escape with only minor injuries."

Unlike the last time I was in a hospital, this one's expression conveys only concern and protectiveness, not animosity.

"Visiting hours are almost over. Are you expecting anyone else?"

Jameson's face appears in my mind, a question and an answer at once. I'm longing to see him come around the corner. My friends are here but there's a hole in my chest their laughter can't fill.

I swear I heard his voice at the accident. Steady, urgent. But it's possible I saw what I wanted to see, heard what I wanted to hear.

The nurse is still waiting, and I shake my head. With my response, she walks out.

A knock on the door has us looking up.

"How are we feeling?" Theo's disembodied voice accompanies a massive bouquet of balloons.

He passes the ribbons to Bree, who ties them to the arm of her chair.

"Wow. That is a lot of helium, Ashford," Megan says.

Theo comes to the bed, bending to wrap me in a gentle hug. "That hurt?" he asks when my nose wrinkles.

"Nah. Just trying not to swoon that *the* Theo Ashford deigned to visit me in the hospital." My voice is a croak, my throat feeling about as healthy as it sounds.

The girls exchange a look then Bree stands, tugging Megan. "We're going to get coffee. You want?"

"Juice?" Holding off on the caffeine until my head stops pounding feels like a smart move. "Thanks."

They disappear down the hall, talking about Bree's date that she had to reschedule.

Theo grimaces. "I assume you've heard what happened in the race."

I shake my head.

"Jamie pulled right off the track and was gone. He was worried about you. Turns out he was right to be." Those blue eyes lock on mine, and I feel his helplessness.

I wet my lips that feel dry as a desert. "There was nothing either of you could have done. My brakes failed."

"Not on their own, they didn't." He tells me what Jameson told him—that he suspected Luca was involved, as a desperate ploy to keep me from talking about how ARI tanked its own car. That's why he came after me.

I shiver despite the sunlight streaming in the windows.

"Jamie knew," Theo says after a moment, his voice rough. "I think he knew even before the race."

Theo's words settle into my bones as the nurse pokes her head in again.

"You really should rest . . ." She trails off when she spots my visitor. "Theo Ashford. Can I get a picture?" She looks hopefully between us.

"How about an autograph." Theo signs a piece of paper from the pad by the bed and hands it over. She scampers off.

"See? You're halfway to being a superstar already," I tease, and he grins. "Does that mean you won the seat?" My voice sounds more even this time, and evidently, I am capable of formulating a question. Progress.

Theo shoves his hands in his pockets and crosses to the window. "ARI issued a press release today," he confirms. "But everyone's demanding an explanation for why Jamie left. There's speculation his withdrawal had to do with Dekker. They don't know the truth . . . yet."

"You deserved to win, Theo," I tell him.

"But Jamie didn't deserve to lose." Theo crosses to my side again. "When I found out what happened to you, I should have stopped it. Or fixed it." He curses. "It's fucked up, but I won and I still wish I'd been Jamie. I'd die if anything happened to you on my watch."

"I'm proud of you," I say softly. "I might not be the one for you, Theo Ashford, but she's out there."

His fingers squeeze mine. "I'll make it up to you. To you and Jamie."

I'm glad he's here, but it's not enough. I can't stay here. This place feels oppressive. I start to get out of bed, but Megan and Bree come back and catch me.

"Excuse me. I don't think the doctors approved that," Megan says.

"You can't stop me."

"No, but I can." Theo blocks the way.

I size him up. "I can take you."

"I'll use my enormous fan base to clog the hallways. Did you see how that lady just busted in here for a photo?" He hitches a thumb toward the hall, flashing that Theo grin.

Damn it. I drop back onto the bed.

51

Shay

GETTING DISCHARGED FROM the hospital is easier than I expected. Being home, where my dad dotes on me as if I might slip away at any moment, is harder.

He won't let me out of sight for a second. The first night, he makes me the biggest stack of star-shaped pancakes I've ever seen and sleeps on the couch so he'll hear me call if I need anything.

My brain fog clears the next day. The awkward yet adorable pep talk Dad gives me for surviving the first semester of school is heartwarming.

Still, for a moment, I think he won't let me go to my exams a week after the crash, but when I remind him Megan's going to pick me up and I won't be alone for even a second, he releases me to my friends.

"That was cruel and unusual punishment," Megan groans as we head out of our first exam, rubbing her fists over her bleary eyes, smearing makeup in the corner.

"Like I got hit by a truck," Raj agrees, shaking his head.

I shoot him a look.

"Too soon?" Zane asks, shouldering his book bag.

Our feet shuffle along the shiny marble floors lining the academy. We're a tired little army heading down the hall together after spending all morning hunched over desks and paper. Other students look over and whisper, and I know it's me they're talking about. But they have their own shit to deal with too, so I tell myself the gossip will pass.

"Let's go to The Junction and celebrate by mainlining sugar." Megan loops an arm through mine.

We pass the theater where Luca gave his Legacy Day address. The spot by the lockers where Theo gave me my AirPods. The door of the classroom where my legs brushed Jameson's more than once, where I'd dream up ways to sabotage his car and pretend I didn't crave him as much as I wanted revenge.

My phone vibrates in my jeans and I swipe for it. But it's only Bree looking for updates on my exam.

"Not him?" Megan asks, sympathetic, as I tuck the phone away again.

After the accident, police came to take my statement. Dad said they were looking at my car for signs of tampering. But there's so much I don't know, and piecing together who was involved and how I crashed feels way outside my capabilities right now.

"If it makes you feel better, nobody's heard from Jameson," Megan informs me. "He's probably holed up with lawyers trying to overturn the decision about Theo's seat."

"Or he's afraid to come near you because he fucked up your life," Zane chimes in.

We all look over at him.

"He did," he says defensively.

I remind myself the last time we spoke, Jameson pushed me

away. He wanted me gone and was willing to use whatever means necessary to do it.

By the time we reach the front doors, Zane and Raj are a few steps ahead, arguing over changes to the cars for the new F1 season.

This place used to feel so foreign. Now, all I see are the memories and the friends I made. Even if I walked out today and never returned, I'd have accomplished more than I expected to.

I've always felt safer depending on myself, but with Jameson, I could never keep the walls up. He made me fight until I realized I wasn't fighting him at all, but the fear I'd been hiding behind.

On impulse, I hit his contact on my phone. Each ring on the line has my stomach flipping over. When his voicemail kicks in, I don't hang up.

"It's me. I don't know how you knew to come after me, but I'm glad you did. Particularly given the horribly inconvenient timing."

I take a breath and force myself to keep talking.

"When you told me to leave, it hurt like hell. But it also made me take a hard look at why I wanted to stay." I swallow, my throat suddenly tight.

"I like this place, these people. How everyone wants so badly and isn't ashamed of it. How they find a way to do what's never been done. I like who I am here. Who I have to be, and who I'm allowed to be.

"I need you to know . . ." My feet feel heavier with each step. "It's not the same. I miss walking down the hall and seeing you coming the other way. I miss checking my phone knowing you're the one texting. I miss the way you look at me like I'm the answer to every question in the whole world."

A tear slips down my cheek.

"I'm still here, but nothing is the same without you."

52

Shay

I FIGURED THE Mustang would be in rough shape, but not this rough.

The police returned it to us a week after the accident. The tow truck driver shot me a skeptical look as he helped me and Dad wheel it back into the garage.

I've been assessing for more than an hour, trying to salvage what I can from the engine without much encouragement. Finally, I poke at the edge of the dented bumper and the entire piece clatters to the floor with a metallic clunk.

"That's it. Time of death. I'm calling it," Dad says from the doorway.

"Oh, so now you're a doctor?" I shift up off my knees and straighten. Sweat covers my arms, plus streaks of dirt.

"Nope, but I am a pretty good mechanic. Even I know you can't fix everything." He offers me a hand and helps me up. "You ready for supper? I've got bacon in the fridge."

"Sure."

But he stops me before we get to the door.

"Shay, I need to tell you something." He huffs out a breath as he comes and sits next to me on the workbench.

I expect a caution about taking it easy. I'm totally unprepared for what follows.

"I'm proud of you. Beyond proud." He reaches an arm around my shoulders, and I hesitate before leaning into him. "Just when I think you can't get any better, you prove me wrong. You're smart and capable and caring. In case I don't say it enough . . . you've always been the best thing to ever happen to me."

I blink, my eyes burning even before he continues.

"I wanted to make your life easier, especially since the first few years were so full of pain and grief. I thought keeping the truth from you was a gift, but I've realized you're not the child who needed protecting anymore. Which is why I need to tell you this."

He takes a deep breath and I straighten, my shoulder blades stiffening as I take him in.

"I'd been working on the grid for ARI for five years when Luca called me one night—he'd hit another car on a back road and didn't know what to do. His car was barely damaged, but the other one flipped."

I wrap my arms around myself, fingers digging into my biceps. "Dad, you don't have to—"

"I told him to stay put and called the ambulance. But by the time it arrived, he was gone." Dad rubs his chin, his face pale. "It wasn't until the next day I learned your parents didn't make it. You were taken to the hospital with non-life-threatening injuries.

"I confronted Luca. He figured I would take his side, but I wouldn't. Not on this. He had been going through difficulties in his personal life, grappling with his team who wanted him to retire. He offered to pay me to make it disappear."

My stomach is roiling, but he keeps talking.

"I should have brought what I knew to the police, but I wanted to take care of you. I offered to take you in. You didn't have any family, and I couldn't stand the thought of you alone going into the system.

"Luca pulled some strings to help make it possible, but I told him that after this, we weren't friends. We never would be. The last thing I did was make him put the money he tried to give me into a trust for you, one you can access when you turn twenty-one."

Next year.

I'd only ever had half the picture of what happened with my parents, filling in the gaps myself. Fitting in these new truths alongside what I thought I knew feels like trying to repair a bone that already healed crookedly.

"I understand if you blame me," Dad says. "I couldn't bring them back, but I wanted to take care of you. This was the best way I knew how. I know now that it wasn't right.

"When you took an interest in cars as a child, I thought, what father doesn't want his child to follow in his footsteps? But the closer you got to the industry, to Ashford, the more I realized it was dangerous. I tried to stop you. I tried so many times."

It makes sense, in a way. How angry he got when I wanted to pursue racing. It was fear underneath.

A question lurks at the back of my mind that I don't want to ask, but I can't stop myself.

"How much is in the trust?"

"Half a million dollars."

The air whooshes out of my lungs.

That's more money than I've seen in my life. It should be harder to say what comes next.

"I don't want it."

"Shay," he goes on cautiously at my expression. "It's enough for you to start over doing anything you want. Forget starting a garage with me or working for ARI. You could go to any college in the country. Buy a house in a new town. Go anywhere. Be anything. Think about it, honey."

I don't want to think about it.

I'm spared having to respond when the doorbell rings and Dad heads through the door to the house to answer it.

I turn back to the Mustang to deal with my feelings.

Luca paid for my silence. Or my future, depending on how you see it. There's a whole world of possibility now. But it was paid for in blood.

Winning at all costs is a romantic idea, until you're the one paying the price.

"Shay. Door." Dad's wearing a strange expression.

I want to tell him I'm busy, but there's a tug deep in my chest amid the grief and shock.

I head past him out to the front porch. No one's there, but the Corvette Stingray Jameson restored idles in front of our house.

The heaviness of moments ago slips away, pushed to the back of my mind.

It's all breathtaking curves and beautiful design. My heart kicks as I run out onto the street and around the hood.

I feel like a kid seeing a unicorn. It's painted the palest mint green. Like budding leaves on the first day of spring.

"It's finished," I say to no one. Not only restored, but a work of art.

"Been working on it around the clock." Jameson's voice from behind me sends tremors through every inch of my body.

He's here.

I spin to face him.

After two weeks without seeing him, his presence is overwhelming. His athletic frame, strong shoulders, and lean hips defined even through his jacket and jeans. His hard jaw and full mouth. The dark lashes framing blue eyes and the hair that falls into them.

For a second, I wonder if I'm imagining him. Except I wouldn't imagine him like this—the worry etched on his face, or the way he stands like he's bracing for impact.

Jameson nods to the car without breaking my gaze. "What do you think?"

That's like asking if I like sunshine or rainbows or the feel of the wind in my hair.

"It's incredible," I murmur, running a hand over the hood.

"It's yours." Jameson's words have my gaze snapping up to him. "I built it for you."

"Jameson . . ." I trail off because there are no words for what I'm feeling. It seems impossible to be surprised again this week. Somehow, I am.

"It has some safety modifications. Three-point seat belts. Roll cage in the frame. Disc brakes."

"That's very responsible of you," I whisper, trying to make light of it.

Still, he looks lost. "I should have come sooner. I pushed you away when I found out what my father did. I couldn't believe you would want anything to do with me, or that I deserved you, after what he cost you."

His expression fills with guarded hope. "But I listened to your voicemail. I decided even if I can't forgive what Luca did—to you, to Theo, to my mom—I didn't have to own it. My father's failings don't have to be mine."

I step closer and he tips my chin up, his breath light on my skin.

His forehead leans against mine, and it's overwhelming to touch him again. I haven't felt real these last few days.

"When I said you should leave"—his blue eyes bore into me—"it was only because I couldn't ask you to stay. If you still want to go to college, I'll carry your books. If you want to waitress at The Junction, I'll rub your feet after every shift. If you want to work on cars, I'll drive anything you touch. But no matter what, I'm going to be there.

"I told you once there wouldn't be a happy ending for you and my brother," he goes on. "But I hope to hell there can still be one for us."

My chest expands until it feels like my ribs could crack. He's here, and all I want is another second with him.

Another hour.

Another lifetime.

He waits me out, pulling back an inch.

"I spent my entire life thinking letting someone in was the dangerous part," I say finally.

Jameson goes still. His expression softens, like I've handed him something fragile.

"But"—my voice wavers—"you're the first person I ever needed who didn't make me feel broken for it."

His hands tighten on me. "You're the only one I'd choose. Over everything."

His lips fuse to mine, hot and sweet at once, like he's been starving for exactly this. He tastes like salt and him and everything I let myself want these past months.

I kiss him back, tugging on his hair. I shift my hips on the front of the car, looping my legs around him. He groans and presses into me.

There's a sharp knock on the window.

"Shit, that's my dad," I pant.

"So we can't do what we did the last time we were on this car?" Jameson asks.

A rush of desire competes with the storm of emotions filling my chest. "Unfortunately not."

His thumb brushes my lip, and I wrestle with the urge to suck it into my mouth.

"Come back after dark," I say.

He grins, and it's the most beautiful thing I've ever seen. "Damn right I will."

"And, Jameson? Drive fast."

53

Shay

"**GET READY TO** lose," Jameson tells Knox, his voice low with malice.

"Would you be that sure for one large?"

Jameson doesn't hesitate. "Make it two."

"I'm out." Mateo lifts both hands. "You fucking idiots."

The indoor karting venue has swirling lights and graffitied murals on the walls. The ten-car track is admittedly cute compared to where we usually race, but that does nothing to diminish the adrenaline pumping through my veins.

"Why not five?" Megan tosses as she squeezes into her kart.

The guys exchange a look. Then nod.

Megan swears. "It was a joke."

"Don't fuck this up," Knox calls to Zane, who ignores him as he gets into his own vehicle.

"Let's go over the strategy again," Jameson says, fastening my helmet.

I shake my head. "No. I've got this."

Exams wrapped up last week and we're officially on break. With all the time I've spent working on cars this year, it's my first chance to race from behind the wheel.

I climb into my own kart next to the other engineers.

It doesn't occur to me to ask permission.

I'm in the driver's seat. And I'm determined to win.

We take off.

Zane takes the early lead. He's duking it out with a few other engineers from our class, until two of them collide and get taken out.

The academy drivers are hollering from the sidelines, jerking and waving. Clearly, they're not used to watching.

Megan cuts in front of me. We swoop around the next turn and I get her back.

"She's a fucking Ashford!" Knox hollers as Eden cuts in front of Zane as we finish our lap.

"Rules just said no drivers," she tosses, flipping him off.

Megan and Eden go head-to-head on the next lap.

Out of nowhere, another car appears. "Raj?!" we exclaim in unison.

He's hooting with delight, but it's short-lived as the girls team up against him.

At the last minute, I sneak through and over the finish line.

"Knew you had it in you," Jameson says proudly, dragging me into his arms after we all pull to a stop.

"I'm sweaty," I protest as I drag my helmet off, my hair falling down around my sticky neck.

"You'll be sweatier when I'm done with you."

He kisses me and it's game over.

"I love you," he says against my mouth, like it's the easiest truth in the world.

I don't hesitate. "I love you too."

The only thing better than being in the driver's seat surrounded by my friends and a little healthy competition is having this kind of welcoming committee at the finish line.

Bree's there with her new boyfriend, Trevor. Eden stayed for the holidays, I think because she has some school drama she wants to avoid.

"My vote is to replace Legacy Day with this," I say to no one. Though this isn't an officially sanctioned school event, the third years surprised us all by organizing it.

"Who knows if there will be another Legacy Day." I look up to find Vogel perched over the railing. "I wanted to deliver the news in person that you passed all your exams."

I'm relieved but still thinking about something else. "Any news about Luca?"

"Nothing public." Her expression is regretful.

The police are investigating my crash, but so far it's been nearly impossible to link it to Luca personally.

However, thanks to a new tip, the federation has reopened Dekker's dismissal complaint against ARI. It was enough to trigger a no-confidence vote by the ARI board. Luca was put on probation and removed from the CEO role indefinitely.

Keane is keeping a close eye to ensure no one interferes with how he runs his shop. After learning about the sabotage, he swore no one would ever get close enough to do it again.

What I do in the future is still undecided, but at least in the meantime, Dad's job at ARI is protected.

"What happens to the academy while Luca's on probation?" I ask Vogel.

"There's an endowment to continue its operations, but it's under the purview of the board."

"Which includes Jameson and Theo," I guess.

Her head inclines.

Competition makes you hungry, so after karting, we all head to the diner. Bree and I are off the clock, but her brother takes orders and runs food as I shift into a seat next to Eden.

"Have you heard anything from Theo?" I ask.

She shakes her head. "I think he's keeping his distance from the carnage."

Everyone is eating and laughing, but Jameson's standing by the doors staring at his phone. I slip out of the booth and cross to him. He holds out his phone.

THEO: I wanted to win but not like that. Let's have a rematch.

"What do you think?" Jameson asks evenly.

I'll make it up to you. To you and Jamie.

Theo's words come back and I feel my chest light up.

"I think you should do it."

54

Jameson

WE DON'T WASTE time scheduling the rematch. Whatever my brother's shortcomings, postponing the inevitable isn't one of them.

The do-over race is on the same track. A few dozen witnesses only, key ARI personnel and classmates from the academy.

No cameras. A rule we decided together.

Theo and I look at each other before we start.

"Feel different this time?" he calls to me.

I nod. "You and me."

I don't mean the lack of other drivers. I mean that for the first time, it's on our terms.

The lights go off and we're speeding down the track.

Each curve, I take from memory. I don't fight my brother or my father or my expectations. I drive the best I know how.

The rest is faith.

When we cross the line, I'm first by less than a second. There's no ceremony, only relief in my chest twinged with regret for my brother.

At least Shay's there when I get out. If I hadn't noticed her waiting near the finish line, I would've spotted Megan's fuzzy pink jacket.

"You did it!" She launches herself into my arms.

"We did it," I correct.

"Come on, I didn't give you any strategy this time." Her hands find my hair. If she minds that I'm sweaty, she doesn't show it.

"You gave me exactly what I needed." I kiss her hard.

Being with her has changed me. She's made me better, kinder, more open.

Forced me to challenge the things I want. It's not all about winning, though that's still pretty fucking fantastic.

In a few months, I'll get to test myself against a whole new field.

I love that she'll be there with me. I just love her.

The rest of the engineers crowd us to celebrate.

"What is that?" My eyes narrow at Megan, who produces a giant bottle from behind her back. "We said no champagne."

Zane produces one, too. Raj looks guilty but does the same.

"You think everyone does everything you say just because you're an Ashford?" Shay teases, reaching out as someone passes her a bottle. Her hand moves toward the cork. "One, two, three!"

Then I'm ducking as a dozen bottles spray at once.

EPILOGUE

Shay

WHEN I POP my earbuds in and start down the street, it's barely eight a.m. Somehow, though, the sun is already beating down on the city.

The weather is warmer here than home, the birds flitting in the trees. Melbourne is beautiful in March.

I hear the car before I see it. The purr of the engine is noticeable over the music in my earbuds as the vehicle pulls up next to me. Convertible, top down. Beautiful curves. Slick paint job. I'm a fan before I look over to the driver's seat.

Dark hair. Sunglasses. Don't-fuck-with-me jawline. If the car had me hooked, its driver has me sunk.

"Where are you going?"

I tug out a headphone as he speaks. "Wherever I want," I say pleasantly.

"I have an all-access VIP pass for the first F1 race of the season with your name on it."

I fish inside my bag for a lanyard, slipping it around my neck. "What, like this? Already got one."

"If I have to get out of the car and carry you, it's going to cause a scene."

"Might be worth it."

Jameson smiles and that curve of his beautiful mouth decides it.

Playing hard to get is fun.

Being his is even better.

I shift into the car, hauling my cross-body bag with all my gear.

"Fuck. You must have an F2 car in there."

"Not quite." I laugh.

He leans over to brush his lips over mine. Every thought about the day ahead evaporates from my mind as he kisses me. It's him and me and how insanely good this feels. He was mine last night, and win or lose, he's mine again tonight.

I'm excited for the first race of the season, to watch him drive, to cheer for him to win.

I had a text from Dad this morning wishing us luck. He decided Australia was too far, so despite an invitation from Jameson to travel with us on the ARI jet, he said he'd be watching from home.

Someone behind us honks. Jameson ignores it, coming back for another pass.

"You're due at the track," I murmur against his mouth.

"Your fault I'm late. You snuck out early," he accuses.

It's actually remarkable I woke up at all given how late he kept me up.

"Any advice?" he asks, turning those steady blue eyes on me.

I laugh. "Just drive your race. You qualified third."

"Which means I have a lot of work ahead of me."

“Qualifying third is the highest debut by a rookie driver in two decades,” I correct, reminding him of the stats.

“It’s not first. I want to win.” His eyes flash with competitiveness.

Damn, he’s sexy. This guy is everything I never knew I wanted.

He makes me proud of being bold, not ashamed of it. He helps me believe in my dreams and push past my limitations. At the same time, he’s there for me in a way that makes me feel like I can lean on him. Like I’m already enough.

It’s like the story my mother used to read me, the one with the prince and the dragon.

Jameson Ashford isn’t the haughty prince at all. He’s the dragon—defiant, dangerous, uncompromising. The path my bravest self would choose every time.

“Before I forget.” He tugs off the ring from around his neck and passes it to me. “Since I can’t race with it.”

“I’ve never had a guy give me a ring before,” I tease as I put it on.

“Don’t give me any ideas.”

My mouth falls open. “I’m twenty-one, Ashford. Slow your roll.”

“Fine.” He reaches for my hand as he hits the gas. “But I’m not going anywhere.”

✥

Jameson is whisked away by PR the second we reach the ARI garage.

“This is for you!” Megan descends on me with coffee, looking utterly at home in her new ARI jacket and staff pass. I expected the grid to be a sea of strangers, but it's amazing to see familiar faces.

"I figured you'd be too busy to stop for food," I tease.

"Food, yes. Friends, no."

My smile widens.

"Anyone seen Raj?" Megan asks.

"He's been busy all week. He couldn't be happier. He and Zane are arguing over who's working harder."

Raj decided why stop at U of M and started building his dream list of grad schools, and Zane's had virtual meetings with two teams already, one of which offered to fly him to their headquarters in the summer for an in-person meeting.

Megan scored the ARI internship. I expected to feel jealousy, or disappointment. Instead, all I feel is pride.

That and relief that the dream didn't vanish for me; it only changed form.

After the holidays, Vogel came to me with an offer—she'd mentor me personally if I stayed another semester at the academy. Plus, she would get me access to work with Keane on the F1 cars under development in the top-secret ARI garage.

Since I was a late transfer in the first place and still felt pressure to catch up, she explained it would give me a chance to absorb the world of experienced techs before I traded it in for the "different country every weekend" pressures of the grid.

I'll still get unprecedented access to the best teachers, cars, and opportunities. Luca's influence and methods aside, the company really does recruit and train the best.

I said I'd agree on one condition: that I could fly to Jameson's races when I wanted. Vogel grudgingly signed off, even mentioning there might be a spot on the company jet as long as I didn't fall behind in my classes. For now, it's the best of both worlds.

Eden, who wouldn't miss her brother's first F1 race for anything, descends wearing a short dress that probably cost thousands of dollars. The drink in her hand has ice cubes in it.

"That's not coffee," Megan observes.

"No, it's not." She smiles sweetly. "Well, Shay. You're officially a WAG now. How does it feel?"

"Sweaty," I say honestly, shielding my face from the sun with a hand.

Luca's probation has been extended since the renewed inquiry surfaced files at ARI that cast more doubt on his business practices with not only federation guidelines but possibly state and federal laws.

Jameson told the police his father was behind my crash. They claimed to take it seriously, but it was difficult to turn up evidence of sabotage in the hollowed-out Fastback.

Still, he's not ready to give up on justice for my birth parents and me.

I'm not, either, but it helps that control of ARI now sits with the board. In some ways, removing Luca from the company he lied to, manipulated, and almost killed for feels like the cruelest punishment.

Despite the warmth of the day and the excitement of my friends, someone's missing.

I text Theo. **You coming today?**

"He's probably drinking his feelings," Eden says, not unkindly. "I'll keep tabs on him. He'll bounce back."

The grid takes their warm-up lap, then lines up for the start of the race.

Jameson's in the car, his expression grimly determined. I can feel how badly he wants this. But more than wanting it, he's earned the right to race the best in the world. I'm so proud of him.

My fingers dig into the railing.

One.

The first light blinks on.

Two.

My heart hammers in my chest, too fast to be healthy.

Three.

Four.

This is just the beginning. The start of a new act for ARI. For Jameson. For me.

Five.

My hand grips the ring around my neck.

The starting lights go out.

Theo

"THAT'S ANOTHER WIN," the dealer proclaims as poker chips form a small mountain in the center of the table.

"Sir?"

Finally, I sweep them.

The pile in front of me is growing by the minute.

Don't ask how long I've been here. I can't remember a time before my ass was in this seat, surrounded by the air conditioned red and gold backdrop of the finest casino in the world.

"You don't look like someone who won big." The woman next to me is perfectly put together in contrast to my disheveled, undone bow tie look, the collar of my shirt unfastened.

There are casinos where you don't have to wear a suit. Monte Carlo isn't one of them, but they give me some leeway.

I'm an Ashford, after all.

"What time is it?" I blink, the buzz of alcohol wearing off.

"Nearly noon."

"What day?"

She and the dealer exchange a look.

"Thursday."

Not that far off from what I thought.

"What do you do when you're not here?" the woman asks as I start to stack my chips.

"I used to drive cars."

"Like a chauffeur."

I cock my head. "Sure."

Shay's called more times than I've answered, trying to reconcile me to the fact that I did the right thing.

There was no way I could race in the seat I only won after my brother left to chase after the girl he loved. The one who loved him back.

And maybe . . .

Maybe for once, I wanted to be the hero.

My chest aches. From the outside, it might appear that women are interchangeable for me. When it was about companionship and distraction, they probably were.

She was different. She made me question whether the story everyone had about me, my family included, was even true. Thanks to her, I not only wanted more but for the first time, I tried more.

If I had won the seat and the girl, I wouldn't have held it over Jamie. I would have been generous in victory, not advertising the fact that I got everything I wanted at his expense.

But he had to one-up me there too.

Work with me. We can rebuild together.

Ha. Only Jamie would think it would be better for me to go back into the belly of the company, spend days right next to the brother who was more everything than I was.

Fuck. If this is what heartbreak feels like, I see why people become alcoholics.

"And now?" the woman next to me asks.

"I'm in between opportunities," I say, taking a sip of my drink. Whatever number I'm on.

At least Ignite has been having a good season. I shouldn't be pleased but I am. They're competing against my company. I make money when ARI does well. When my brother succeeds.

"I know what you should do."

"Yeah?"

"Poker." The woman nods to my stacks of chips.

I take a second to appreciate the winnings I've accumulated as the dealer begins a new hand.

Growing up, Jameson was brilliant with cars. Eden, when she was around, was a social mastermind.

I've always been good at cards. I know the rules, watch the players, smile, and wait.

I know when to bet big, and when to fold.

I lift the two cards in front of me. Nod for another.

We're still playing the hand when my phone vibrates in my pocket. I'm about to hit ignore when the number scratches a touch of recognition in my brain.

I answer. "Shay, I swear to God, if this is you, stop calling—"

"It's the Team Principal for Ignite racing."

No fucking way. But I've heard the voice of the top dog at ARI's biggest rival before, so I'm not questioning if it's true.

"You know why I'm calling."

I toss back the rest of my drink. "You missed my birthday by months."

He doesn't laugh. "We have the best car on the grid."

"Second best."

He pauses only a second. “No. We have new upgrades to roll out next weekend.”

Curiosity cuts through my buzz and my indifference. “Why are you telling me?”

“We want you to drive for us.”

I’ve swallowed my last sip, and thank fuck, because I would’ve choked on it.

An F1 team is calling to offer me a seat. It’s so ludicrous I could laugh.

“Because I’m an Ashford?”

“Despite it. If you had any other name, we could’ve called sooner.”

I click off and look up at the dealer, whose brows pull together. “Good news, sir?”

“I’m out.” I drop my cards, a full house, on the table with a flourish and grab my jacket off the chair.

The dealer blinks at me in shock. “But . . . why?”

My heart thuds against my ribs as I shrug into my jacket, smoothing down the lapels.

“I got a better offer.”

YOUR

ASHFORD ACADEMY

ADVENTURE CONTINUES WITH

THEO'S STORY IN

Running Hot

ACKNOWLEDGMENTS

TO THE READERS who have followed my stories over the years: Thank you. Your messages, enthusiasm, and love for these characters are the reason books like this exist. I've wanted to write this story for a long time, and it's been thrilling to dive into the world of racing through *Crash Course*—with all its complicated legacies, buried secrets, and delicious rivalries.

My gratitude to the incredible team at Berkley XO and Penguin Random House for welcoming Ashford Academy into the world and for the care you've already poured into this series. I'm especially grateful to my editor, Tiara Kittrell, whose insight and enthusiasm have shaped this story in countless ways.

Thank you to my wonderful agent, Georgana Grinstead, for believing in my work and helping guide this next chapter.

Becca Hensley Mysoor, thank you for being my creative coconspirator and favorite "yes, and" partner for all these years.

Gina Azzi and Annette Brignac, thank you for sharing your love of cars and racing, and for your enthusiasm for Ashford Academy.

Kate Tilton, thank you for keeping all the bookish details running smoothly through this process and never batting an eye when I propose something new.

Finally, thank you to the friends and family who support this strange and wonderful career. I appreciate you cheering me on every step of the way.

Photo credit: Ariana del Mundo

PIPER LAWSON is a *Wall Street Journal* and *USA Today* bestselling author of smart and steamy romance. She writes women who follow their dreams, best friends who know your dirty secrets and love you anyway, and complex heroes you'll fall hard for. Piper lives in Canada with her tall and brilliant husband. She's a sucker for dark eyes, dark coffee, and dark chocolate.